Advance Reviews

"Newcomer Kate Brandes delivers honest, shades-of-gray storytelling in *The Promise of Pierson Orchard*. This is a nuanced tale about the rise of poison in one fractured family, and how high-pressure situations can clarify what's most important to us. You'll remember these complex characters long after you've finished the book."

– **Therese Walsh**, author of *The Moon Sisters* and *The Last Will of Moira Leahy*

"A well-tended story about two brothers who love the same girl and were disappointed by the same woman—their mother. When life brings them all back together again, old wounds are re-opened and regrets bubble to the surface. As sweet and tart as the apples grown in an orchard so vivid I felt as if I had been there, this novel is sure to please fans of family-driven fiction."

– **Catherine McKenzie**, bestselling author of *Hidden* and *Fractured*

"In her impressive debut set in a small U.S. farming town, Kate Brandes expertly portrays the conflict between single-minded corporate interests and those who unite in their struggle to challenge it. Brandes' characters demonstrate the heart and strength of everyday people leading complex lives. You will be touched by their honesty and root for them to see past their flaws. Deeply relevant to our times, *The Promise of Pierson Orchard* quickly builds momentum and will have you invested from the first insightful chapter to the whirlwind of an ending."

– **Renee Rutledge**, author of *The Hour of Daydreams*

"A multi-generational family finds themselves conflicted as they debate the best future for their land and orchard when Green Energy offers to lease property in their town, promising financial relief, but also bringing the risks of drilling for natural gas: destruction of the land they love. I consider myself a friend of the environment, so the story appealed to me. At the same time, I appreciated that the story was not a one-sided, predictable description of the damage done by drilling. Instead, it was a balanced telling of both sides of the story. It was thought-provoking and well done. I'll remember this story a long time."

– **SANDY WARD**, author of *The Astonishing Thing*

"Brandes tells the story through the POV of two brothers, the woman they both love, and the mother that left them as young boys. The portrait she created of this small family, as they too struggled with compromise, was well done, emotional, and heartfelt. Their motivations, passions, and fears were evident on the page, and I held my breath during the last few chapters to see how their stories would end."

– **JENNI WALSH**, author of *Becoming Bonnie*

"*The Promise of Pierson Orchard* is a wonderful read, compelling, and surprising, and sparkling with insight. I devoured it in a single afternoon, and my guess is that you will do the same. Or you may decide to savor Kate Brandes's fine writing over time. Either way, I envy you the treat of reading it fresh."

– **ROBIN BLACK**, award-winning author of *Life Drawing*

"Kate Brandes' beautifully crafted story maps the town of Minden, PA with compassion and insight. Her characters feel as real as people you know, and as their lives are tested, broken, and patched together, she evokes the enduring bonds that tie us to our families, our communities, and nature itself. This is a lovely, stirring novel."

– **ALIX OHLIN**, highly acclaimed author of *The Missing Person* and *Babylon and Other Stories*

"Capably following in the footsteps of Barbara Kingsolver's *Prodigal Summer,* Brandes marries flora and family in *The Promise of Pierson Orchard* to craft an unmistakable sense of place in an evolving environment. This paean to pastoral roots torn asunder by capitalist yearnings is equal parts promise and prediction for our fast-changing future."

– **ELLEN URBANI**, author of *Landfall* and *When I Was Elena*

The PROMISE of PIERSON ORCHARD

The PROMISE of PIERSON ORCHARD

a novel

Kate Brandes

The Promise of Pierson Orchard
Kate Brandes

ISBN: 978-1-942545-51-4
Library of Congress Control Number: 2016942105

The characters and events in this book are fictitious. Any similarity to real persons, living or dead, is coincidental and not intended by the author.

Wyatt-MacKenzie Publishing, Inc.
www.WyattMacKenzie.com
Contact us: info@wyattmackenzie.com

Dedication

For my mom, Joan.

PART ONE

NOVEMBER

CHAPTER 1

Jack

November 3—Cold. Wind coming. Working the harvest all hours, without her. Little sleep. Can't keep up. Need a fight today like I need breath.

HARVEST HAD BEGUN as it did every year in Minden, Pennsylvania. McIntosh and Liberty first, on through Cortland, Empire, Jonagold, and Gala. And now, in November, Braeburn.

Jack looked out over the forked trunks of the trees extending into branches bent with fruit. Fallen apples littered the frosty ground.

Rubbing the back of his neck, he checked his watch, anxious, counting the hours until he'd be able to find some peace with his fists.

He'd been at it since the first arc of light to the east shone through the early morning mist lying low in the hills, before the mist gave way to blue sky. Morrigan Mountain stood steady to the north, accompanied by the constant flow of Silver Creek running beside the orchard. Yet Jack's home, the place of his grandfather and great-grandfather, where he'd lived all his life, felt unfamiliar.

Down the row LeeAnn picked apples from her trees. She worked harder than she needed to with those organic sprays and sticky traps and whatnot. Just a short time ago they'd helped each other get from one day to the next. Starting again each morning had made sense. But that was before she'd left him two weeks ago. Now when he went into the house alone each night, the long hours seemed pointless.

Reaching for the fruit with practiced hands, chapped and stiff with cold, the wind in the forecast prodded Jack to work even faster. He couldn't sell apples that fell to the ground.

When he looked over at his wife again, the sunlight streamed through her dark hair, bringing out a deep auburn hue he'd seen only in this kind of late day fall light.

He couldn't take it another second and abandoned his tree. He walked toward her down the grassy strip between the rows of apples and waited below, unnoticed, as she stood on her tiptoes to pluck from the highest arching branches. The ladder, situated on soft ground, shifted slightly. His reflexes put him instantly in position to catch her when she fell.

She screamed in surprise. And then in his arms her face reddened—whether from anger or embarrassment, he didn't know. What he did know was, with her so close, pressed against him, smelling of apples and hard work, he didn't want to let go, even though he already had.

"Put me down," she said stiffly.

He looked into her eyes, that striking shade of violet, and stalled for only a moment before placing her on her feet.

LeeAnn picked up a shovel and held it between them a moment before unloading mulch from a wagon, shoveling it around the base of the tree as though nothing had passed between them. Maybe for her, nothing had.

Reaching into his coat pocket, he produced five small apples. "These are for Itch." Their cat, which had gone with her, liked to play fetch with the little fruit.

"Thanks." She quickly tucked them into her pocket and continued shoveling.

He bent and picked up a branch broken by LeeAnn's fall. It looked surprisingly healthy, still holding onto the last of the season's fruit, although her apples were smaller and more blemished than his.

"You still using that organic spray with clay?"

"Yep." She straightened and faced him, wiping the sweat from her face with her sleeve. "You're welcome to try it if you want. I think I've finally got the timing down."

"I'll go by my own methods. I know what works."

"Suit yourself." LeeAnn brushed off her hands on her pants. "I'm glad you're here because I want to talk to you about something."

"Oh?" Hope welled in his chest.

"I'm thinking about expanding my organic operation."

"You've already got three acres," he said.

"And you've got fifty."

She knew as well as he did how much they'd given up for these trees. All those hours over so many years. They'd put too much thought and energy into the orchard to change things now. "Those fifty are yours, too. I'm taking care of them like we always have."

"I want to use my techniques on more acreage," she said. "I thought I could start with the trees closest to these three acres and then expand. We should really come up with a five-year plan."

"For my family's land?"

LeeAnn looked at him hard. "As you said, it's my property, too. And I don't want to work at the diner forever. This is what I love to do."

It was easy to be optimistic now about next year's harvest, with the trees full of promise and this year's apples filling the barn. Soon enough the trees would be bare-branched with next year's buds folded tight to the twig, protected against the cold of winter. But so much could go wrong come spring. The chances of a good year were already low enough. The last thing they needed was a gamble.

"You're asking me to give up trees that make money for something untried. We can't afford to experiment. These three acres you're playing with are already a risk."

"It's about more than money, Jack. My way of growing apples is honest. Like nature intended. And if you want to focus on the money, you'll remember my fruit paid off last year."

"Just barely. What about all you lost to codling moth?"

She picked up her shovel and began moving mulch again. "I learned in the process. I'm only asking for a small expansion."

"You want to take good acreage out of regular production to try new ways when the old ones work just fine."

"It's our acreage, together."

"I don't know, LeeAnn." Jack dropped the branch.

She stopped shoveling and met his eye. "It's been your way all these years. Isn't it time for something different?"

"I'll think about it." Jack turned and headed back to his trees.

From his ladder he stuffed his sack full and emptied it again and again into a large cart, working fast. When the cart was full, he walked to the barn down the rows of fruit trees casting late day shadows over the ground.

Lack of sleep and double-time work had caught up with him. He'd been trying to fill in for what LeeAnn had always done in addition to his jobs, picking and selling apples by day and packing the fruit while running the cider press way past dark. All his life, work made Jack put one foot in front of the other, even when his dad died and Wade left in the same twelve hours. Focus got him through.

In the barn, Jack climbed onto the mud-crusted tractor and drove it to the orchard to retrieve the full apple cart. He pulled out a slim notebook from his back pocket to update his picking estimate for the day. In search of a clean page, he flipped past notes of apples picked, sold, planted, grafted, equipment repairs, bloom times, spray times, and harvest dates.

January 17—A foot of snow last night. Shoveled walks. Repaired tractor. Tried to talk to LeeAnn about plans for putting in new trees in the spring, but she's distracted. Always distracted.

February 23—Bitter cold. No snow. Just gray. Ordered seedlings. Figured budget for next year. Winter's too long, too hard. Not getting anywhere.

April 14—Chilly mornings. Starting to warm up during the day. Hard to plan when LeeAnn won't talk business.

September 30—Hot and sticky. Apples on target. She's thinking of going.

The care of the apples and disintegration of their marriage, right on the same page. Fate had played its hand.

As Jack reached the barn his cell rang. LeeAnn didn't sound angry anymore. "I'm headed out," she said, "but I want to talk again before too long. We need to figure out how to move forward."

"I could make dinner. We could talk more about what you want for the orchard." Maybe he could still somehow make it up to her. All those years of trying to have a baby while their marriage unraveled. He hadn't needed a doctor to tell him it was his fault.

"I can't stay, Jack."

A short while later he heard the crunch of tires on the drive and assumed she was leaving, again.

But then a man's voice called his name.

He stepped into the doorway of the apple barn. Everything stopped.

A brand new black pickup was parked between LeeAnn's red Chevy and Jack's old beater. A man stood beside it, with his hand raised in greeting, but he said nothing more. Coming from the bright light of the barn into the dusk prevented Jack from making out the man's face.

Jack stared in his direction. Some tug of memory caused him to hesitate. There was something familiar about the slight curl in his shoulders.

LeeAnn emerged from the edge of the orchard and the man turned at the sound of her boots on the gravel drive.

"LeeAnn?" the man said.

She stopped. Her mouth opened and closed. "Wade Pierson?" She hesitated a moment more and then walked slowly toward him. "Is it really you?"

There, right in front of him, was his brother. Wade. Back after twenty years.

He was still alive, at least. Wade's arms encircled LeeAnn. Jack clenched his fists and went back into the barn. He offloaded the fruit from the wagon, bruising most of it. He washed apples with shaky hands and then crushed them for the cider press. LeeAnn and Wade came through the doorway.

"Jack, look who's here."

Jack glanced up and then couldn't take his eyes from his brother's face for a long moment. He wasn't a sixteen-year-old kid anymore. He'd grown taller than Jack and filled out. Damn if he didn't look even more like their dad now, with that same dark red hair and fair skin. That curl of the shoulder used to give Wade the look of someone unsure of whether he belonged.

But now Wade stood there smiling, like he would be welcome. Like he could just show up after all this time with as much warning as he gave on the night he left. His clothes were not the kind worn by men who worked with their hands. His face was unmarked by the lines that years spent outdoors etched into a person.

LeeAnn smiled up at Wade as though trying to reassure him.

Jack stood, out of duty, and wiped his hands on his pants. He walked toward his brother and offered his hand.

Wade took it but not before eyeing the dirt and apple bits Jack had not quite wiped away. "Welcome back," Jack said, unsure of what to say next. Wade had never even sent so much as a Christmas card.

"It's good to be back," Wade said, checking Jack over. "Geez, what happened to your eye?"

Jack looked away. "It's nothin," he muttered.

"Working hard, I see."

"Especially this time of year," Jack said, returning to the apple press. "But you probably don't remember much about harvest time." Jack fed in one apple after another. He could not stop.

From the doorway, LeeAnn looked back at Jack with even more distance. Probably pissed that he couldn't stop working, not even for this.

"I've gotten a job here in town," Wade said. "I'll be staying awhile."

"That's good news," LeeAnn said.

Jack's hands stilled. Long-capped anger roiled in the pit of his stomach. He'd worked his whole life to keep this orchard from going to the bank, while Wade had run away to do who knew what.

LeeAnn hung her hand on Wade's shoulder, the same way she had when they'd been a couple before Wade left.

Jack began to feed the press more pulp, which squeezed into a bucket on the other side. The walls of the apple barn seemed to close in on him. "What job?"

"I'm working for Green Energy. I'll be offering money for land leases, for natural-gas drilling."

"Oh?" Gas prices were high now that the pipeline network was complete. People had been waiting a long time for natural gas drilling to finally come to eastern Pennsylvania and they would be eager to do business, but not with someone they didn't trust.

Jack picked up another apple, gripping it so hard he dented the flesh under the skin. "LeeAnn, you think we should lease the orchard? You'd be able to expand your operation like you want. And Wade could get something out of this place once and for all."

"Why are you being like this, Jack?" Her voice was sharp with warning and all-too-familiar disappointment.

He knew he was being an ass but couldn't stop. Everything felt mixed up. He'd wanted his brother to come back for so many years. But he hadn't. Now LeeAnn was gone, too.

She turned to Wade. "Sorry, it's not the best time."

She sounded as if she'd already chosen sides.

Or . . . what if she was thinking the thing that had just occurred to him: leasing might be a way to get money for the in vitro procedure she'd wanted?

Jack stood, hands on his hips. "I do want to talk more," he said. But later, after he'd had time to think. "After the worst of the harvest is over."

"Sure . . . I understand," Wade said. "Listen, I'm sorry I haven't been in touch."

Jack didn't reply.

"When you have time, I owe you an explanation."

Jack shrugged.

"I'll leave this for now." Wade pulled a card from his wallet. He walked over to Jack and laid it beside Jack's hand. "I'm staying at the Red Leaf if you want to reach me."

LeeAnn glanced at the clock hanging above his head. "I need to run to the store before it gets late."

The sound of two car engines faded, draining Jack's gumption for work. He left the press full of pulp. It would be ruined. He'd have to dump it in the morning. For once he didn't care.

Wade's card fell to the floor. Jack picked it up and looked at it: WADE PIERSON, LANDMAN, GREEN ENERGY. He'd written in his phone number at the bottom.

Landman. What did Wade know about land? He'd left Jack holding everything: grief, an orchard on the verge of bankruptcy, an empty bank account. And he'd chosen now to show up, when Jack's relationship with LeeAnn was at its weakest.

Jack was past exhaustion but rest was not an option. Not with the coil so tightly turned in his body. The caged thing living inside him scratched. It was Thursday and it wanted out.

Not bothering to change clothes, he climbed into his pickup and drove to the barn he'd visited every Thursday over the last eight years. When things between him and LeeAnn had started to go bad.

Standing outside the barn that housed the fistfights, he felt a calming in his soul even as his body anticipated pain.

The barn sat at the end of a long lane. Gray, weathered wood lit by a single pole light. Only the cars parked in the grass on Thursdays differentiated it from any other barn. Inside the smells were not of hay and animals, but the stink of sweat and adrenaline, stale beer and cheap perfume. Two spotlights illuminated the ring, which was bordered by a rectangle of straw bales and surrounded by metal folding chairs five deep.

The crowd included a few girlfriends, but mostly men coming to watch and bet on what they were too afraid to try themselves. Jack didn't know or care why the other fighters came. Fate brought him to this barn to fight.

Some sat and others stood, money and beer cans in hand. Two young kids were at it in the ring. Both fighters were so intent on not getting hurt that they took more of a beating than necessary. The blonder one favored his right side, probably because of a previous punch to the ribs. Another left jab would finish him. And the darker-haired boy couldn't see well out of his right eye, making him wide open on that side. These two were here for the money, paid to fight by the guy who owned the barn.

But Jack wasn't there for cash.

Rage sheltered in him, like it did in anyone. Except his had been drawn to the surface by love held out of reach.

He looked for the John Deere hat and headed toward

Bob, the man who owned the barn, ran the fights, and, judging by his belly, drank most of the beer. Jack told Bob who he wanted to fight. Bob would do what he said. Jack was the reason people came. All eyes were on him now, sizing him up. People counted on him. Bet on Jack, they said, and you're gonna win.

Last time, when he'd sensed that LeeAnn would leave him, he'd wanted the beating. At his request he'd been paired with a newcomer, a man with cold, dark eyes and JESUS tattooed across the fingers of his right hand. The man outweighed him by seventy-five pounds. Jack had defended himself enough to stay alive. Every punch he took had a kind of sweetness, the physical pain blocking the deeper ache that threatened to bury him. Everyone betting on Jack lost that night but he could have told them that ahead of time.

Tonight the same man stood across the room. Jack nodded; the man stared back with a leer. Jack stripped off his shirt and waited, bare-chested and bare-fisted.

CHAPTER 2

Wade

WADE STOOD IN the heart of the Tic-Toc diner feeling like a preacher at a tent meeting surrounded by weathered faces tipped his way.

"They'll start by sending out a geologist who'll do some tests," he said. "If they decide to drill, they'll prepare the site and bring in the rig. That's the noisy, messy part. Then it quiets down and your property returns to normal." He took a sip of water and cleared his throat. "And a lot of times they don't drill from your property at all, just underneath it—come in horizontally. If gas prices drop, nothing will likely happen until the market comes back. Heck, a lot of times they never drill. Green Energy is paying for the option."

Small landowners were there. Most of the families, many of whom Wade had known growing up, needed the money. Since he'd arrived a week ago he'd heard one story after another about unemployment and dwindling relief benefits.

So far Wade had secured five leases during one-on-one

meetings with people needing to earn fast. He'd taken some clues from a list of names taped to the cash register in the diner, with the word TAB across the top. He'd started with people he didn't know from before, to avoid having to talk about the past.

This job offered him a position in this community, a chance to help make it better and make up for his sins. If he could help folks in need, they would return the favor by letting him build community trust. He hoped he might have just enough goodwill now to make deals with some people he *did* know standing before him. Because he would also eventually have to go after the bigger pieces of property that Green Energy wanted, including Elzer's land and the orchard.

"But what are the risks?" LeeAnn asked.

She'd kept her distance all morning but now stood close by with a coffee pot in hand. Wisps of dark hair curled around her face, framing violet-blue eyes that, Wade thought, reflected the person you wished you were. Just as he remembered from back when they were younger. God, he still couldn't think of her as Jack's wife. He'd wanted her to be closer all morning. Even now in the diner with all these people, in her presence, he felt like he could be freed from the past. She'd been the one to welcome him back, even if Jack hadn't been able to. At least she didn't seem to hold onto what had happened—not the bad parts, anyway. With her he'd felt nothing of his brother's unspoken accusations and questions.

"Seems like we'll have enough money to fix anything that might go wrong," Reverend Joe said from over her shoulder.

LeeAnn turned toward the reverend. "Some changes can't be fixed."

So far, only LeeAnn seemed undecided about the benefits of gas leasing, and Wade wanted to convince her more than anybody. The history they'd shared had been short, but it shaped both their lives. It seemed only right they be on the same side.

Doc Black, at his usual place at the counter, handed a Sudoku puzzle to Stu and spoke up. "This gas drilling is more than about what may or may not be good for this town. It helps us get off foreign oil. This is an opportunity to help our country."

"And no one can argue with that. Except LeeAnn." Stu winked at her before filling in the rest of the Sudoku puzzle that had stumped Doc.

Wade put his hands on his knees and leaned forward. "I know many of you have been waiting for the opportunity to lease your land for a long time." He looked up at LeeAnn. "But the advantage of having to wait is that drilling is safer now. There've been accidents in the past, but we've learned from them and the chance of those being repeated is small. The process is better than ever."

Some people nodded in his direction, but not LeeAnn.

"Makes sense," she said. "But no one's asking how Minden will change because of the drilling. There'll be more money and I know that seems good, but what comes along with it that we haven't thought about?"

"Elzer better watch out – sounds like LeeAnn's ready to run for mayor," Franny said, from behind the counter.

"I just know nothing's easy. Not even this."

"But," Reverend Joe said, "for the first time in years we can plan for a future instead of slowly fading. And think how much a little extra money could help families in need. Like your folks, LeeAnn."

LeeAnn's look told Wade she wasn't entirely convinced. He clapped his hands. "That's right, Reverend," he said. "We can make this a win-win. Anybody who wants to sign on now, take a number." He offered a stack of cards numbered one through thirty he'd cut and labeled that morning. "That way you can sit and enjoy your breakfast or coffee while I work through the line. If you can't stay, sign this paper and I'll be out to see you over the next couple days."

Two lines formed. Eighteen people took a number, and a few more than that signed up for a later visit.

Wade felt a rush of excitement. He could provide something desperately needed. If ever a town begged for change, it was Minden. Gun raffles, Friday night football, and monthly fire hall breakfasts still provided the only entertainment. The place had been gathering dust since the coal days. Steady work was a good thirty-minute drive. Same with any kind of grocery or drug store. In his room at the Red Leaf he'd been able to stock only milk, bread, and pudding from the Stop-N-Go at the edge of town. Luckily the Red Leaf's bar offered a steady supply of bottled beer.

With only a short time in Minden, he needed to make it count. After that, Green Energy would send him off to new territory. Elzer, Minden's mayor and lawyer, still owned a good chunk of land around town. Maybe, if Wade could get Elzer's property and the family orchard, Green Energy would be happy. Maybe he could even talk them into letting him work from Minden as a home base.

Doc Black was the first one to sit across from Wade. He wouldn't be like the others Wade had already signed who couldn't turn down fast money. Doc would make a choice. He had that face Wade often confronted as a salesman, resigned to the conversation required to get the desired information. Despite his words of support about foreign oil, Doc wasn't going to be talked into anything.

"Stu always finish your Sudokus?"

Doc pushed up the sleeves of his flannel shirt and shrugged. "The man is aggressively logical. It's that mechanic's mind of his. I used to study strategies trying to get a leg up, but it never helped much. I get those black-belt puzzles and, at this point, I just try to find ones I think he won't be able to solve. That's what the game's become for me. But it hasn't happened yet. And we've been at this for ten years."

Wade started most deals on the outside, at odds with the potential customer. Comfortable territory for him. People took note of his ease and usually let down their guard. A sale was based on a good feeling between him and the potential buyer more than anything. Building that connection was the key.

"How long you been in Minden now?"

"Twelve years or so. The wife and I have twenty acres at the foot of the mountain."

"East or west of town?"

"Couple miles west."

"The place with the round barn?"

Doc nodded.

Wade hadn't missed the topic of conversation between Stu and Doc at the counter over the last week. "There used to be a good fishing hole right around back."

Doc smiled, looking him in the eye for the first time. "Still is."

"Bass as big as my forearm swam that hole when Elzer's dad still owned the place," Wade said.

"And the fish have only gotten bigger," Doc said, "since you've been gone."

"You don't say," Wade leaned back in his chair, crossing his arms and forcing a smile.

Doc cleared his throat, ready to get down to business, since it was clear, Wade guessed, that he wasn't going to say more about why he'd been gone.

"How much do you think my twenty acres is worth?"

The sweet part was watching the change come over people: suspicious to cautious to interested, and then, most times, grateful for the opportunity to accept what he offered. Wade told Doc how much he could make. He could retire early and spend more time fishing if he wanted. Doc didn't sign right then, but he would. He took Wade's card and a few extra to display in his office.

Next, Stu sat down. They'd been friends in high school. He was still a wiry guy, mostly unchanged except for the age in his face. Wade's hands shook with nerves and he put them into his lap. Stu had always been a good guy. Not one to throw things in your face.

"I sure was surprised to hear you were back in town."

"It's good to see you," Wade said, offering a hand that he did his best to steady. "How you been, Stu?"

"Real good. Thanks. I married Franny over there." He pointed to the blonde behind the counter. "We've got three kids now."

"And you're still fishing."

"That's right. Sometimes Jack comes along. You've been out to see him, I guess . . ."

"First place I went when I got to Minden."

"He's wondered over the years about what you've been up to."

"I should have been in touch. I know it. I'm gonna explain things when Jack's ready to talk."

Stu nodded and seemed to accept this as explanation enough. They moved on to discuss the ten acres he owned with his brother. Stu wanted to sign, anxious to buy a house for the family, but his brother wanted to hold out for more money. Wade agreed to sit down with both of them the next day.

Two hours later Franny brought Wade a sandwich while he talked with Reverend Joe, who'd waited patiently for everyone else to have their say.

"We've been trying to sell off some of it for over a year now," the reverend said of the church's thirty acres. "Funds are low. People can't afford to give much. The church roof is leaking and we need a new furnace. Would Green Energy have any use for the property?"

"I can mention it to them." Wade said, glancing up to find LeeAnn at the end of her shift, going out the door.

"Pardon me, Reverend, I've got to take care of something. I'll come see you about the church's property once I talk with the boss." He stood up, leaving his sandwich untouched.

"I hope we'll see you in church now that you're back."

Wade put his coat on. "I haven't been in a while. But maybe." He put some bills on the table and stuffed his pocket with the list of potential leases. Outside the diner he caught a glimpse of LeeAnn right before she turned the corner. He followed. As he passed by the back of the diner he saw her again to his left, going up a flight of steps and then through a doorway.

Long ago that door led to an apartment. Was that where she lived, instead of the orchard? She'd left the orchard the same time he had the other night, saying something about grocery shopping. But maybe that had just been a cover for where she was really headed.

Maybe she and Jack weren't together anymore?

He stopped at the base of her stairs, thinking about what he might say to allay her fears about the drilling. Whatever the situation with Jack, the decision to lease the orchard would have to be mutual. And why wouldn't they want to make some real money from the place?

The thought of having to talk to Jack and her about plans for the orchard made him risk a look at Morrigan Mountain, which stood just to the north. About three quarters of the way up, Table Rock loomed, marking the place where it had happened. The place where his life had fallen apart. He wasn't going to be able to continue to work in Minden much longer until he faced the moment he'd accidently shot his father.

He needed to go up there. Maybe LeeAnn would agree to go with him. He sure couldn't ask Jack.

He knocked softly.

She looked surprised and maybe a little uncomfortable to see him on her doorstep. He didn't miss the packing boxes lining the kitchen wall behind her.

Hearing a meow, he looked down at a white cat swirling around LeeAnn's ankles. She bent down and picked up the cat, cradling him.

"This is Itch."

The cat had no eyes, only lids shut over empty sockets. "How does it survive like that?" Wade asked, trying not to appear as repelled as he felt.

"Born this way. He senses more than you might imagine. Watch this."

She let her hand hover above the cat's left ear, until he extended his head. "Somehow he knows my hand is there."

Wade reached out to pet the cat since that's what LeeAnn seemed to want. "I hope you don't mind me stopping by here without an invitation. I . . . I need to drive along the ridge to the gap. Wondered if you would ride along?"

She put Itch gently on the ground and nudged him back inside the door. "I'm not sure that's such a good idea."

He swallowed. "The truth is I can barely even look in that direction." He stared at the ground and then found the courage to meet her eyes. "I don't want to go alone."

She drummed her fingers on the doorframe, considering him. "I'll get my coat."

"Wade! Watch out!"

Driving north up the mountain, he swerved out of the way of an oncoming logging truck driving too close to the middle. Wade held tight to his side of the road and they passed each other with only inches to spare.

"Lousy out-of-town drivers," LeeAnn said, shaking her head.

If she were not with him, he would have turned around right then. Instead he drove on and, at the top of the mountain, turned left onto old Ridge Road. His hands gripped the steering wheel. He stared straight ahead, still rattled.

"Are you sure you're ready to do this?"

Wade saw the orchard in the valley below.

"In two weeks, I'll be my Dad's age when he died."

"Is that why you came back here now?"

He ran his hand through his hair.

"There's a pressure inside me that keeps getting stronger. Anxiety, I suppose. This job might be a way back to a more normal feeling. That's what I want to happen, anyway."

Since he'd been gone, he'd spent his time trying to become someone else. Running away from a single gunshot.

He'd made a habit of talking to people and reading everything he could find. No sales training could be better than knowing how to chat it up with anyone from redneck to CEO. Listening was key. Finding out what mattered to someone and starting with that.

Now he had his chance to make a life that mattered. He could finally prove himself. Soon other gas companies would arrive in town and he didn't want to give up his opportunity to make a difference.

Wade peered through the leafless branches, down into the valley squared off in shorn corn and soybean fields, clouded by wood smoke. He rolled down the window, gulping at the fresh air.

"You all right?" LeeAnn asked.

He nodded. Beads of sweat tickled his back uncomfortably. LeeAnn shivered in the autumn chill, but he didn't roll up his window. He couldn't.

He parked at the top of the gap beside a small feeder stream that flowed down the mountain, but he didn't let go of the wheel. "Damn, I'm a wreck," he said, trying to smile. "I should have come here alone. Sorry."

She squeezed his arm and he wished she wouldn't let go.

"Maybe this is far enough for today."

He looked out at the bruised sky, interrupted by the yellow and brown in the trees, just like that day. Even the same smell of decaying leaves. It was almost the anniversary now, with a few days until hunting season. He opened the door and stepped out of the truck. "Let's go."

They set off down the gap. A thin layer of ice coated the rocky slope and Wade lost his footing several times. He'd always climbed up to Table Rock from the orchard during hunting season; he'd never come down to it from the ridge. This felt wrong, as though he were sneaking up from behind instead of approaching head-on like a man.

They walked down along the little feeder stream overgrown with hemlock and rhododendron. If they chose to follow the rivulet all the way down, they would come to Silver Creek at the edge of the orchard. It sat catty-corner from LeeAnn's parents, the Moore place, along the base of the mountain.

A raven flew over, its lonely croaking call invoking the desolation that had never left him. A raven that day long ago had soared overhead as a witness to a spot of orange collapsed in grief in the brush.

Wade stopped walking. There'd been no one to talk to then or after. No one to teach him how to forgive himself, the sixteen-year-old boy whose bullet had taken his dad's life. That hunting accident had been like an earthquake in the lives of all who'd been there, ripping them apart. It was as if he'd just squeezed the trigger.

"Wade?" LeeAnn said, from somewhere in front of him.

He felt the recoil and smelled the smoke. He clutched at his chest, remembering his dad's head flopping crookedly when Jack picked him up and walked him down the mountain, LeeAnn beside him.

LeeAnn spoke again. He nodded, not really hearing.

She took his hand like he'd needed someone to do so long ago. "I'm here, Wade."

He sucked in a deep breath as if he'd been too long under water. His head cleared.

"I think we should turn back," she said.

"I need to do this."

It was now or never. He set off again down the mountain, checking over his shoulder to see that she was close behind. When they came to Table Rock, LeeAnn climbed on top and extended a hand. They stood beside one another looking down over the place where his dad, Jack, and LeeAnn had been standing. As if the memories triggered by the raven had flown off with the bird, it was not the reckoning he'd expected.

LeeAnn sat down on the rock and he beside her.

In the valley below smoke drifted from their chimney. Jack's chimney.

"Beautiful, isn't it?" LeeAnn said.

He gazed down at the trees in the orchard, but he couldn't see beauty.

"Sometimes I think about what this rock has seen," she said.

"What do you mean?" Wade tensed for the accusation he both expected and dreaded.

"It's here. Always the same. People come and go, but it watches and keeps on, like the rest of the land. I always thought about myself that way, like that kind of constant. But maybe I'm not." She gave him a sad smile.

"How long have you and Jack been separated?" he said.

"Just."

"But you're still working the orchard?"

"I care for my trees a few times a week. My experimental plot, Jack likes to call it. I don't use chemical spray. He thinks it's a waste of time. But I love the work of growing fruit naturally. I know it probably sounds corny, but it makes me happy to be able to nurture something simply that brings people nourishment and enjoyment. In the summer I make jam from a big strawberry patch I planted for extra money. People start placing orders months ahead of time. Every time I hand someone a new jar I always hold it up to the sun to show how the light comes through, like a red jewel."

Listening to her soothed him. Things with her were simple and pure. He could almost forget.

"How's Jack doing? He didn't seem too happy to see me the other night. Understandably, I guess."

"Works too hard. It's his way. After your dad died, he nearly worked himself to death."

"I suppose you came over to help him out, back then," he said, trying to imagine the time when his brother had replaced him in her heart.

"Someone had to. Mom and Dad helped. That's what I love about Minden—people stick together."

Was that blame or hometown love in her voice?

"He's put his whole life into saving that orchard," she said. "Caring for the place is his way of holding on to family."

"What family?" Wade asked, too quickly. He took a breath trying to calm himself. "Stella made us feel like we didn't matter by leaving and then never coming back. Dad was no picnic. And the rest of them were all dead by the time Jack and I were about nine or ten."

LeeAnn didn't reply. When he glanced at her, she wiped her eyes.

"There were people here for you, Wade."

But not the one he'd needed. Stella had not come, despite the fact that he'd called her and asked. Dad was right to exclude her from his definition of family, even if she was their mother. Instead Dad had tried to make every square foot of the orchard valuable by connecting it to some family story. Meanwhile, he never had so much as the time of day for his own sons. The rift between Wade and his dad could be crossed only during hunting season. Yet here, in this place, he felt awful thinking ill of the man. "I'm sorry. You were telling me how Jack managed."

"Jack wants to hold on to where he came from," LeeAnn said. "After the accident he started keeping these notebooks. He had to learn so much and seeing his days written down helped. You know he's not a big talker. Words on paper are easy for him, though. He likes to read about where he's been. It's his way of trying to work out life, I guess. He still keeps notebooks."

She turned to him. "And now, in the last few minutes, we've said more about what that day meant to us than Jack did with me in twenty years."

Like their father, Jack could be stubborn. If his reaction to seeing Wade back at the orchard was any measure, Jack had grown into a version of their father, angry and resentful. Getting him to say yes to a lease would be difficult, even if LeeAnn agreed.

A shadow passed over them. The raven again.

"How are you feeling, being back here?" she asked.

"What I want now is to get some peace. I'm hoping it works out."

"What have you been doing all these years?"

"This and that." Nothing had ever held him. Not yet. "I've always been good at sales. I'm excited about how this new job of mine might let me help Minden."

She turned to him. "I have to be honest. I'm not sure what I think of the drilling."

"What are you worried about?"

"My home, my community. I'm worried about what might go wrong."

"But drilling brings opportunity for the people here."

"I know. And change can be good. It's how I see the orchard. We have to change how we do things if the place is going to be successful over the long run. But, still . . ."

"If I can help people here get a better life, maybe over time they'll forget what happened all those years ago."

"They don't blame you."

He watched the clouds chug past overhead. So heavy, but no rain so far. LeeAnn had believed in him once. His happiest days had been with her. Maybe it was still possible to get back to feeling like that again. She'd always been his promise of something better, before the worst had happened. He turned to her. "I never stopped thinking about you."

She gave him a weary smile, shifting her gaze to the orchard.

CHAPTER 3

Jack

November 9. Picking the last of the apples. Dreading the winter break. Cherry picker needs a new hydraulic line. At least that's something I can fix.

TWIST AND LIFT, twist and lift. These were the words Jack spoke over and over again to the workers who'd come to help during the harvest. Keep the stem on the apple, he'd tell them, so they last. Twist and lift. Stems needed to be pulled, not snapped. They must be handled gently. Each little cluster of leaves on the tree contained the bud for next year's fruit, so if too many twigs broke, fruit spurs would be lost. One picker who didn't know these simple rules could damage the apples and the tree, and he could afford neither.

Before she'd moved to town, LeeAnn had trained the workers. She had a way of making everyone feel a part of the operation. They wanted to work well, for her. Jack didn't have her touch and it showed in how they treated the trees this season, no matter what he said. And what could he expect? Even he couldn't seem to pick a tree clean without bruising the fruit.

Jack climbed down the ladder and took a bite from a small apple in his sack, seeking the balance of sweet and tart that the Piersons had cultivated over generations. All these years, he and LeeAnn had been part of that balance, pushing through the harvest by leaning on each other. They were a perfect complement: she handled the crowds, drafting cider and ringing up sales all at once; he maintained a singular focus on the harvest, seeing it through no matter what. Year after year the flow of their work followed the trees. Pale pink blossoms in the spring followed by the swell of the fruit, and then pruning for next year's crop. Always knowing they'd see it through together.

Jack spit out the apple. These days, everything tasted bitter.

He worked the rest of the day without stopping for lunch. Dinner was a can of soup he didn't bother to warm.

Afterward, he headed toward Silver Creek to get away from his empty house. The full moon lit the sycamore trees a ghostly white. He crossed the creek over to Stella's property using a few stones jutting out of the water.

Out of the corner of his eye he saw a dark form move past behind him. He turned, but the branches of a tree swaying in the breeze left behind a familiar vague disappointment.

While he'd never seen one for sure, ghosts roamed the orchard. Maybe it was his great grandfather who'd planted the first apple tree, or his grandfather who'd expanded the operation, checking on the progress of the work they'd started. Or his dad, who probably thought Jack wasn't upholding the Pierson reputation. Nothing had ever been good enough for that man. But still, Jack wanted to know what his father would think of the place now. Even he would have to admit it had prospered over the last twenty years.

He stood on the water's edge, looking back toward his house. The warm glow of the windows should have been inviting, but he could hardly stand being inside anymore.

He rested his back against the trunk of the large sycamore on Stella's side of the creek. Reaching up the trunk, he slid his fingers along the curling bark until they ran across the carving. Migrating over more than thirty-five years, what Stella had once carved low to the ground was now almost out of reach. Her message, Mom Loves You, had widened with the growth of the tree like the big X Wade had made through it. His last act before leaving Minden had ruined the only message they had from their mother. Jack had tried retracing her words with a knife, but the slash through them couldn't be fixed.

Opening his wallet, he pulled out a black-and-white photo he'd taped together after Wade had ripped it in two before he'd left town. In the photo he and Wade appeared happy to be next to each other on their mother's lap. Wade looked up at Stella with obvious love. The picture was taken just before she walked out.

Jack sank now to the ground with his back at the base of the tree, angling his body and head as she had in the photo. What had she been staring at?

He turned and looked at the marks on the tree. His brother had always defended Stella to their dad and believed she would come back. But the deep X in the tree said everything about how he felt when she hadn't. And that had been Jack's fault.

He'd made a promise to himself, should Wade ever return. Now he had to keep it.

The next morning Jack parked his truck at the Feed and Seed, avoiding the diner, and walked down Main Street. It had changed little over the course of his life. Built mostly by Welsh ancestors, who'd seen Minden's potential because of its similarity to the landscape back home, they'd already known how to unearth its coal. Coal had given people a reason to settle. The valley carved by Silver Creek made a fertile place for early farms once the trees were cleared. The cut-stone façade on the bank and the library showed the European-inspired architecture paid for by long-ago coal money and left intact through lack of progress. The nostalgic charm didn't register for newcomers who mostly found Minden invisible and beside the point.

And maybe Minden didn't seem like much, but what those passing through didn't see made the place special: the connection between people and the land. A community built on the hardship of mining coal and living with the consequences. Most stayed because of the bond that sacrifice forges not only to place but between people. Jack wondered if the gas drilling would weaken that bond or make it stronger.

Just past Doc Black's practice was Elzer's office. Jack's lawyer looked up from his desk, the smell of wintergreen and old paper thick in the air. The dark wood-paneled room, lit only by Elzer's green desk light, made him wonder, not for the first time, why Elzer didn't put in some overhead lights. But then again, Elzer also preferred things the way they were.

"Jack. What brings you?"

"I need advice."

Elzer motioned to a chair.

Jack sat on its edge, not entirely comfortable in an office even if it was Elzer's. "Wade's back."

"So I heard."

"He'll want to talk to me and LeeAnn about leasing the orchard."

"Probably."

"I figure since he's working for the energy company, we're only going to hear one side of the story."

"It's not my area of expertise, and I'm not in a position to offer legal advice, if that's what you're asking."

"Because you're mayor?"

"Yes," he said.

"Do you know anyone else who could?"

Elzer's chair squeaked as he leaned back. "No one really comes to mind."

"What about Stella Pierson?"

Elzer raised an eyebrow. He straightened a stack of papers lying between them. "You don't want to go there, Jack."

Elzer's opinion normally carried weight, but not on this topic. Jack didn't feel he owed Wade much, but there was this. When it would have mattered a great deal to Wade, Jack had kept Stella from coming to Minden. Now Wade had returned and it was time to make up for that.

"She's an environmental lawyer, as I understand it," Jack said. "Bringing her here could help people figure out what to do with their property. You just said you can't give legal advice."

"She's going to stir up trouble. The past tells the future," Elzer said, crossing his arms. "I was around when she left you boys. What good would come of bringing her here?"

Jack took off his ball cap and held it in his hands. "I want to tell you something, Elzer. Something I never told anyone."

Elzer leaned forward. "All right."

"The night after the hunting accident, me and Wade stayed at the Moore house."

Elzer nodded.

"I heard Wade on the phone in the kitchen. He'd called Stella to ask her if she'd come."

Elzer rested his chin in his hands. "Why would he have done that?"

"You know how Wade and Dad were always at odds. So he figured that Dad drove her away. And he believed she'd come back for us if we ever really needed her."

"And what did she say?"

"She told him she would. But only after a long drawn-out conversation that had Wade so upset, Gabriel and Rose pulled him away from the phone and put him back in bed.

I was there in the kitchen at the time and picked up the receiver he'd left dangling."

"And?"

"I saw how hard she made that call for him. How long it took him to convince her to make that simple two-hour drive. I didn't want her here. I didn't see her as the savior Wade did. I thought she'd make things worse. So I picked up the phone and told her Wade had changed his mind and she shouldn't come to Minden."

"I see."

"Wade left the next morning, before I could explain what I'd done. I believe he left because she didn't show."

"You don't know that." Elzer cleared his throat. He pulled out a can of chewing tobacco from his desk drawer. "And so now you want to bring her to town?"

"I know it seems crazy."

"Yep, it does."

"But the time is right. Wade's back. Drilling's about to start—and Stella might have information this community needs. It's also a chance to make up for what I did. I don't know how to talk to Wade about it now. But maybe if she were here, too . . . At least I could go see her and talk it over."

Elzer stuffed a large wad of tobacco in his lower lip and considered Jack for a long moment. "She was involved in a case against Green Energy. Did you know?"

Jack shook his head and crossed his arms. "That's what I'm talking about. Information we need to know."

"Green Energy is a huge company. They go to court just like any corporation their size and less often than most."

"What was the case about?"

Elzer let out a long breath. "Polluted water. I don't know much beyond that."

"I'm going to go see her to find out more."

"I still don't think it's a good idea, Jack."

"Maybe not." Jack stood. "But I'm going anyway. It's

something I need to do now that Wade's back. Over the last few days I've been thinking about it. She's held onto her land all these years next to the orchard. That's got to mean something."

"Wade doesn't want her here in Minden. Not with what he's trying to do. She'll be against the drilling."

"Maybe. But Wade never got to make amends with Dad. He's had to carry that around. Me, too. It could be different with Stella. That could matter to Wade. It could have made the difference to him all those years ago."

Elzer spit into a cup on his desk. "You should know her name's Brantley now." He turned toward the file cabinets lining one of the office walls, filled with information about Minden's people. "Let me get you her address."

Jack decided not to call Stella first. He spent the two-hour drive to northern Philadelphia with his mind firmly on the orchard. He'd left it in the charge of a new hired man. Jack called him twice from the road with reminders.

When he arrived at the address Elzer had given him, he found a relic stone farmhouse sitting in the middle of suburbia. Jack drove past slowly, studying the house perched along the Delaware River, with the sign Brantley & Brantley out front. He still had half a tank, but headed to the gas station he could see up ahead on the left.

He topped off his tank, then parked his truck under an oak tree at the station. He sat for a long time looking back at the farmhouse. No one came in or out. A white Volvo and red Subaru were parked out front, so he assumed she was there.

He'd been telling himself he could treat this like a client approaching a lawyer—sort of like he talked to Elzer about the orchard. He and Stella didn't even know each other. Not really. This was just business.

Except that it wasn't.

What would he say to her? They weren't even starting off on the common ground that strangers shared. She had a past she'd run from. And he was part of it. By all signs, she didn't want to see him now. Why had this seemed like a good idea?

The wind blew, raising goose bumps on his arms. He rolled up the truck window. The oak tree above him shed so many leaves he had to turn his wipers on to clear them from his windshield.

What was the worst thing that could happen?

She could throw him out of her office. Basically, he'd be in the same place he was now. Except that he would have tried.

If he didn't do this, nothing would change. Not for him. Probably not for Wade. And he'd made that promise to himself.

Jack drove the short distance to the law office and pulled in next to the Volvo. Getting out of his truck he felt stiff, his body rebelling at what he was forcing it to do. Even breathing felt like work.

He knocked on the door, and when no one answered, he went inside and a bell dinged. No receptionist. Instead, a tall, middle-aged man dressed in a coat and tie walked out to greet him.

"Patrick Brantley," the man said. The new husband extended his hand, revealing a braided leather bracelet. "How can I help you?" His grip was warm and firm. Jack liked him instantly and relaxed a little.

"I'm here to see Stella Brantley. She's not expecting me. I hope it's okay." These people were busy. He'd been foolish to think that he could walk in without making an appointment.

"Of course. Follow me," Patrick said, as if drop-ins were a regular occurrence.

He led Jack down a narrow hallway past a tidy office Jack assumed was Patrick's to a door a little farther down.

"Stella? Can you spare a few moments?"

She stood at a filing cabinet with her back to them. Without even looking around she said, "Sure, have a seat."

"Make yourself comfortable," Patrick said, removing a stack of files from the only chair in the room and placing it among the others that checkered the floor.

"I'm sorry, I'm looking for a letter," Stella said, her back still turned. "I shouldn't have put it in here. Once something goes into a drawer, that's it—*pfft!*—gone."

"Take your time," Jack said, grateful for the opportunity to assess this woman in stages. Her dark hair streaked with gray and the lines on the back of her neck suggested both wisdom and vulnerability. She was still relatively slim and dressed like a lawyer who should have never tried a life at the orchard: wool pants, a blouse, and loafers, complemented by simple jewelry. She was a far cry from his childhood memory. She looked capable.

Sliding the file drawer shut, Stella turned toward him.

Jack's stomach tugged. They looked alike with the same olive skin. And the hazel eyes Wade also shared. Fate confirming that he also was never meant to be a parent.

"Now," Stella said, smiling and taking a seat at her desk. "I'm sorry to have kept you waiting. What are you here to see me about?" She took a long sip of her coffee, not yet meeting his eye.

She didn't recognize him, even given the resemblance. He couldn't speak for a moment and cleared his throat to cover his nerves. Grit and adrenaline would get him through this. This moment was just another kind of fight. "My name's Jack. Pierson." He let those words hang in the air between them.

There was a soft intake of breath. She leaned toward him, overturning her coffee cup. Black coffee ran over the side of her desk onto the floor. She didn't seem to notice. "Jack?"

Maybe she did care something about him and Wade. She remembered him at least. But he didn't want to think about that kind of thing now. He had to treat this as business as much as possible if he was going to make this work.

Stella stood. She put out her hand and then shook her head as though deciding that was the wrong thing to do. She went to sit back down and bumped the desk with her leg, sending a stack of files over the edge.

"I'm just going to get the door," she said, limping around the fallen files. She glanced down the hall toward Patrick's office, then pushed the door closed.

Jack bent to gather the fallen files and handed them to her. She picked up her spilled mug and placed the files on the corner of her desk, before mopping up the pool of coffee on the floor. Her hands shook.

"I'm surprised you're here. I'm glad you're here, but it's unexpected. Let me get us some coffee."

Stella moved to a Keurig machine. "Anything in it?"

"Just black."

"Me, too," she said.

They liked their coffee the same. Was she really glad he'd come? She'd closed that door awfully fast.

Stella seemed to collect herself as the machine hissed, but after handing Jack a cup she gripped the handle of hers with a marble fist. "So, what is it you're here to see me about?"

"I'm here for legal advice. About gas drilling."

He thought he saw a look of relief on her face, but he couldn't be sure.

"Elzer told me you've worked on a case against Green Energy."

"Elzer."

Jack noted the familiarity in the way she said his name. "Can you tell me about the case?"

Stella nodded, the furrow in her brow relaxing. She stood and looked out the window toward the river and Jack could see the same curl in her shoulders that Wade had. She turned back toward him. "I worked on it for a year. It ended in a payout and nondisclosure agreement."

"What does that mean?"

"My clients got money but had to agree to keep quiet about what happened to them. They needed the money. I don't blame them for settling with Green Energy. But the details stay hidden. It was a toxic trespass case."

Stella's voice struck a rhythm. She clearly lived and breathed her work. Was she trying to talk above him on purpose? Did she want to make sure he knew she was a smart lawyer? "Toxic trespass?"

"My clients' water was contaminated by gas, but they'd never leased their land. Leaking wells next door were to blame, so I argued the contaminated water from the neighbor's property was a form of dumping. The law says that if dumping occurs, it's considered a form of trespass. I had solid data and experts ready to testify, but in the end my clients wanted the cash."

"Sounds like you weren't happy with the compromise."

"I didn't like falling in line with the nondisclosure agreement. I would rather have brought the case to trial and taken it all the way, no matter how long and hard the road."

Fighting words. And yet she could leave her sons when they were just four and five. Jack sipped his coffee to hide his anger.

She played the game better than he could, keeping the topic safe and far away. "Listen," he said, "drilling is going to start in Minden and we need legal advice. Wade's working for Green Energy buying leases. My wife and I own property we could lease. And the whole community is in need of another opinion besides the energy company's."

"*You're* suggesting I come to Minden?"

"Yes."

"I don't understand."

"People need to know the other considerations besides the money. You can open our eyes."

"Such as the fact that fracking isn't regulated by the Safe Drinking Water Act, and the industry doesn't disclose the chemicals they use. That the process is industrial. That water and land have been contaminated and they will be again. And beyond that, Minden will never be the same."

If Stella agreed to help, it was because her work entitled her to return to Minden, not her sons. That might be best, for now. At least she wasn't planning to resume a role she'd never played.

"Does Wade know you're here?"

"No one does. Except Elzer."

Stella sat back. She started to speak several times but couldn't seem to find the right words. She reached into her purse and pulled something from her wallet. After studying it for a moment she passed it to Jack.

A black and white photo, creased and worn soft. The same one Wade had left behind and Jack now carried in his wallet: Stella with them both, near Silver Creek.

So she did think about them. Jack tried to read the sad eyes of the woman in the photo, looking off into the distance. He suddenly saw the picture differently. He and his brother—their boyish faces so sweet, so trusting—sat on her lap, clinging to her slack arms as if sensing she was about to leave.

Jack handed back the photo, stood and pulled out the bills he'd stuffed into his back pocket before leaving Minden. He laid the crumpled money on Stella's desk. "It's all I have. But the harvest isn't over yet, so I'll get you more as soon as I can."

He met Stella's eye, but could read nothing. Less than fifty dollars lay on the table. "If you're going to say no, do it quick because I'll need to find someone else to give the town legal advice."

Stella, still holding the photo in her hand, handed back the money. Jack put on his coat. He turned to leave, but paused by the door, struck by another picture hanging on the wall. Stella stood with her arm around Patrick next to the Brantley & Brantley sign. She looked right into the camera, her face content. This was not the same woman who stared blankly into the distance in the older photograph.

Whatever had been missing with her sons, she'd found with Patrick.

Jack pulled open the door.

"I'll do it," Stella said.

Jack hesitated and then turned back toward her. "You will?"

"I'll do what I can. I can't take your money, though."

Jack nodded, fear closing his throat. This was what he'd come to do. But it could very well make everything much worse between him and Wade. And between him and LeeAnn.

CHAPTER 4

Stella

JACK WOULD SPEND all his savings to protect the place Stella had abandoned.

The front door chimed as he left the building. Patrick came into her office.

"I know that passion in your eye," he said.

Stella straightened. "You do?"

"And I admire you for it. But no more pro bono work for the time being—we agreed. Our other cases need attention. From the clients who can pay." He nodded toward the stack on her desk that had so recently been scattered on the floor.

"This one's right up my alley, though. It will give me another shot at exposing Green Energy for what they are. He's prepared to give me a retainer, but he doesn't have much. Still, I want to help him."

Patrick was a good man, practical about their workload and bottom line because he had to be. But he wouldn't stand in her way. He gave an exasperated look and then smiled. "It took him a lot to come in here. He was so nervous at the door. I guess another small case can't hurt as long as it doesn't take you away from the work we already have on the books."

He'd always believed in her, even though she deserved less. "I should be able to handle it."

The truth was Jack had already given her a retainer she wasn't yet ready to mention. He believed she might be able to offer something after all these years. It was an invitation when she'd assumed there could never be one.

"Listen, I have to fly out tonight." Patrick leaned against her doorway and crossed his long arms. "Sunrise Solar called. They're acquiring a new panel manufacturer in Spain and need me at a meeting tomorrow morning."

"But you were just there."

"They pay the bills."

She walked to the door and hugged him.

"You okay?" he said. "You look a little peaked."

"I'm fine." She stood on tiptoes and he bent down so she could kiss him on the cheek. "See you when you get back."

When she heard his car leave the drive, Stella looked up a number and dialed.

A man she pictured with a large wad of tobacco in his lower lip answered her call. Her insides were like jelly. She felt like a trespasser.

"Elzer Hawk."

"It's Stella Brantley."

She waited for him to respond and half expected him to hang up, but he said nothing.

"I wondered if I could drive up to talk in person. I . . . I'd like to get a sense of things."

"Jack came to see you, then?"

"Yes."

He let out a sigh. "I hope this isn't a big mistake." He was quiet for a long moment. "We better meet at my house. That far south of town you won't run much chance of seeing anybody who's not ready to see you."

After hanging up, she sat in front of her computer considering her screen saver, the same picture of her and Patrick that hung on the wall. Such a proud moment the day they'd opened the law office, their world full of hope and potential.

She'd left her sons when she hadn't been able to be a good mother. Then she'd found success as a lawyer. Every day she worked hard to make her work count. To prove it had been worth it.

She moved the cursor and the picture disappeared. She typed her sons' names into Google. She found nothing new.

Many times she'd wanted to explain her past to Patrick, but she'd done the unspeakable. She was sure he'd leave if he learned the truth. And the longer she'd gone without telling Patrick about her sons the more impossible it was to bring it up. He also didn't know about the property she owned beside the orchard. She paid taxes every year with money that could have supported their firm. She'd kept these secrets and lived with the shame, as penance. But the secrets took from her marriage. She'd agreed to help Jack because she owed him, yes, but she also owed Patrick. Now she'd be forced to share the truth.

She went to the window in her office. The Delaware River flowed beneath a moon emerging on the horizon. Jack had always been the more self-possessed child, trying back then to take up her considerable slack.

Silver Creek wound through Minden to feed the Delaware. Springs on her property were the source of some of the water that now flowed past. Its surface reflected bits of moonlight in the otherwise inky darkness. The reflections were spotty, as though the river were fading, giving her the feeling that time was running out. And that Jack probably offered a last chance to come clean.

CHAPTER 5

LeeAnn

THE STARS WERE still visible in the dawn sky when LeeAnn left her apartment to visit her parents for the first time since leaving Jack.

The morning was cold, even for November, and she said a small prayer before turning the key. Her temperamental car grumbled more and more lately. The engine choked despite the prayer. She tried again and after a promising rev, it quit.

The last time Jack tinkered with her car, neither one of them realized she'd use it to drive out of his life. Couldn't he see how much she'd rather have stayed? But he'd watched her pack from the kitchen table, his breakfast sitting untouched, and then gone out to the apple trees. Instead of asking her to stay, he'd gone out to work.

Another turn of the key proved useless. She opened the door of the red Chevrolet and slammed it shut before giving it a kick. "Damn it!" Fixing the car had been Jack's thing, not hers. Now she was stuck until she could call Stu, who she probably couldn't pay.

"Need some help?"

She jumped at the sound of a male voice and spun to see Wade standing behind her.

"I couldn't sleep, so I decided to take a walk," he said.

The paleness of his skin glowed in the breaking light. A stark contrast to Jack's dark hair and tan.

"I can't get the car started," she said.

"Let me take a look."

She rubbed her ring finger. Part of her wanted to defend Jack's role. But Wade had already leaned in next to her and popped the hood.

LeeAnn reached into the glove box for a flashlight as Wade bent toward the engine. She noticed the tattoo on Wade's forearm for the first time: a raven, cheaply done.

"You like this old car?"

She shrugged. "It's what I can afford."

He stood back. "Try now."

LeeAnn climbed in and turned the key. It started without hesitation.

She rolled down the window. "How'd you do that?"

He shrugged. "Not sure what they might say at the Red Leaf when I come back from a walk looking like this." He held up hands streaked with black grease.

"They'll wonder why you've been out walking."

Smiling, he waved as she drove off.

She crossed the bridge in town, reminded for the first time in years of her first kiss with Jack at that spot. He'd been happy that day. So had she. She remembered thinking how nice it was to see his smile. That had been almost two years after Wade left town.

She passed her church on the left and the house Franny rented from Elzer. The wind pulled leaves from the sugar maples lining the road, sending them in a colorful spray across the pavement in front of her. The reds and pinks of the dawn lit the countryside. She tried to memorize the beauty of that moment because she sensed a quickening of the land, as though readying itself. But she would leave reading signs to others. She was no good at it. Her mom's cancer had shown her that.

She pulled into the drive of her parents' small house, its gray asphalt shingles as old as the nearby coal mine and buckled from too many years. There'd never been enough money to do more than maintain, especially with the most recent batch of medical bills.

She reached for the coffee cake she'd made the day before while waiting for Jack to leave her apartment. He'd arrived after her morning shift. His left eye was puffy from a recent fight, but he looked much better than he had the day she left him, when she woke to find him on the couch so beaten that she worried he might not wake.

Standing on her doorstep, Jack held out her red coffee cup, the one with the chipped rim she always used at home. "I thought you might want this," he said. "You forgot it."

She didn't take the mug.

"You don't want it?"

"What I want is for you to stop." She pointed to his bruised eye.

He turned away.

Why did he do it? Even now, his bruises hurt her as much as they ever had.

When she'd opened her apartment door, Itch jumped into Jack's arms. The cat missed him. He stroked her head with hands so gentle that she couldn't understand how he used them every week to punch people. She'd had to lift Itch out of Jack's arms before going into her apartment. She thought about falling from the ladder and him catching her. If only their marriage could have been more like that moment.

Inside, the cat went right to the kitchen window that overlooked the front stoop. Jack stood there still holding the damn coffee cup. When he finally climbed into his truck, parked next to her car, he just sat there. She made a coffee cake to pass the time, to stop from feeling like he'd trapped her inside.

She'd spied on him from the kitchen window, looking past the pot of violets Jack had given her years ago. It was the one extra she'd brought to the apartment. He'd scooped them up from the woods with his bare hands and carried them to the house because, he'd said, they matched the color of her eyes. Now the flowers drooped. She hadn't watered them and didn't do it then. When the coffee cake came out of the oven, Itch jumped down from the window and LeeAnn saw he'd finally gone.

Now, when she stepped out of the car, her dad's dog, Nell, rushed toward her in greeting. The few remaining cows lowed in the old stanchion barn, having been milked and fed. Her mother's laughter came bubbling from the house. She closed her eyes to take it in, wanting to imprint the sound on her mind, just like the rosy light of the morning. She and her dad counted on that laughter like the apple blossoms needed the bees. With the cancer back for a third time, neither of them could guess how much longer it would be part of their days.

LeeAnn slipped off her sneakers in the mudroom and took in the familiar scents of a dairy farmer—the hay on her father's jacket, the sharp odor of manure on his boots.

She opened the kitchen door to more welcome smells of her childhood home and paused a moment to take them in. The smokiness of the wood stove. The store-bought powdered sugar donuts her parents loved. The burnt coffee made hours ago by her dad. True of most every morning at this time, Rose and Gabriel Moore were sitting at the dining room table, beyond the kitchen, heads bent together over the paper.

"Hi," LeeAnn said. They glanced up surprised, so focused on each other they hadn't heard her come through the door. This is what she'd expected marriage to be.

"Hello, sweetheart," her mom said. Only tiredness around her eyes signaled the spread of the cancer to her lymph nodes and God knew where else.

"I brought a coffee cake," LeeAnn said.

Gabriel stood. "I'm going to wash up the milk house. I won't be long." He leaned down to kiss Rose. "Let you girls talk."

Still in her robe, Rose put on the teakettle. LeeAnn settled on the couch in the living room, over-warmed by the wood stove. The wind outside came through the single-pane windows and nudged the lace curtains, frayed from too many washes and yellowed by years of sun.

Rose brought two cups and slices of coffee cake on a tray and sat down across from LeeAnn in the same overstuffed armchair that had been there since LeeAnn was a child. "So tell me," she said.

LeeAnn shrugged.

"How do you feel now that you're in your own place?"

"Like I'm supposed to be someplace else. Like I have no idea what happens next." LeeAnn added sugar and milk to her tea. "I could still move in here," she said. "To help you and Dad."

"Stay where you are. Right now you need the separation from Jack and us so you can think clearly. We've got lots of help from the church for the household things."

Her mother left her tea and cake untouched. She never ate or drank much these days.

"Gabriel told me Jack looked bad a couple weeks back. Worse than the usual split lip. That was part of your decision to leave, I imagine."

LeeAnn nodded. "When I saw him, Mom, I had to go."

"I guess that's been his way of dealing."

"Or giving up."

Her mother gave her a sad smile. "You seemed happy for so long."

They had been. Until she'd gone off birth control. Days, months, then eight years passed hoping for a dream that never came. When her mother had first gotten cancer and they all thought she might die, LeeAnn had wanted so much to keep some of Rose Moore alive in her own child, before it was too late.

"You don't love him anymore?"

"It doesn't seem to matter."

"Give it time," her mom said.

LeeAnn shook her head.

Time had run out. Doc Black had confirmed her perimenopause only a few weeks before.

"I wish Jack had said he didn't want kids a long time ago."

"How can you know he doesn't?"

"Because even though he seems to love fighting, he never fought for our baby. You know how he is. Fate is everything. It's all through those notebooks he keeps. Remember at first how he wanted to name the baby William if it was a boy?" LeeAnn wiped her eyes. "But then it was like he looked for signs that a baby would never arrive—the unhatched bluebird eggs, the frozen spider case, frost on the apple blossoms, and on and on. He stopped sleeping in our bedroom. And then he refused to sell the land down by the creek that could have paid for fertility treatments. Not his family's orchard, heavens no. The dead are more important to Jack than the living."

Her mother suddenly appeared tired and ill. LeeAnn wanted desperately to take back the outburst.

"I'm not second-guessing you," her mom said gently. "I'm sure some distance between you two is right for now." Her mother let out a long sigh. "I'm sorry, I feel so sleepy. I'm going upstairs to lie down a little. Do you mind?"

"Of course not. Do you need help up the stairs?"

"No, I'll be fine."

She looked so tired. "Mom?"

She turned back from where she stood at the foot of the stairs.

"I'm so unsure about what's happened to me and Jack. Giving it time is good advice. Thanks."

She nodded and gave LeeAnn a real smile before shuffling up the wooden staircase.

When her father came into the kitchen, LeAnn joined him. He leaned against the counter with a cup of coffee in his hand. Beside him the answering machine blinked rapidly. She stared at the number displayed on the machine.

"Dad, you've got eleven messages here."

He set his coffee down a little too hard, some of it sloshing onto the counter. "Debt collectors."

The sound of defeat in his voice was unusual.

"Do you want me to talk to them?"

"Won't do any good."

"How bad is it?"

When he spoke, he whispered, perhaps afraid her mother might hear, or still wanting it to remain hidden from everyone but him. "I hate the thought of you not having this place someday. Guess I could sell off the last of the cows."

A lifelong dairy farmer, these last few animals gave him a sense of himself now that he had to work at the landfill for money. Selling the cows wouldn't make any difference if they were about to lose the house.

He put his arms around her and pulled her close. "Your mom—she wants to die at home." His voice cracked. "I want to give her that at least."

She hugged him tighter. "Dad," LeeAnn said, trying to hold back the tears he couldn't anymore, wanting to be strong for him in the way he'd always been for her.

"It's bad this time, LeeAnn," he said, barely getting the words out.

They held each other. She'd been clinging to the idea that her mother would make it through somehow, like before.

Leaning back she looked into his eyes. Her parents needed as much peace of mind as they could get right now. She would start by making sure they kept their house. She'd ask Wade to talk to them.

CHAPTER 6

Stella

THE ALARM WENT off and Stella opened one eye. She turned toward Patrick's pillow. Empty.

The morning light came in around the blinds, casting long shadows on the otherwise blank wall facing her bed. Each blind made a separate line on the wall. She imagined her life chopped into distinct pieces of past and present—what Patrick knew about her and what he didn't. The shadow lines stretched to the corner of the room where the light bent and the lines merged into an amorphous shape on the adjacent wall, giving no indication of what would happen when past met present.

She got out of bed and opened the blinds, stripping the shadows away. A thin layer of snow covered the ground, as if the world had gone blank. Just as, for all the years she'd known Patrick, she'd omitted Minden from her storyline.

Her work meant protecting places like Minden, because by protecting the land and water she looked out for Wade and Jack. That's what she told herself, anyway. When she'd first heard about the drilling years ago, Stella had known this time might come. And she'd been working harder than ever to avoid thinking about the consequences.

Later that morning, as she drove toward Elzer's place, the same old arguments played out in her head. She was a lawyer, after all. She could be convincing, even to herself, about why her sons wouldn't want her in their lives. She told herself she had no right to meddle. She'd made her bed. She'd built a wall between them that could never be torn down. Brick by brick, with Patrick as the mortar.

Suburbia gave way to woods and rural farmland, and billboards disappeared. Strip malls were replaced with fields studded with rusted farm equipment, failing split rail, and bales wrapped in white plastic. The roads grew narrower. As the houses became sparse and forests crowded in, Stella fought off encroaching claustrophobia fed by self-doubt. She slowed down. Angry drivers passed, leaning on their horns with the occasional middle finger extended.

The closer she got to Minden, the less she felt she could justify all the reasons she'd never returned.

When she finally reached Elzer Hawk's dirt drive, she didn't turn off the engine. Anxiety sat heavy on her chest. For the first time she allowed her eyes to go to the gap in Morrigan Mountain, to her land. God, it had been so long since she'd last seen it. That had been another time altogether.

Table Rock was visible about three quarters of the way up. Should she turn her car around, return home, and forget Minden? She had a good life.

Except. Except Patrick deserved better.

Engine off, she unfastened her seatbelt and opened her car door.

Elzer's was a simple house with log siding. Smoke

drifted from the chimney and birds surrounded the ornate feeders hanging outside. She'd expected a more impressive home to fit the image she had of the man who lived there. One who was all-powerful in her mind, since he knew her sons.

Elzer, the first lawyer she'd known, handled the deed work on her acreage when she and Steve Pierson married. She'd called him a few times over the years to ask about Jack and Wade. He'd done her the kindness of telling her what he knew. It felt odd to have never been to his house. But theirs was a false kinship, not unlike the one between her, Jack, and Wade.

Now, when he opened his front door, Elzer didn't seem happy to see her. He smelled like the chewing tobacco she remembered. Reluctantly, he shook the hand she offered. She quelled the urge to hug him to make more of a connection.

"I'm going out for a walk. Why don't you come along," Elzer said.

He slipped on his coat and Stetson and she followed him around to the back of the house onto a path. She took care to keep her loafers on it, flanked as it was on both sides by wet, soggy ground. Tufts of grass and sedge stuck up through white patches, with small areas of standing water and low shrubs interspersed.

He stepped over a low spot in the path. "Watch yourself."

Elzer was at least ten years her senior, but she found that she was out of breath trying to keep up with him and had to fall back a few strides. When they came to a small pond, he pulled a bag filled with bread out of his pocket as a group of ducks hurried toward them. They snapped up what he tossed, fighting over the larger pieces. He turned to her, ready to talk. But she suddenly wasn't prepared and looked past him up to a clear view of her land.

"So?" he asked.

"I told Jack I'd come to Minden and be another voice

in the community besides Green Energy. But I also need to try to explain things to Wade and Jack. I hoped you might be able to offer some advice in how to broach that topic with them."

"Broach that topic?" He buried his hands in his pockets and stared off toward the pond. "I can't help you with that."

"But you know them." She took a step toward him.

He met her eyes. "They're not characters in a storybook you can open and close. They're real people. Folks I care about. If you want to know how to talk to them, then you should have come back here long ago. Jack told me what happened when Wade called you after their dad died. He's asked you to Minden now, as a way of making it up to Wade. Only I can't figure why Jack feels responsible for you not showing up. He was a kid. You were the adult who chose to stay away."

She shivered in the cold, damp air. "I'm here now."

"It's too late now." He shook his head.

He had to understand she was back for good reason. She'd come to him for guidance because he was like her, a lawyer.

"Why butt in?" He stuffed the empty bag in his pocket.

She didn't know what to say.

"We'd better head back." He turned and walked back toward the house. They went along in silence, her trying to keep stride. Finally, he said, "Tell me about your involvement with the water contamination case a couple counties over."

So he was interested in what she knew, if nothing else. "It was faulty well construction. I thought it might lead to a toxic trespass case. But it didn't," she huffed, trying to keep up.

"Is that what you want to tell Wade and Jack? We don't even have any wells in yet."

"Can you slow down a little?"

He stopped and turned toward her. "Sorry."

She took a moment to catch her breath. "They should

know what the possibilities are for Minden and the orchard."

Elzer began walking again, at a pace she could easily match.

"How are they?" The humiliation of not knowing burned her cheeks.

"Jack tell you he and LeeAnn split?"

"No."

"She's living in an apartment above the diner where she works."

Stella kept her face passive even though she struggled with the overwhelming feeling of being in over her head. How much had Jack's troubled marriage motivated him to seek her out?

"How long has Wade been back?" Stella asked.

"Just over a week. He's staying at the bar in town, the Red Leaf. Not with his brother."

So they weren't close. Even now, with Wade back after so long. "Do they know anything about me?"

"They don't know we ever communicated. That was never for me to tell them."

Stella wanted to say she hadn't meant for it to turn out this way, that she wasn't a bad person, but what was the point? He wasn't going to believe her.

Back at his house, he walked her to her car.

"You need to think about this, Stella. Think about what's best for Wade and Jack."

"Jack asked me to come here. I can't refuse him."

Elzer shook his head. "Suit yourself." He turned back toward his house, leaving Stella with a sinking feeling.

At the end of his drive, instead of heading home, she turned toward Morrigan Mountain. She wanted to step on her property again. If this was her last time in Minden, she needed to see the stretch of Silver Creek that had meant so much. Did it still look like it did in her mind? Was the sycamore still standing on her side of the creek?

Driving past the volunteer fire department, Stella

skirted the west end of town and stopped at the intersection with Main Street where the bridge crossed over Silver Creek. She remembered standing on that bridge with her dad right after they'd moved to Minden. Flood waters rushed under them. The swelling creek shook the bridge and her dad led her quickly back to their car. That was the only time she'd seen him scared.

To the right she saw dingy storefronts and a few old cars and trucks lining the street that looked as down on its luck as she remembered. Forgotten. Poor. Desperate. A place ripe for drilling exploitation, she thought. There was the diner. LeeAnn might be there now. Jack was less than two miles away. Wade could be nearby. She put on large sunglasses. She wasn't ready to see any of them. Maybe she never would be.

Reluctantly she looked left. In the distance was her father's old church and the parsonage they'd once shared. Her last conversation with him had been in that house. She'd been sixteen sitting at the kitchen table across from him, with a rubber band stretched between the buttons of her jeans.

On impulse she turned the wheel and hit the gas. The parsonage grew bigger as she approached. Stella parked and stared up at the small Cape Cod. Painted the same white, the shutters blue now instead of black. When she lived there she imagined the upper windows, framed by dormers, were eyes watching. She jumped when a man appeared in one of them.

She wondered for a moment, irrationally, if the man could be her father. But he'd died long ago. She sat entranced by a mix of anticipation and dread, unable to take her eyes away. The man stepped out onto the porch and waved, as though he'd been expecting her.

She rolled down the car window. "I used to live in this house and wanted to see it once more. I shouldn't have intruded."

"Not at all. I'm Reverend Joe," he said, walking to her

car and extending his hand.

He had a warm, friendly face and a bit of a paunch under his sweater vest. The kind of man who would be right at home in all the places her father hadn't, at potlucks and fire station breakfasts. She imagined him listening to problems over coffee and cookies offered in kitchens all over Minden. He struck her as more kind than keen, also unlike her father.

"Did your dad serve the church?"

"For a short time, many years ago."

"Come in then. Take a look."

"That's not necessary." She reached for the car key.

"Please, I insist." He opened her car door.

Her eyes went to the windows. She didn't want to go inside. But he reached in and took her hand and she followed him, obediently, like she was sixteen again.

She stopped midway up the porch steps. "I really don't need to come inside."

Holding the front door for her, he said, "Just take a quick peek. It's good to revisit your roots."

When she stepped in the door, the house looked much smaller than she remembered. But aside from some different furniture, it was the same.

"I'll leave you to it," Reverend Joe said. "Take your time. I'll be on the porch."

She wished he would stay but felt too scattered to ask. And it would take an explanation she wasn't prepared to give. Walking through the living room, she made it only as far as the kitchen doorway, facing the same table where she and her father had last seen each other.

He hadn't answered her that day, but he often didn't. He focused deeply on his work, which had everything to do with the church and little to do with her.

"Dad," she tried again.

"Hmm," he said without raising his head.

"I need to tell you something."

"Hmm," he said again, his eyes on his Bible.

"It's important," she said, trying not to cry. "Please look at me."

He took off his reading glasses and regarded her like a preoccupied minister, not a father. She wondered if he'd ever been young. Could he understand that sometimes people made mistakes? That sometimes when you're so terribly lonely in a new place, you take comfort where you can?

"What is it? I need to finish this."

"Dad . . . I don't know if I can say it."

"Say what?" he'd snapped.

She pushed the words out. "I'm . . . I'm pregnant. It was an accident," she blurted. "I'm sorry."

He picked up his reading glasses and put them back on as if she hadn't spoken. He went back to his Bible and his notes.

"Dad?"

When he didn't answer this time, she took the pen from his wrinkled hand and closed his Bible. Her hands shook.

"What do you think you're doing?"

"I need to see a doctor. I need new clothes. Mine don't fit." Her voice trembled as much as her hands.

"You're on your own." He reopened his Bible and flipped to the page he wanted.

"But . . . I need your help."

He removed his glasses again, and spoke to her slowly as though she were not his daughter. Not even one of his congregation. "Your condition is your doing. Don't mention this to me again."

He stood and walked toward the living room. When he reached the same doorway Stella stood in now, he turned toward her. For a moment she thought he realized how scared she was and how much she needed him.

"There's another thing you should know," he said. "I've been offered a job at our old church in Wisconsin. The new minister didn't work out. I'm going back in two weeks.

Given what you've told me, you'll stay here."

She dared to hope. "But Dad, we have friends in Wisconsin who could help. Here there's nothing."

"You've made your bed."

He turned his back on her and left the room.

The memory was painful. Stella wiped her eyes. Only recently had she considered that maybe her father had done the only thing he could at the time. He'd lived by a set of rules that didn't allow for daughters pregnant out of wedlock.

Stella shut her eyes. They'd never spoken again. Could she at least do better than that?

"Is it as you remember?" the reverend asked from his rocking chair when she came onto the porch.

"Yes and no. It helped to see the place again. Thank you."

He walked her to her car before returning to the house.

She drove back toward town, glimpsing the diner again before she took a left up to the top of the mountain and then left again along Ridge Road, which she followed until she came to the gap. Here she parked the car and walked alongside the little rivulet edged with hemlock and rhododendron running toward Silver Creek below. Her loafers grew soggier which each step, until she came to the large piece of flat-lying sandstone everyone used to call Table Rock.

Climbing onto it she ran her hand over the rough grain of the stone where Jack had been conceived. She, the new girl in town, suffering from an outsider's loneliness. Steve, trying to fill a hole in her he couldn't possibly understand. He'd tried to love her and he'd given her this land. Her sons had been the reason she'd kept it.

She sat, drew her knees up and looked down at the valley. The air smelled of burning leaves. Her vantage from the rock gave her a good view of the orchard. Its end-of-fall beauty surprised her. The sunlight shone on the trees, their upper reddish branches reaching to the sky, promising what they would become in the spring. The whole place lay before her like a distant story. She'd seen the orchard in her mind like this, from above. From this distance it seemed approachable.

Someone drove a tractor out of the barn. She squinted as she leaned forward, straining to take in any details. It could have been anyone, but she sensed it was Jack.

His wife had left him and still he did what needed to be done. Like his father.

She stood up on the rock, wanting to get a better view. Part of her wanted to walk down the gap toward Jack right then and emerge through the tangle of brush and forest. She would explain to him how much she'd always cared, even though she'd never said so.

But the forest had grown dense and the thicket so tangled that she couldn't see a way through. Instead, she stood still, listening to the low hum of the machinery.

She couldn't see Silver Creek from Table Rock. She would never have been able to see it. But in her mind it had been clearly visible, just like the love she'd sent to this vista for the creek to carry to her sons.

CHAPTER 7

Jack

November 17 – Harvest finished. Need to stock supplies.

At the Feed and Seed, Jack loaded bags of fertilizer and pesticides into his pickup from the loading dock. It was cheap this time of year.

Moving the fifty-pound bags, one after another, sweat dripping from his face, he thought about his wife.

He wished he didn't know exactly how she'd felt when a baby never came. Growing up he'd kept watch for a mother who never returned home. Daily disappointment closed off a little more hope. So losing that hope between him and LeeAnn—watching it go, knowing it was his fault—

"How's it going, Jack?"

He jumped, so lost in thought that he hadn't sensed anyone around. He relaxed his fists when he saw it was only Franny and Stu looking up at him from beside the truck. Franny frowned at the cut above his eye.

"You okay?" Franny said.

"Not really."

"Anything we can do?" Stu asked.

"If I knew what to do I'd have done it by now." Jack started moving bags again.

"She might just need some time away. That can help a person see things with fresh eyes," Franny said.

"I hold on to that hope," Jack said.

He finished loading the bags and brushed the dust from his hands before jumping down from the truck.

"Has she said much about Rose and Gabriel? I don't even feel like I can go check on them. Don't want to put them in a difficult position, feeling like they have to pick sides or something. But I worry."

Franny put her hand on his arm. "It's worse than before."

He wiped his eyes. "Christ, I hate this."

"They're being cared for, Jack," Franny said. "The church is there. LeeAnn's helping, of course. And they'll call if they need you. You know that."

"I just feel terrible. For LeeAnn. For feeling like I can't do anything."

"LeeAnn's trying to see if they might lease. For extra money. So they can keep the farm."

Why hadn't she said anything to him? He kicked his tire hard enough to dent the rim.

"Pull yourself together, Jack." Franny said. "You hear me. If you want LeeAnn back in your life, you have to sort yourself out. You think LeeAnn wants to come back to that?" She pointed to the cut above his eye.

Jack thought of Stella. "I'm taking steps."

"Have you had an actual conversation with your brother since he got back?"

Jack shrugged.

"That would be taking steps," Franny said.

"All right now, Franny," Stu said.

But she was right. Jack would call his brother. He'd promised a meeting. LeeAnn should come, too.

"Take care, buddy, okay?" Stu offered his hand and Jack shook it. "Let's go fishing sometime soon, you hear?

Me and Doc are out there every week. We're bored with each other. You come and join us."

Jack said he would even though he wouldn't.

He went into the Feed and Seed to pay. Just inside the door, still out of sight of the register, he heard LeeAnn's name. He stopped to listen.

"Wade's in that diner every day. And you know it's not just cause it's a good place for business."

Jack slipped out the way he'd come. He left a wad of bills tucked under a pallet on the loading dock.

At least it was Thursday.

CHAPTER 8

LeeAnn

WADE, REVEREND JOE, Doc Black, and Stu sat at the counter at their typical early hour.

"Your usual, Reverend?" LeeAnn asked, already reaching for a blueberry muffin.

"Yes, ma'am."

"How's that new furnace working out?" Wade asked the reverend as he bit into the muffin.

"Wonderfully." He wiped his face with a napkin, missing a smear of blueberry at the corner of his mouth. "The church is comfortable, even when it dips below fifty. Don't you agree, LeeAnn?"

"It is." She refilled creamers wondering how the new furnace was related to Green Energy.

LeeAnn wiped down tables and set down fresh paper placemats and silverware. In a town this small you knew all kinds: ones you liked and ones you didn't. But family, neighbors, and the land were all you had. You relied on what you knew. By leaving and staying away for so long, Wade had become an outsider, an unknown. But since he'd returned, he earned credibility quick.

Elzer walked in.

"Mayor's arrived," said Stu. "Sit up straight everybody."

"I was starting to worry," Franny said.

"Can't sleep worth a damn. There's so much to work out with this drilling starting up," Elzer said.

"You thinking about leasing?" Wade asked.

"I'm not in any hurry," Elzer said. "But I am hungry. Franny, how about some pancakes?"

"The cook's late. The mix is next to the stove," she said, pointing. "Make me some, too, while you're at it."

Elzer didn't move. "Coffee then. Could I get that at least?"

LeeAnn poured him a cup. "I made this pot strong."

The door opened and a large group entered, followed by the cook who arrived just in time. LeeAnn pasted a smile on her face and grabbed a stack of menus. Franny hurried to help her move a couple tables together. The first wave of the gas industry had arrived for breakfast. More kept coming. Landmen from competing gas companies. Businessmen looking to set up shop as they had in other boomtowns to offer the needed supplies and services: piping, sand, heavy equipment, and housing for the drillers. And geologists who'd already begun prospecting leased properties.

LeeAnn refilled coffee and refused one highfalutin order after another—egg-white omelets, steel-cut oatmeal, whole-grain pancakes—none of which they had on the menu. At some point Wade left and she waved goodbye.

Talk of drilling came from all directions. Reckless excitement, full of promise, dismissed possible consequences. These newcomers saw only what they could take. Still, so many in Minden, like her parents, needed extra money.

Dishes piled up and LeeAnn helped the dishwasher unload the sterilizer so they could run another cycle. The cook worked frantically at the stove, so many green slips of paper hanging above him that LeeAnn couldn't see his face.

She turned with her coffee pot and found Wade back at the counter. She glanced at the clock. Hours had passed.

"Lunch," he said.

"I guess you were right about drilling being good for business," she replied, nodding at the packed restaurant.

He winked.

Franny came up beside her. "I've got tables five, ten, and nine. Can you get two and three? They just sat down."

"Hey, while I have you two together," Wade said, pushing a stack of flyers across the counter to LeeAnn. "My boss agreed to host a fishing contest this weekend. Show our support for the community. Franny, I thought your kids might enjoy it. Biggest fish earns you five hundred dollars."

The flyers on the counter were printed on thick glossy paper with Silver Creek in full autumn color pictured across the top. On the right side, the Green Energy logo overlaid the creek, as though staking a claim.

"What a great idea," Franny said.

LeeAnn hoped Franny could also see the ploy behind this fishing contest. Franny took the flyers and laid them beside the register before hurrying off with menus.

When they'd served the last lunchtime tuna melts and cheeseburgers, Franny and LeeAnn closed the door and collapsed into a couple empty chairs.

Franny took off her shoes. "Whew!" She rubbed her feet. "I made a week's worth of tips by noon. Have you seen the cash drawer?"

LeeAnn stood heavily and walked to the register. She opened it and stared, thumbing through the money. "If this keeps up, we'll be able to hire another waitress. Looks like we're gonna need one."

"We should set up for tomorrow," LeeAnn said, not wanting to sit down again for fear she wouldn't be able to get up. Franny groaned but stood and they got back to work.

On the way out the door, Franny asked LeeAnn to come

to her place that evening. "The house will be quiet and you need to get out of that apartment. Also, it's tree time." For years she and Franny had cut down Christmas trees a few days after Thanksgiving from the property Franny rented from Elzer. It once operated as a Christmas tree farm.

"I don't want a tree this year."

"Yes you will."

"I'm tired after this shift, aren't you?"

"I also have beer and can't drink it alone."

Thinking about her empty apartment, where a clock ticking in one of the unpacked boxes made the only sound, LeeAnn said, "I'll be over after dinner."

"Get there before dark, so you can pick a nice tree for once." Franny's pager went off. "Ambulance run. See you tonight."

LeeAnn watched her run across the street, jump into her truck, switch on the blue emergency lights, and speed off to rescue somebody they probably both knew.

When LeeAnn arrived that evening, she walked into Franny's house and found her in the living room. After grabbing a hand saw from the garage, they went behind the house where the trees, planted long ago, now grew wild and untrimmed. Most were now too tall, but the tops could be cut off.

"I'm going to wait for Stu and the kids. Let's get you one."

Franny walked just ahead of her, leading the way. The sun lay low and orange under a violet sky. LeeAnn scanned the weedy rows as they wove their way through the fields. A small leggy tree, bending slightly to one side in the soft breeze, caught her eye. "What about this one?"

Franny turned and seeing the tree, put her hands on her hips. "Predictable."

"What?"

"Who else would want that tiny crooked tree?"

"But it speaks to me."

"Oh, all right," Franny said, cutting the thin trunk midway. "Probably didn't even need the saw. I could have just snapped it off. You complain every year when all the needles fall off. I hope I won't have to remind you this one started with only half."

"It'll be fine."

Franny handed LeeAnn the spindly tree. "Let's get some water for the poor thing."

Inside the house with the tree soaking, LeeAnn took a good look around her friend's place, the opposite of her own present life. Franny lived in a whirl of activity and loved ones, her living room overflowing with toys and books. Nothing in boxes.

LeeAnn took her place next to Franny on the couch and Franny handed her a beer and placed a bowl of salted peanuts on LeeAnn's lap.

"Everything go okay with that call?"

"Car wreck. Luckily no serious injuries." Franny, always respectful of people's privacy, never mentioned names of those she encountered as a volunteer for the ambulance crew. Not even to LeeAnn.

"How are the kids?" LeeAnn asked, passing the bowl of peanuts to Franny.

"Fine for the most part. Little Ben's having trouble in school with his reading, but we're working with him as best we can."

"Don't they have a reading specialist?"

"Most of the 'extra' teachers were cut two years ago because of budget problems."

Franny opened her beer and cleared her throat dramatically. "So, Wade . . ."

"What about him?"

"There was something between you two once."

LeeAnn shook her head. Surely, it couldn't be so obvious. "He's been gone for twenty years," she said as offhandedly as possible, but felt the heat climb her neck. Franny wouldn't miss this, which only made it worse.

Franny raised her eyebrows.

"We were young. First love. You know how that is. And then he left town and I married Jack. I've heard nothing from him, or about him, since."

"And?"

"And he was a handsome bad boy back then. Leather-jacket rebel. Angry with his parents. The kind of guy no teenage girl can resist."

"So you slept with him, but ended up marrying the good brother?"

"I didn't sleep with him."

"But there was something. How far did you make it? Has he seen you naked?"

LeeAnn rolled her eyes. "Franny."

"Well?"

"He's seen me."

"Have you seen him?"

"Do you always need every detail?"

"Yes."

"Oh, for God's sake . . . "

"What *did* happen?"

"He came to my window one night."

"That's when he saw you naked?"

LeeAnn gave her an exasperated look. "I wore my nightgown."

"Color?"

"Pale blue."

"Long or short?"

"Medium."

Franny pursed her lips. "So you remember every detail. Go on."

It was all so long ago, but LeeAnn had to admit she enjoyed thinking about it. Speaking of that moment aloud pulled the story from memory and made it real again. Made her feel young. She had loved Wade then. "I opened the window and told him to leave."

"But you didn't really want him to leave."

"Maybe not."

"Then?"

"Then he asked to come in. But I said no."

Franny clapped her hands together. "But you didn't really want to say no."

"*Then* he said if I wasn't going to let him in, he wanted me to take off my nightgown."

"And you said no, but you did it anyway?"

LeeAnn gave her a sly smile.

"I knew it! And then?"

"He left town the next night," LeeAnn said, her excitement deflating like a punctured balloon. She hoped they could leave this conversation.

"*The next night?* No wonder."

"What?"

"Unfinished business. You, naked at seventeen, on one side of the window and him on the other. He's never forgotten it. Since then he's been stuck halfway through that window. You too, maybe?"

Even though she was sure they were the only two in the room, LeeAnn checked over her shoulder. "It was forever ago. And no one knew about us back then. Except Jack, since he was around so much and we couldn't hide from him."

"No one knew? Why not?"

LeeAnn dusted peanut salt from her fingers, thinking back to those days.

"Their dad, Steve, suspected me and Wade were interested in each other. He saw me give Wade a small pink stone down by the bridge in town. Steve took the stone from Wade and hid it, although Wade found it later. There was always something between Steve and my dad. When Steve found out Wade planned to work at my parent's dairy instead of the orchard, he barred Wade from seeing me as long as he was still living at home. So we planned to keep our relationship a secret until Wade could get his own place."

Franny took a long swig from her bottle, grabbed the bowl of peanuts from LeeAnn's lap, and ate another handful. After a moment she said, "I've heard about that terrible accident. With his father. Is that why Wade left town?"

LeeAnn wished now that Stu and the kids would appear. In all these years, she'd never really talked about that day, and although she knew she probably needed to, the prospect of having to remember it twice in such a short time felt overwhelming. But she couldn't avoid it with Franny. "I was there."

Franny's eyes widened. "What? How could I not know this?"

"Jack and I agreed right after the accident that we wouldn't talk about it with anyone. My dad and Elzer felt the same. When it happened, so many people wanted to hear the details, including reporters from all over. Honestly, nobody but Wade knows what really happened. Jack didn't want to speculate. Neither did I. We wanted to protect Wade, wherever he'd gone. We hoped he would come back and explain when he was ready. We just didn't figure it would take him so long."

"What do you remember about the accident?"

LeeAnn put her bottle on the coffee table. She hadn't planned to go down this path. But maybe Franny should know her part of the story now that Wade was back. The words were untried, though. She didn't know how far she'd get. She took a deep breath.

"It was the first day of buck season. The only day of the year when Steve Pierson would set foot in our house because the deer were a problem at the orchard and the dairy. That was something my dad and Steve could agree on. So we were over at my house that morning for breakfast, all of us with long johns, Carhartts, orange. You know."

"You hunted?"

"Back then I did. With Dad."

"Interesting. Go on."

LeeAnn hesitated, attempting to line up events in her mind she'd tried to forget. "Mom had made a big breakfast, a heap of scrambled eggs, bacon, the whole bit. Jack was in a bad mood."

"Why?"

"He never liked hunting. Mostly I think he was jealous of the attention Wade got from their dad during hunting season."

Franny grabbed another big handful of peanuts and crunched them. She offered LeeAnn the bowl. LeeAnn shook her head, then took a drink to help steady herself for the rest of the story.

"Steve wanted us to drive the deer up to Table Rock, where Wade would wait to take the shot. That's what we'd always done. Wade was all for it. He'd been in his dad's bad graces with wanting to work at the dairy, and hunting was always a way to make things right between him and his dad, at least for a while. But then Jack asked if he could be the one to shoot instead of Wade."

"I'm guessing Steve didn't like that idea," said Franny.

"No. He brushed Jack off. Jack said he had a bad feeling and Steve told him to shut his mouth."

"Nice guy."

Unable to sit any longer, LeeAnn walked to the window. A branch, moved by the wind, scraped against the glass. Clouds covered the half moon. She turned back toward Franny. "He was a hard man. Thing is, he preferred Jack and he never would talk to him like that usually. But Steve could be hard on both his sons, in different ways. My dad wanted to make Jack feel better and took his side. Steve got angry and told my dad to get his nose out of Pierson business once and for all. The conversation turned Dad off and he went to the barn, where he stayed." LeeAnn crossed her arms in front of her, shivering for a moment. "If only we'd all done the same."

LeeAnn sat down and finished her beer.

Franny went into the kitchen and came back with two more. "So Jack was jealous of Wade?"

"They needed the meat, and fewer deer meant less damage to the orchard. Steve would tell anyone who would listen how great a shot Wade was. It made Jack mad since Wade never did much at the orchard otherwise. Hunting was the one thing the three of them did together. It was the only time Steve took time off to be with them."

"So you all went up the gap as planned, driving the deer toward Wade?"

LeeAnn nodded. "Wade went up the mountain about a half hour ahead of us and we all took a different path toward him."

LeeAnn opened the second beer and took a sip, but it left her stomach feeling sour. She put her bottle on the table, abandoned.

"And?" Franny asked quietly.

LeeAnn blew out a long frustrated breath. "All I know is what I saw after the gun went off. Jack yelled. I thought he'd been shot from the way he sounded. I ran straight up the mountain towards Jack's voice. That's when I saw him leaning over his dad. And Wade sat on the ground a short distance away, holding his gun."

"Jesus," Franny said.

LeeAnn ran a hand through her hair. She wished the conversation were over, wished she'd just stayed home. She took a deep breath. She could barely talk now without choking up. "Of all the damn trees in the woods that could have taken that bullet. But it hit his dad."

"Oh, God, honey." Franny shook her head.

In a near whisper, needing to finish the whole story now, LeeAnn said, "By the time I got there Jack was trying to find his dad's pulse. The deer crashing through the woods made the only noise. Wade never moved."

"Lord." Franny held the beer and a handful of forgotten nuts in her hands.

"Jack threw his dad over his shoulder and started walking

down the hill toward help, blood everywhere. I don't know how he did it, since he was smaller than his dad back then."

"What did you do?"

"I didn't know who to go to—Jack, doing everything he could to carry his father either dead or dying, or Wade, all alone after . . ." LeeAnn took the tissue Franny offered and dabbed her eyes. "I went over to Wade and said, 'Let's get your dad down the mountain.' I wanted us to stay together. But he shut his eyes and wouldn't open them, even when I asked him to look at me. He shook his head and squeezed his eyes tighter. So I told him I'd send somebody and then I followed Jack. I looked back once. This time Wade met my eyes, and he seemed so lost. But I turned away."

Franny scooted herself close to LeeAnn on the couch and put her arm around her shoulder.

"We learned later Steve died up there," LeeAnn said, wiping tears away. "Probably as soon as he was shot. I think Jack knew that before he carried him down the mountain."

"What happened to Wade?"

"I don't know. I should have stayed with him. I'm sorry for that." LeeAnn covered her face with her hands. "Maybe then he wouldn't have left. Maybe . . ."

Franny reached up and took LeeAnn's hands in her own. "But you needed to help Jack. And Steve. You didn't know he was dead."

She shrugged. "Elzer and my dad had to go up later to get Wade. They found him still sitting with his gun, talking to it, like the gun had been responsible."

"Did you have to see that, too?"

"No. Dad told me later. But I've seen Wade in my head so many times since, looking at me as I headed down the mountain with Jack."

"And you never saw him again until he came back here?"

LeeAnn shook her head.

The only thing she'd found was the torn picture of Stella, Wade, and Jack on the bed Wade had slept in that night. She'd watched Jack carefully tape it back together and put it in his wallet, where it still was.

"Should have never left him alone up there." The branch scratched at the window again and LeeAnn wiped her eyes dry. She'd always wanted to tell him that, but he'd left before she could.

Franny hugged her close. "Jesus, LeeAnn. You were doing your best trying to protect, not hurt. And who knows," she said. "Maybe he's here now for a reason."

Groaning, LeeAnn dropped her head in her hands. "Not you, too. Fate sure didn't take care of me and Jack."

"Maybe. Maybe not."

LeeAnn let out a long breath and dried her face with her sleeve. "At least now with Wade back, maybe there's a chance to sort through what happened."

They both turned toward the noise in the kitchen. Stu and the three boys roared in like a cheerful tornado flinging off coats and shoes, everyone talking at once.

Franny's kids were the closest thing LeeAnn had to her own. But tonight their presence made her feel lonely. LeeAnn gathered her coat and small tree. If only Wade and Jack had known the love of a close family.

CHAPTER 9

Stella

OUTSIDE THE WIND blew in great gusts. A chair on the back porch they never used toppled over.

Inside Stella sat alone on the couch in the dark waiting for Patrick to come home from his trip. Now that she'd made the decision to return to Minden, it was time to tell him the truth. When she heard his key turn in the front door, she switched on the floor lamp. Her stomach did a dangerous flip. She'd rehearsed what to say to him dozens of times, so much so that parts of the conversation had shown up in her dreams the last few nights. But now that he was here, walking in the door, she forgot everything she'd practiced.

He put down his suitcase and took a seat next to her.

She reached up and smoothed his windblown hair.

"We sure don't do this much," he said, putting his hand on her knee. She couldn't think of a time they'd sat there. They spent more time at the office than at home.

"How was your trip?" Her voice sounded too robotic. She felt removed from him, like he'd already learned the truth and decided to leave her.

"Not what I expected. Sunrise Solar is talking about a potential merger."

"Are you worried about losing them as a client?" As usual, she could lean, for a moment, into their business relationship, which had always provided shelter from her hidden truths.

"Not terribly. I hold the company's legal knowledge. It would be nearly impossible for someone to step into my shoes."

It was now or never.

He studied her. "What's wrong?"

The wind rattled the windows.

When she told him about her past, he would see her as less. He would understand how well she'd shut herself off and closed doors. She'd amputated whole parts of her life. Patrick knew less about her than the solar company he represented.

"There are some things I need to say." She had a vision of herself at the edge of a bottomless Silver Creek, poised to dive. She'd never learned to swim. Her throat closed, as though she was already drowning.

"Okay," he said, sounding afraid.

Did he suspect an affair? Part of her wished it was that. She could dismiss and leave an affair. But motherhood abandoned was elemental, and her husband had no idea about this part of her life.

She moved away from him a bit, which only seemed to project the rift that was about to split open between them.

He put his arm around her, drawing her back. Another gift she didn't merit. "When I was a teenager I lived in a town north of here called Minden."

"Where that man was from, who showed up in the office the other day?"

"That's right." She paused. "The truth is . . ."

God, how could she say it?

"Yes? Whatever it is, just tell me."

"I have two children living in Minden. I was seventeen when Jack was born, and less than eleven months later, Wade came. That man from Minden—that was Jack."

She stopped to let this sink in. Patrick stiffened and said nothing, but he kept his arm around her. So many years of tension she didn't know she'd been holding released and she sagged against him. Tears ran down her face, and he wiped them away.

"I'm sure you must have had your reasons for keeping this from me."

Hearing the empathy in his voice allowed her to keep going.

"I left them with their father when they were four and five. And I haven't talked to them since." She thought of the picture of them in her wallet. Their smallness, the look on their faces, said more about what she'd probably done by leaving them than she could confess. It said too much. She would not show it to him.

"Why are you telling me about this now?" He sounded more cautious and she wished for more of the understanding she'd heard in his voice a moment before.

"Gas drilling is about to start in Minden. Jack and his wife, LeeAnn, own a sizeable piece of land they may consider leasing. My other son, Wade, works for Green Energy. Jack asked me to come to Minden to talk about what I know, in case it might help them."

"Uh huh."

A distance stretched between them that had never been there before. "I was afraid to tell you. Afraid what you would think of me."

She waited for him to look at her, and when he finally did, she searched his face for a sign of what he felt. His hand was limp in hers. He did not return her squeeze. She took a deep breath. It all needed to be said now.

"There's more, Patrick. I own property in Minden, adjacent to the orchard where Jack lives. I've held on to it, even though we could have used the money had I sold. I've paid taxes on the land every year. Part of it is along a creek running between my property and Jack's. It probably doesn't make sense to you, it hardly does to me, but that property has been my only connection to Jack and Wade."

She waited for him to say anything. "What are you thinking?"

He sat very still. "I don't understand why you didn't tell me."

"I was afraid you'd turn away."

"I deserved to make that decision."

She flinched at the sharpness in his voice, but his arm remained firmly around her. "It's just . . . when I left Minden I needed so much to talk to someone, to have someone understand, to make sense of it myself. But it turns out people can't understand a woman who would leave her children. It seemed like I couldn't talk about my past unless I wanted to break ties. I didn't want to break ties with you. But I also never wanted to hurt you. You haven't deserved my dishonesty. I agreed to help Jack, in part, because it forces me to tell you all of this."

He pulled her closer, but the tone of his voice turned more toward his lawyer self. Removed. Objective. "How are you hoping to help?"

"I lost my last fight with Green Energy. Here's another chance. Maybe it's an opening with my sons. One that I really didn't understand I was waiting for until Jack walked into my office."

"It's messy, Stella. It's personal. It's a borderline conflict of interest. Is this for you or them?"

"I've had nothing personal with these boys—these men. I want to do what's best for all of us."

"Do you have the answers they'll need?"

"It wasn't their fault. It was me, so young and in the wrong life."

"And what about why you've never returned until now. When Green Energy has just arrived, a company you have a history with and a grudge against."

"I can help them protect what they have. The land has always been a priority for me, one I believe I share with them."

Patrick sighed and looked at her. Another gust of wind reminded her of the stormy night they'd met. He was sitting beside her in the law library muttering to himself about a case. She helped him develop his argument. Then they raced through wind and rain to a diner around the corner and talked all night, both of them knowing they'd finally found the one.

However he might feel about her shameful behavior, maybe the love and commitment between them would be enough to see them through.

"Do what you have to do," he said.

CHAPTER 10

Wade

WADE TIED HIS boots in his room at the Red Leaf.

He stood and studied the map he'd tacked to a board on the wall. He stuck two more pins through Minden. A green one to mark another property he'd leased. A red one to mark a new place he was after.

Later, outside next to Silver Creek, Wade's boss handed him a rod as new as the fishing vest he must have bought for the occasion. Wade sat on one of the picnic benches they'd rented. Balloons with the Green Energy logo were tied to trees along the creek marking the section for the contest.

Wade checked for LeeAnn among the few people starting to gather, but didn't see her. Jack wasn't in sight either. He probably wouldn't come.

His boss cast with surprising skill. Harrington Price could handle a rod. Thank God. Wade didn't want to lose the headway he'd already made in Minden.

Given the fine weather, he expected a good crowd. He scanned the pickups and cars beginning to park along the street. This contest would help Minden see him for who he wanted to be–someone trying to do right by his town and ease their trouble.

The local band they'd hired set up their instruments and Wade looked again for LeeAnn.

"How are the leases coming?" Harrington asked.

"Right on track."

"We need more landowners with large acreage." Harrington reeled in his line.

Green Energy wanted contiguous pieces and Wade would build them, but he needed time. "I'm working on those. I hope to have the Moore property, soon, which is fifty acres."

"What about your brother?"

Wade looked over the crowd, avoiding Harrington's eyes. The chatter of so many people made a low droning pierced by the occasional high pitch of a child and the screech of tuning guitars. For all Harrington knew, nabbing the Pierson lease should be as easy as showing up at the orchard and telling his brother where to sign. He'd been hired because he'd hinted as much. "I'll see Jack this week. He called–wants to talk. Catch up mostly. We haven't seen each other in a while. But I'll see how he and his wife feel about the possibility of leasing. I've also talked to Elzer. These folks need time to feel like they've made the decision."

The fifty-acre Moore property would provide a key connection and give him real credibility with the community. If he could get it, so would the orchard.

All the years between the accident and getting the job with Green Energy had been time passing. But his return to Minden had taken on the importance of a pilgrimage. It was hard being back and knocking on people's doors, asking them for something. But doing so gave him the opportunity to reinvent himself.

Harrington checked his watch. "Can you point out the mayor so I can introduce myself before it gets busy?"

Wade looked over the crowd and nodded toward Elzer. He noticed that LeeAnn and Franny and her family had also arrived. Harrington set off toward Elzer and Wade followed.

Under the brilliant sky, Silver Creek appeared as beautiful as it had on their flyer. Harrington started the contest by telling everyone Green Energy liked to celebrate the places they worked. "Natural gas is helping to reduce emissions from coal burning plants and that's helping fish stay healthy across the country. Here in Minden, we want to bring jobs. We'll make improvements to the roads and infrastructure. We value the opportunity to invest in this place and enrich your lives. Today, we also want to have fun and show how much we care."

For the first time Wade believed what he'd told every property owner he'd met with so far: Minden had potential. He could see beyond the narrow houses with plywood windows, the tarped roofs, the damaged barns overtaken by vines and wind, and the rusted equipment that showed Minden's neglect. The creek sparkled with vitality. A fish even jumped as his boss spoke.

The next two hours were a blur. Half the town showed up with their families. Wade, charged with weighing and recording the fish, never sat down. Others from Green Energy ran the food tent, serving free hot dogs and hot chocolate.

People enjoyed the band. Wade liked giving and not asking anything in return, even for one day. Folks stood nearly elbow to elbow lining the creek. Franny's son, Ben, caught a good-sized fish.

"Twelve inches. That might put you in the running for a prize," Wade told the freckled boy, who resembled his mother.

LeeAnn, who was standing nearby, laughed out loud and Wade felt high.

When the contest ended and they'd handed out prizes, Harrington called up Elzer and Wade to make the announcement.

Elzer stood in front of the crowd between Wade and Harrington. "Green Energy let me know today they'll make a sizable donation to Minden Elementary. It will mean improvements to the building and more teachers, including a reading specialist." Elzer put his hands together. "Let's hear it for these gentlemen representing Green Energy, and for their generosity today."

Elzer shook hands with Harrington, and then Wade, as people clapped and whistled. LeeAnn had mentioned Ben's reading trouble. Wade was impressed by how quickly Harrington had put his suggestion into action. Wade found LeeAnn in the crowd. She and Franny were hugging, with Ben squeezed happily between. Too bad Jack wasn't there to see it all.

At long last he was set to be the hero instead of the pawn.

CHAPTER 11

LeeAnn

Despite the cold November air, LeeAnn rode with her window down to the orchard for the meeting with Wade and Jack, doubt and misgiving growing about whether it made sense for her to be there. She wanted the brothers to talk alone, but they seemed to need her as a bridge between them.

As she passed by her church, Reverend Joe hung new letters on the sign in front to read Autumn Leaves, Church Don't.

Just beyond the sign, heavy equipment scraped away the meadow and topsoil in the field on the west side of the church. She hit the brakes. On Sunday mornings she liked to sit in the pew that allowed her a view of that meadow. Now it seemed there would be no more goldenrod or aster or finches. What instead? She almost didn't want to know. She made a quick U-turn and pulled into the church lot.

She called to the reverend.

"LeeAnn," he said, smiling. "I was just thinking about your mom and dad. I'm planning to visit tomorrow. Do they need anything?"

"They're all right. Looking forward to your visit."

She pointed toward the machinery working not more than three hundred yards away. "What's going on?"

"It's good news, really. Green Energy bought the acreage to build a support complex. It's paid for the church's furnace. No one wanted to wear parkas during services again this winter. And we have enough left to pay for our new roof. That goes on next week."

She felt sheepish for having missed these decisions the church must have made over the last weeks.

"What kind of complex?"

"A trucking facility to receive and store pipe, sand, chemicals, and other supplies. It'll serve the whole region, as I understand. There will be a hotel and new restaurant to house and help feed the drillers. I know it's a change." He looked over at a dozer stripping topsoil from the ground. "You heard about Green Energy's donation to the school?"

"Yes." LeeAnn watched sumac and joe-pye weed yield to the machinery's blade. Who would eat at the "support complex" when workers left Minden, and would it take business from the Tic-Toc while they were here?

"Don't you think it will be out of place?"

"The new facility? Perhaps at first. But sooner or later it will be a part of Minden. Just like the buildings we have now."

These new buildings would be grafted onto Minden, for better or for worse. An experiment like the ones that she and Jack did with the apple trees over the years—crossing one breed with another, with mixed results. If a graft failed in the orchard, it could easily be gotten rid of. Not so with the changes in Minden, and it remained to be seen how this graft would take.

"The church was in real trouble, LeeAnn."

"I know," she said, starting her car. And it wasn't like she had better answers. But she drove off relieved to put the scene behind her.

When she got to the orchard, golden autumn light glinted off the bit of shellac still clinging to the faded wooden sign she'd designed and Jack had carved, that hung on the apple barn. It said Pierson Orchard in bold letters. She knew Jack read the sign with the possessive: "Piersons' Orchard." But LeeAnn had always thought of her and Jack as a part of the orchard. The trees were, after all, somewhere between natural and family made, shaped by hand, weather and soil. The trees taught them over time how to grow apples. And she and Jack and the Piersons before them had done the apples' bidding. The bugs ate the fruit and so they sprayed or found other ways to protect the apples. The suckers took energy from the crop, so they pruned. They trucked in bees to pollinate. During spring, after the flowers were on, they prayed in church for no frosts so they could get more apples. "Be fruitful and multiply" was the creed of every living thing. At least the trees had managed that.

She saw limbs that needed pruning. Her hands twitched to fix what she could see wasn't quite right, to do the trees' bidding, even now. The strawberry patch also needed to be mulched. That kind of work resulted in something concrete, rather than the emotional quicksand that lay ahead.

Wade's truck was not yet there.

She listened for and then heard Jack in the apple barn.

As she reached the barn door she heard the pop of Wade's tires on the gravel behind her. She turned. Wade's eyes met hers and he nodded as though to say, "I'm ready for this." She hoped so, because she realized she wasn't prepared.

She went into the barn ahead of Wade. Jack was bent over, working on the cherry picker. He no doubt wanted to avoid being cornered in the house.

He looked up at her. Even with a streak of grease down the side of his face, dressed in an old stained sweatshirt and jeans patched in the knees, he was handsome. She was relieved to see only a small Band-Aid above his eye from his most recent fight. She felt the pull of him even now and rubbed her finger over the place her wedding ring had been. He seemed to read her thoughts as he often had. Hope sparked in his eyes.

"LeeAnn?"

"Wade's here." She turned away, not wanting to encourage him. She stacked some apple crates into a corner, making an excuse about needing more room for all of them to talk.

"I need to fix this hydraulic line so I can get this picker back out this afternoon. The high limbs need pruning."

Jack would avoid this as long as possible. He bent his head down into the heart of the machine as soon as Wade walked into the barn. He'd asked his brother to the orchard, but he didn't acknowledge Wade and instead let him stand there, as though to say he could deal with his brother when he was good and ready. LeeAnn pulled up two chairs, one for Wade and one for herself. If Jack chose sides, then so would she.

LeeAnn said, "Is it all right if we talk in here? Jack needs to get the picker going."

"Whatever works."

She sat, but instead of following suit Wade put a folder he'd brought on the chair. It looked like one of his gas lease information packs. The papers appeared too crisp and clean in the barn, like his aftershave seemed out of place next to the smell of pressed apples and Jack's sweat. She hoped Wade wasn't going to try to steer the conversation toward gas leasing right away. There was so much more they needed to talk about.

Wade pulled a pen out of his pocket. He clicked it nervously.

Jack finally stopped what he was doing and wiped his greasy hands on a rag. He shook his brother's hand. "Thanks for coming. I figured we should talk some, now that you're back and settled in."

"Yeah," Wade said, with a nervous laugh.

Jack stood there with his hands on his hips.

"Minden sure hasn't changed much in all these years." Wade made it sound as though this counted as a negative.

"Oh?"

"Except this orchard. You always felt for this place, and it shows. Looks better than when I left. You and LeeAnn both deserve credit for that, I guess." He turned toward her for a moment, as though they were also just meeting for the first time.

Wade's words fell awkwardly. Jack called this meeting. He had to start the conversation they needed to have. Where could either of them even begin? LeeAnn tried to think of something helpful to say but came up empty.

Jack picked up a hacksaw from the ground and went back to the picker. He started cutting away at the damaged hydraulic line. "Why don't we start by you telling us what you know about the drilling?"

Wade crossed his arms and turned so he could talk to both of them. "You're sitting on millions of dollars in gas rights and royalties."

Jack put down the saw and picked up a rasp, as though Wade had only mentioned an eighty-percent chance of sunshine. He flared the ends of the line he'd cut. "Is that right?"

Wade clicked his pen a few more times and then put it back into his pocket.

This wasn't the conversation these two men needed to have. Still, maybe if they started with this, then the stuff that mattered would follow.

"How does it work? I mean, what's the process?" LeeAnn asked. She could at least learn for her parents' sake.

"You sign a deal to lease your gas rights," Wade said. "I can help you with that. That gets you money up front. If they decide to drill a well, and they don't always, then you get money on top of that from the gas that's taken from the ground. Those are the royalties."

Jack looked at LeeAnn. "How fast do we get the money?"

She wished he wouldn't toy with Wade by pretending to consider leasing.

"You'd have a check less than two weeks after signing. You could hire more help, do improvements, take a vacation, get a retirement plan, and whatever else would make your life easier."

Jack put down the rasp he'd been using. He asked LeeAnn what she thought, as though actually considering the idea of leasing his family's orchard.

"I . . . I'm not sure," she replied, confused.

Wade leaned toward Jack and said in a low voice, "I would love to be able to help you after all this time. I know I haven't been here. This job gave me a way to return."

"You didn't need this job to come back here," Jack said.

Wade flinched. If Jack noticed, he ignored it. Typical.

"You know the orchard was never my thing. This is my way of being able to help."

Jack came over to speak to LeeAnn—but not so close that Wade couldn't hear. "We'd have money. I know you don't want to adopt. But maybe this gives us a way. And you could have those extra acres you want."

His candor now, in front of Wade, embarrassed her. Was he trying to claim her in front of his brother? How had she slept next to this man for twenty years of her life? He seemed completely foreign to her now.

She looked at her husband and shook her head. She'd heard other women talk about labor pains and how it wasn't that each spasm was so painful, but you had to endure them for so long and in the end with your tolerance gone, they became unbearable. She'd often thought of her relationship with Jack that way. It had been good and solid for a long time, like a pregnancy in which you can only look forward to how happy your life will be.

Then her infertility.

Their problems had started out as an ache, a dull pain that could be breathed through. But when Jack stopped talking to her about anything that mattered and took up his Thursday night fistfights, she was left with endless time to think about how much she wanted a baby to love. A child to pass the land on to, a child to carry part of her mother on in this life, a child to bring her and Jack back together. And then she watched that possibility dwindle, alone. After two, three, four barren years she couldn't look past it anymore, a pain she could no longer talk through. In time her relationship with Jack had become unbearable. Years five, six, seven, and eight passed. Her only choice had been to leave him to cut the pain—both his and hers. Freeze him out of her life, along with any hope of a child, before nothing remained of either of them to save.

Back when she'd still had hope, she'd suggested the one possibility that might have saved them—to sell some of their property to get money for fertility treatments—and he'd said no.

And now, *now*, he wanted to lease their land for drilling?

Jack crouched down before her, so that they were eye to eye. He pressed on, oblivious. "I want to find out more. I want to know if it's safe. But maybe we should consider it."

LeeAnn didn't respond. Given that her chances of conceiving at her age were so small, his proposal now felt insincere—and too late.

"We should think about it, is all I'm saying," Jack turned back to the picker.

Wade sat beside LeeAnn and she desperately needed to go outside for air. She wished she'd never pulled up the two chairs or agreed to this meeting in the first place.

Wade said, "What about the land on either side of the creek? It's not part of the existing orchard and probably won't ever be. You could start small, see how it goes, and then lease more later if you want."

That land was the same piece LeeAnn had asked Jack about selling. Part of it sat at the base of the gap, where they'd all started up the mountain that fateful day. She'd thought Jack would be glad to be rid of it.

Jack had an odd look on his face she couldn't read.

"What do you think?" Wade said.

Jack stood up from the picker, looking directly at Wade for the first time. "The property across the creek is not mine."

LeeAnn stood. "Whose is it, then?"

CHAPTER 12

Jack

"IT'S STELLA'S LAND," Jack said.

As soon as the words were out of his mouth, Jack knew he'd gone too far. He focused on the hydraulic lines in front of him, slipping clamps over the ends he'd flared.

"You're kidding, right?" Wade said.

Jack replied, eyes still on his work. "Dad gave it to her. A wedding present."

LeeAnn would not take this well. He wished he hadn't brought it up. He glanced up to see Wade standing too close to her.

Tightening the clamps on the line, his hands never stopped. Wade should see that work on the orchard never ended. It was hard every day, requiring hands and energy that stood by. Not just when it felt right or opportunities arose. He worked as hard as he could, every day. Anybody could see that. Especially LeeAnn.

"You didn't want to sell our land because it connected to hers?" LeeAnn said.

"Partly." The truth now in front of his brother shamed

him. Wade shouldn't see inside their lives like this.

"Why did you keep that from me?"

He cringed. This was a private conversation. One they should have had a long time ago. Stella had held onto that acreage for a reason and so had Jack until she could tell him why she'd kept it. LeeAnn had been right about one thing: for them, adoption had never been the right answer. Children were meant to know who they came from.

"I can try to explain, but not now." Not in front of Wade.

"How did you find out?" Wade asked.

He answered only to buy himself time to think about what he might say to LeeAnn to help her understand. "I logged a bunch of land right after Dad died. To make ends meet. When I had to get the deeds together for the permit, I asked Elzer to help me. He's the one that told me."

"You've known, all this time?" LeeAnn asked.

Jack nodded. He'd let his anger get the best of him. LeeAnn moved a step closer to Wade.

"She must have gotten a letter from Green Energy, like you did. We contacted every landowner," said Wade.

"If she did, I haven't heard."

"Like that's a surprise," Wade retorted.

"She's a lawyer," Jack said. "Does something with protecting water. Maybe she knows if the drilling is safe."

"You going to ask her?" Wade said with a sarcastic laugh.

"We're done talking about anything useful," LeeAnn said, turning her back on both of them and stalking off, leaving the brothers alone.

Wade's eyes followed her out the door and Jack wondered if he would have the gall to go after her. But instead, Wade walked over to the window, staring out over the old shooting target he and their dad had used for practice before the hunt each year. Including the day before the accident. That target practice and what followed the day after confirmed for Jack what he already knew even back then: their lives were driven by something out of their control.

Jack fitted the hydraulic line back together as the sound of his dad's voice came into his head.

"Left of the bullseye. Now right. Three more times, just like that." Dad had barked and Wade reacted.

Dressed in camo, Dad and Wade looked even more alike than usual. They laughed at jokes just between the two of them. During that last practice, pride showed in their dad's face, despite his grudge against Wade. Jack, who worked by his father's side every day, had never gotten that prideful look. At least Wade had been able to count on it every hunting season.

"Reload," Dad said before walking toward the target. He stapled a new paper bullseye to the tree and then stood next to it. "Go ahead, Wade."

"As soon as you move out of the way," Wade said.

"You hit the target every time. You'll do it again. Challenge yourself. I'm going to stand right here."

"I don't know, Dad. That doesn't seem like a good idea." Wade's voice had a pleading tone Jack knew grated on their father.

The Pierson boys didn't go against their dad. That lesson had been beaten into them. Jack held his breath.

"Take your shot," Dad said, the edge in his voice sharpening.

"Can you move a little farther away?"

"No. Do it now!"

Jack watched his brother raise his gun and then lower it.

"Shoot. The. Gun," Dad snarled.

Wade raised the rifle again. Jack watched his hand shake. Sweat rolled off his temples even in the cold November air.

Wade would do what Dad said in the end. He'd gone against their father as far as either of them ever had, by telling of his plan to leave the home orchard for something "better." And no matter how brave he talked, he would do what he could to regain Dad's approval. Just like Jack would have.

"Don't, Wade," Jack said. He'd never contradicted his father. But if Wade had the guts to tell Dad he wasn't going to stay on at the orchard, Jack could at least muster the courage to speak against his father's lack of empathy for those he was supposed to love. Jack walked over to stand beside his brother.

"Don't listen to that dimwit. Shoot. Now!" Dad yelled.

"No!" Jack yelled back, his gut lending strength to his voice.

Wade lowered the gun and wiped the sweat away.

"What are you *doing*?" Dad yelled.

"It's too dangerous," Jack said.

"The only thing he has to be afraid of is losing his nerve."

"And if he accidentally hits you?" Jack said.

"Quit simpering. You're just like your good-for-nothing mother."

Wade raised the gun and shot the target four times, dead center.

Dad, who'd let his guard down, jumped a foot in the air and cried out in a high pitch. He recovered quickly and checked the target. "What did I tell you? Now you're ready for anything, son."

Oh, but they hadn't been ready when the very next day Jack carried his dead father on his back down the mountain moving fast—because he wanted to outpace the horror, yes, but also to reach a place where it hadn't happened, where his brother was still innocent and his dad was alive. But that was not to be, ever.

The unexpected ruled. One day life was normal and the days endless and the next your dad was dead. Or your wife left because you couldn't father a child. Or your brother was back ready to step in with the woman you loved but had failed.

Wade left the window in the barn and walked toward Jack. He seemed utterly defeated, let down by Jack's silence. Jack wanted to say something to let Wade know he didn't hate him. That he was sorry, too. But no words came. It was a cop out. Still, he could muster no peace offering. He let Wade leave without saying another word, or even glancing in his direction.

Jack switched on the cherry picker to test the hydraulic line. Fluid bubbled from the line and then sprayed his face.

"Shit," he said, turning off the machine. He spat bitter black liquid.

CHAPTER 13

LeeAnn

JACK TRADED THE possibility of a loving family with their child for a mother who'd abandoned him decades ago. Unbelievable. She rubbed at the counter until her shoulder ached.

"LeeAnn?" Doc was squeezed in at the counter next to Stu. "Could I get the check, or are you too busy thinning the Formica?"

While she wrote up his breakfast tab she listened to the conversation between Doc and Stu, which had reached well beyond the types of bait and fishing line they usually discussed. Their Sudoku book sat untouched at its place by the register.

"What did they offer you?" Stu asked Doc.

"There's been different offers made," Doc replied.

"What were the numbers?"

"I'm not even sure."

"My brother wants to hold out," Stu said, "but I say close the deal now. Except I can't get anyone to tell me what they've been offered, so I can't convince him. I just want to be able to buy a house for the family."

"They want all my property," Doc said. "I'm not sure about that. So it's different figures depending on how much I'm willing to lease."

"You holding out on me?"

LeeAnn laid bills in front of Doc and Stu. She reached up to rub the tension from her neck that grew stronger from listening to two old friends argue. She heard that too much these days.

"Stu, I told them I'd keep the lease amount confidential until we had a deal. I gave my word," Doc said.

"But I'm your friend. And me and my brother need this money."

"When I've made a decision, I'll let you know."

"Don't bother." Stu got up and walked toward the door.

"You leaving me with your bill, too?" Doc yelled.

"At least you can afford to pay."

LeeAnn tore up both tabs and dropped them in the trash. "Just forget it," she said.

Wade came in with drizzle clinging to his unusually rumpled hair.

LeeAnn took his order at the counter. His eyes were bloodshot. She hoped he would get himself together by the time he met with her parents later that day.

She poured his coffee. "Looks like you could use this."

"That obvious?" Wade said, looking at her with the thinly veiled adoration that never seemed to waver. She had to admit it felt good.

"Kind of."

"How do you think it went yesterday with Jack?" he said.

"Maybe it was too much too soon."

"I pushed too hard didn't I?"

"We've got a lot to think about. A lot to talk about. All of us."

"I want to help, is all. But I could tell you were uncomfortable. I'm sorry."

She shrugged. "It's complicated. I hadn't really thought about leasing the orchard before our meeting yesterday. I have other stuff on my mind, too."

Franny touched her arm and pointed to two tables of people waiting. LeeAnn handed out menus, then drinks.

"Order's up, LeeAnn," the cook called.

She slid the plate of scrambled eggs in front of Wade.

"You and Jack should take the time you need," Wade said.

"When are you meeting my parents?"

"It's my first stop after breakfast."

When he finished his food, LeeAnn gave him the bill and cleared his plate.

He met her at the register and handed her cash. "I've been thinking, LeeAnn."

"About?"

"Let me make you dinner tonight. Just friendly," he said in a low voice.

She thought it over. Jack had shown how much he cared. She needed to get on with her life. "Maybe."

"I can answer some of those questions you still have about drilling. Or we can talk about whatever you want."

Had anything between her and Jack been as real in his heart as it had hers?

"So how about it? Dinner?"

"I think . . . yes, okay. What time?" LeeAnn said.

"Six?"

She nodded.

"My change?" he said with a smile.

"Sorry." She counted out his money.

"I heard you were ripping up bills this morning. I'm disappointed you're making me pay."

She smiled at him. "Only so many free meals allowed in one day."

CHAPTER 14

Stella

STELLA WORE A pair of jeans and a simple cabled sweater that she hoped didn't announce *lawyer*.

She wanted to start with Wade. To be upfront about why she was in Minden. Otherwise it could look like sabotage.

Elzer had mentioned Wade was staying at the Red Leaf.

First step was to see if he'd agree to talk. She wouldn't try to explain anything right away, just let him know she'd be around. They could sit down together when they were both ready.

After checking at the Red Leaf office she headed toward the steps to Wade's room on the second floor. The parking lot was now nearly empty, all the company reps out to make a deal or laying the groundwork for drilling.

Stella knocked, afraid to hesitate for even a moment, lest she lose her nerve. Wade's door opened. Stella said nothing and neither did Wade for a moment.

"I'm . . . I'm . . ." she said.

"God, you look just like Jack."

"I know this is unexpected—"

"What are you doing here?"

"I should have called first, but I want to talk to you. This isn't the right time and place, but . . ."

His voice rose. "I don't want anything from you. Not now. Not ever."

"Please. Can we talk later? When you have time and I can explain? I should have . . ."

"There's nothing to say."

"Wait, don't close the door yet."

"Then you'd better tell me why you're here and you better do it now." He spat the words.

"I understand you're working for Green Energy."

He made no reply.

"I've been working on a case that involves them. Polluted water. Damaged land."

"You're talking about bad well construction. I know all about that. Green Energy has paid for it and learned. They do it differently now. It's not going to happen again."

"Maybe not. But accidents can still happen. And . . . oh, this is coming out all wrong! I'd like to explain."

"Get out of here," he said. "Nobody around here needs an emotionally driven environmental campaign full of misinformation. You'll be run out of town, lady, and I'll be leading the charge." He slammed the door shut.

"I shouldn't have come to you like this, without calling first. I didn't think it through, but if you'd hear me out," Stella tried to explain through the closed door.

"Go to hell!" Wade growled, his loud voice only slightly muffled.

Stella returned to her car and sat unmoving, feeling as inept as she had when her sons were little.

CHAPTER 15

Wade

WADE SPED TOWARD the Moore house, his fear of returning there overridden by anger. Stella's surprise visit—or ambush, more like—replayed in a continual loop. From cold mother to cold lawyer, showing up to save the fucking land and water, without concern for her sons. He shifted from third into fifth, grinding the gears of the company truck. Screw her.

Just when he was getting his feet under him again, she returns to sabotage his life. Stella, the curse that would not go away. Rolling down his window to get some air, he turned the radio on full blast. Anything to get her out of his mind.

He pulled into the Moore place with no memory of having driven there. The sad house sat at the base of Morrigan Mountain. Gabriel Moore had been kind and understanding in every way his father and Stella hadn't.

When Wade had made plans to leave the orchard and work on Gabriel's farm, Wade had wanted his father to know his son had chosen the Moore farm, where people loved each other. It had infuriated Dad.

The last time he'd sat in the Moore kitchen had been the last time he'd been together with his dad and Jack, and later that day, the moment he'd lost all faith in Stella. The thought of going into the house now seemed too much on the heels of her visit.

But then Gabriel appeared through the front door. Wade pulled the parcel maps and lease agreement information from his bag. Gabriel was no longer the tall, indestructible force he'd once seemed. But he was still, Wade hoped, an understanding man.

Wade waited for Gabriel and tried to shake off the residue of rage from Stella's visit. A black and white border collie appeared out of nowhere to walk beside Gabriel. The sun came from behind a cloud, leaving few shadows, as if reminding Wade there was nowhere to hide. He took a deep breath and let it out. He needed to be here for this man.

"Place looks great," Wade said, because that's what he always said to new prospects. He forced a smile. He felt capable of nothing more than sticking to his script. But this was LeeAnn's dad, and Wade wasn't some out-of-town flunky buying gas rights. He had history here, if a terrible one. But maybe also a future.

"It's good to see you again, Wade. Long time now." Gabriel offered his hand.

This man was as genuine as Wade remembered. No questions lingered in his eyes about what Wade had been doing or why he'd left. As Wade shook Gabriel's hand, tears came. "I'm sorry," Wade said, turning away. He let out a long breath. "It's hard being in Minden again, even with two weeks gone by already. I'm right back to that day sometimes."

Gabriel patted him on the back. "No need to apologize."

With hot embarrassment, he confessed, "I don't think I can come into your house. The memories." Silver Creek was the only sound between them.

"We'll talk in the barn. Rose is resting. She had a poor night's sleep."

Wade nodded and tried to get hold of himself. He didn't want to add to this man's problems. "I'm sorry, Gabriel. I understand she's not well."

LeeAnn had said little about Rose, but she'd said enough.

Gabriel nodded, almost imperceptibly.

"Good to see Rose's gardens again," Wade said, pointing to the dormant beds surrounding the house on all sides. During Wade's childhood, the flowers lifted the old house out of its desperation, as Gabriel and Rose had lifted him and Jack.

"She loves her flowers, especially zinnias," Gabriel replied, leading the way past the rusty equipment outside the barn and into his office, still a small dusty room crammed to overflowing with *Pennsylvania Dairy Farmer* magazines. The old farmer perched on top of a stack so Wade could have the chair.

"It's kind of you to see me," Wade said.

Sitting across from Gabriel, Wade felt as though he'd taken in a breath the last time he saw him and only now could he exhale. Being with him took Wade back to that day so viscerally. He'd experienced nothing like it since his return, not even when he and LeeAnn had gone to the Gap. The apologies he'd held in for two decades came bubbling up.

"I shouldn't have taken the shot that day, with Dad that close." So much shame poured out of him that he fought to keep sitting upright. Time seemed to bend. He was eighteen again, saying words he'd said only to himself and no other.

He glanced at Gabriel, hands folded, as they'd been when he'd sat down. His head was bowed, but he nodded. "Well. Regret can eat you alive. Best to make what peace you can."

Wade wiped his eyes.

After a moment, Gabriel said, "LeeAnn thinks this land might be worth something to Green Energy, and I've got more bills stacked up than I care to think about."

Wade's training kicked in and he was relieved to put it into automatic. He sat up a little straighter.

"The going rate for leases is a thousand an acre. You've got fifty, so if you leased every acre, you could see about fifty thousand right from the start. On top of that royalties will bring you twelve percent on the gas that's harvested from the well. The royalties last as long as the gas does."

"Would they be interested in every acre?"

"They like to have flexibility as to where they drill."

"I see." Gabriel thought on that. "Can I keep my animals?"

Wade nodded. "They're only after the gas underneath."

"I don't want Rose bothered. She's sensitive now to noise and smells."

Wade looked through the window back at the house. "I'll let them know. Although there are no guarantees where and when—or even if—they drill."

"But you'll tell them about Rose."

"Yes."

"I heard they send out scientists to do tests."

"To see if there's enough gas to make it worth drilling. If not, then they'll be on their way, leaving you with the lease money. If they do drill, the gas company won't take over the whole place, but they'll disturb a few acres. Three, maybe five of your fifty. That only lasts a short while and then your place returns to normal. But you should decide soon. Like I said, we'll go as high as a thousand an acre, and that's probably as high as you're going to see."

"Sounds mostly good. Let me talk to Rose about it, and I'll be in touch."

Wade handed him a contract to look over. "Other energy companies will be by to see if they can get your business."

"You're the first one that's been here in person."

"They'll come, too. If they offer better, let me know and give me a chance to counter. Things can change overnight."

"I'd prefer to deal with you."

For the first time, Wade truly felt like he'd been right to return to Minden.

"I'll leave the lease contract with you. You and Rose would both need to sign. You let me know if you have any questions. I'll check back in a couple days."

"Mind if we shake on what we've discussed?" Gabriel asked.

Wade took the older man's hand. The hand of the father he'd wished had been his.

Getting this lease would be like a vote of confidence to the rest of Minden, but it would mean more to Wade personally. It would be permission to stay.

CHAPTER 16

LeeAnn

LEEANN KNOCKED ON Wade's door feeling a little ill at ease. She reminded herself it was only a dinner between old friends.

He opened the door with a hot mitt on one hand, smelling of aftershave, his hair still wet from the shower and his t-shirt tucked haphazardly into his jeans.

"Welcome." He ushered her in with a flourish of his mitt-free hand.

She took off her coat and laid it on the back of a chair by the door, before taking a seat there. Being in Wade's room, alone with him, suddenly felt too intimate. Telling Franny about the old times with Wade had brought up feelings she'd had for him. She couldn't deny that she liked the attention Wade gave her. There was something about him that made starting over feel possible. Maybe because they'd known each other at a time in their lives when every door was still open.

Wade handed her a glass of wine and finished cooking their dinner over a cook stove he'd set up where the TV usually sat. She sipped the wine and looked around his room. It was tidy with no sign of his work anywhere. She wondered where he'd hidden his suitcase. The only thing on the desk beside her was a little loose pocket change. A few quarters, mostly pennies. That, and what looked like a small pink stone.

She stood and picked up the pebble. She put it in the palm of her hand and held it under the desk light.

"I've kept it all these years," he said, quietly, keeping his eyes on the food cooking in front of him.

She'd found the rounded piece of rose quartz sitting in Silver Creek at the base of the bridge in town one hot day when they'd been swimming. It had been early in their relationship at the peak of first love. That had been the summer before the accident. She'd never found another stone like it. He'd told her at the time that the stone reminded him of her: pure and beautiful. Like an angel. That was right before she'd looked up from the creek at the bridge and noticed Steve Pierson watching them.

"Are you hungry?"

She nodded and placed the stone back where she'd found it. He'd set up a small table covered by a yellow gingham cloth. He pulled out one of the folding chairs. She sat and he pushed her chair in before handing her a napkin that matched the tablecloth.

"Part of your Green Energy training?"

"I worked in a fancy restaurant once." He sat across from her and topped off her glass of wine.

"And as a mechanic. Interesting mix of jobs."

"Mostly I've been a salesman."

"Where was that?"

"Philly."

She rested her chin on one hand. "Is that where you've been all this time?"

"And a few other places." He cleared his throat.

"Maybe you could help at the diner," she half teased.

"I didn't last long in the restaurant business."

He filled two plates and set one before her. "Pork chops, fried apples, and spinach salad. *Bon appetit.*"

He held up his glass. "Cheers."

She touched her glass to his and sipped. "You seem happy," she said, smiling herself.

"I'm glad you're here. For our friendly dinner."

"Me, too."

Looking at her with a half grin, he said, "Can you still whistle real loud, like when we were kids?"

"Funny that you should think of that. I think I can."

She put two fingers in her mouth and blew hard.

He raised his hands to his ears. "It always impressed me that you could whistle louder than the boys."

He sure did make her feel attractive. Nice enough for her to push aside her worries about her parents and Jack for a moment. She took a bite. "This is good. You did this on a camp stove?"

"I learned *some* things in the restaurant business."

Spreading his napkin on his lap, he said, "I saw your dad today about the lease."

"And?"

"He wants to talk to your mom first, of course, but I think they'll lease. If they do, I'm proud to help. I think you know I've always looked up to them."

LeeAnn moved the food around on her plate. They'd be able to keep the house and their property, and for that she was grateful. "My mother was born in that house. She wants to die there. Dad will do whatever he can to make that happen."

"I know their situation," he said gently. He reached across the table and squeezed her hand. His touch soothed her as much as the softness of his voice. "They're good people. Maybe the lease money will give them what they need most—some peace of mind."

He refilled their glasses and grew more serious. "I had a visitor today before I went out to see your mom and dad."

"Oh?"

"Stella."

LeeAnn put down her fork. "Stella Pierson?

He nodded.

"In Minden?"

"That's right. I was as taken aback as you are."

"What did she want?"

"She's against the drilling. Probably lives in a big, fancy house with no worries about money. She's trying to squash opportunity for people like your mom and dad."

"She does something with environmental law? Is that why she wanted to talk?"

"She had a case against Green Energy once. I didn't know that she'd personally been involved, but I'd heard about it. Something to do with water pollution."

LeeAnn crossed her arms. "I hope if there's risk of something like that, my parents know about it up front."

He shook his head. "The way the wells are installed now is completely different. That problem can't happen again. It's safe, LeeAnn. The drilling will be good for this town. I'm hoping to stay around here and see how the changes play out."

She picked up her fork. "Won't you have to go where this job takes you?"

"I'm going to ask them to let me work from here as much as possible."

"You want to stay?"

"I'd like to," he said, holding her gaze. "I want to be a part of something, instead of always on the move. And I can get another job if this one doesn't work out. I've had plenty. I feel accepted here, finally. The meeting with your dad today helped."

She sipped her wine, feeling more at ease.

After they were finished, Wade cleared away their dishes and put on some music.

"Dance with me," he said.

"Wouldn't that be a little more than friendly?"

"Just one dance."

He took her hand, pulled her from her chair, and drew her close. She felt heat in her belly as though she'd just taken a strong drink. She wondered what would have happened if they'd held each other like this after the accident.

When the song ended they stayed together, waiting for the next song to begin.

CHAPTER 17

Stella

WADE HAD BEEN four when Stella last saw him, always calling and searching for her in the darkened rooms she'd preferred back then. He'd needed more than she'd been capable of giving. The rational, lawyer part of her understood his anger now. But another part of her—a part buried so long ago it felt petrified until today—hoped that deep inside Wade still wanted his mother. Instead he'd told her to go to hell.

On her way out of Minden, two out-of-state trucks rumbled past. More geologists working on pre-drilling investigations, their trucks loaded with sensitive equipment that would monitor depth charges they would place in the ground, like little firecrackers, to see where the drill holes should be placed. Just like her, they were after entry points.

She'd tried to talk to Wade in precisely the way she'd wanted to avoid. The problem with offering Jack or Wade an explanation was that she didn't have one that would help. She'd left them because she'd been incapable of giving them a good life.

If she could show them how to protect the orchard and Minden, they would see that she cared. They didn't want the land poisoned, like she'd seen two counties to the west. Those people would never regain their peaceful life. They would forever depend on bottled water and be stuck with property no one wanted. If only Wade had agreed to meet her at another time, when they could have talked in a more objective way.

Stella started her car and headed east out of town. There were no places to stay in or near Minden. All rooms within a forty-mile radius were crammed with people who'd arrived to get the drilling off the ground.

She drove to a hotel about an hour away near the Delaware River. She felt closer to Patrick, now downstream of her, just as her sons had always been upriver. From her window, she imagined she could see lines of tainted frack water in the churn, mixing until it became invisible.

Having had little sleep the night before, and given the emotional expense of the day, she slept most of the afternoon. Her phone woke her as the light faded.

"Stella?" Patrick said.

She sat up in bed. "I decided to stay in a hotel. I need one more day here."

"You could have called. I've been worried sick."

"I fell asleep and lost track of time."

Silence. Stella could hear him tapping his fingers on the wall or his desk at their office. "I don't know about this, Stella."

"It's only one more day. We agreed I needed to come here."

"Did you see your sons?"

"I saw Wade."

"And?"

"It didn't go well," she croaked.

"I'm sorry about that," he said, with real feeling.

"I'm going to see Jack tomorrow and try to explain what went wrong."

He waited for her to say more. He deserved more.

"You know I love you, Stella."

"Yes," she said, bracing herself. She knew the tone in his voice meant an impending shift in their conversation.

"I support you. But I need you here. We've got a case going to trial in a week. As soon as you can, I need you to prepare. I have to go out of town tomorrow again for Sunrise Solar. It's unexpected. The merger deal has turned acrimonious and the execs are keeping the buyer a secret. We desperately need the paycheck. I can't say no or put Sunrise off. We're in a serious financial mess. We could lose the firm. And it's not just that. I need you here with me. Given what you've shared about your past, we need to work through why you've kept so much from me. We haven't talked the way we should. It's not what you told me, but why you've kept it from me that I'm worried about."

"Tomorrow, I promise. After I talk to Jack."

"I won't be here tomorrow."

"I can't leave without seeing Jack. You need me and I want to be there, but I'm here for us. This thing with my sons has been unresolved for too long and it's not good for them or us."

After a long moment he said, "You know I understand what it's like to hide something."

About a year after they'd met, Patrick had fallen into a depression. Something he'd periodically suffered with all his life but had never mentioned to her before then. His depression had ended his first marriage.

"You've always helped me. You've never wavered," he said.

"Thank God you haven't had any trouble lately, Patrick." She wondered if he was warning her he could feel something coming.

"I understand now why you've loved me despite that and maybe even because of it," he said. "You understand what it's like to live with something you want no one else to know. You understand how impossible that is."

"Patrick . . ."

"Just figure yourself out and come back to me, all right?"

He hung up the phone with a soft click, and she hoped it wouldn't become a shut door. One shut so softly he'd be lost to her before she noticed.

She dialed Jack's number, gripping her cell. "I feel awkward talking to you on the phone," she admitted.

"Don't," he said.

She stared out her window at the river. "I tried talking to Wade, but it didn't go well. Can I meet you at the orchard to talk about what happens next?"

He let out a long breath. "I'm around tomorrow. Do you know how to get here?"

"Yes," she said, her voice too high.

CHAPTER 18

Jack

November 29 – Wonder how it would be to stop everything. To quit like Wade. Stella visits today, finally.

GRAY CLOUDS STOOD steady above the orchard dusted white by the first snowfall. The land had the blank look of late November, leaves stripped from the trees and grasses gone pale.

Jack watched for Stella from his ladder perched in a Cortland, pruning shears at work. He lopped off branches and thought about how the Pierson line had also been cut. Starting with Stella and his dad, and then continuing in his relationship with LeeAnn. Wade didn't appear to have children either. The pattern established by his family—with Piersons passing the orchard along to Piersons—was broken. The ghosts Jack sometimes saw out of the corner of his eye were all he had now. Maybe they were the same ones he fought in the ring.

The shears lay heavy in his cold, numbed hands. His nose dripped. His arms ached from years of pushing too hard. In the end, what would it matter? LeeAnn had whispered to him many nights about what would become of the orchard and her parents' place if they had no child. Then it had sounded like blame. But maybe she'd been talking about what mattered to both of them: the legacy of this place and family.

Jack continued to hack away at the apple wood. He looked again for Stella's car.

No matter how much he wanted it to be different, part of him couldn't overcome what he'd once overheard his dad say: "Stella couldn't handle the children. They drove her away." Dad had blamed so much on Stella, but he'd also blamed his sons for her leaving. And Jack did feel responsible. He'd been old enough to remember how miserable she'd been, he and Wade her primary burden.

He climbed down from the tree and collected the downed limbs into a pile.

He'd asked Stella to Minden because she had experience with Green Energy. And even if what she had to say wasn't what Wade wanted to hear, it was part of the whole picture.

But more important, he and Wade needed an explanation from her.

Jack had acted out of anger when he'd picked up the phone Wade had left hanging and told Stella not to come all those years ago. He'd written her off. Told himself she wasn't part of their lives and didn't matter. And it had been a mistake, setting into motion so much heartache.

Her white Volvo crested the top of the drive, a city person's car rarely seen in Minden until recently. He propped his shears against the tree.

Even though Rose and Gabriel had felt more like parents over the years than his own, he'd never called them Mom and Dad. Apple trees were made of two parts. The top of the tree determined the variety, and the rootstock determined the tree's resiliency. Despite how absent they might have been, he was a combination of both his parents. His dad had given him his work ethic and his tendency to shut down when what he offered wasn't good enough. What had Stella given him?

He walked through the orchard toward her car, his feet held up by the land of his forefathers. The ghosts would surely be paying attention now.

Stella parked near the house and got out of her Volvo. She was dressed in jeans and a coat that wouldn't be warm enough, with spotless shoes soon to be muddied and scuffed. She made a full turn from where she stood, looking over the place. Of course the orchard would appear different to her now. A new fruit barn and many more trees. He suddenly ached for her approval like the little boy in the photo who'd wanted her to turn toward him instead of looking away.

"Jack?" she said, putting her hand out. Only a business-like offering, even now. He took her hand. It was dry and cold. He let go after only a moment.

"A handshake seems wrong, I guess," she said.

She said nothing about the orchard, but held on to her briefcase, full of professional purpose. This environmental lawyer was here to talk about the drilling. That's why Wade hadn't wanted to listen.

"What happened to your face?" she asked.

Jack reached up to touch his left cheek, the bruise still tender. "A fight."

Turning and pointing toward Silver Creek, hoping to shift the conversation to something he could talk about, he said, "It's a nice enough day. Why don't we talk by the creek, next to your property?" They needed to start at the place that held the only moment of her life he knew they'd shared.

She put her briefcase down next to her car and followed him over the half-frozen ground toward the sycamore tree. Ice clung to the roots exposed at the sides of the creek. He didn't cross over to her property, but instead stayed on his side.

"Do you mind if we sit?" She pointed toward a couple

of large rocks. She had yet to smile. He took a seat and she sat next to him burying her hands in her pockets, hunched against the cold.

She glanced across the creek, at the tree. She remembered that at least. He saw her wince at the jagged X through the words she'd carved all those years ago: MOM LOVES YOU. He pretended not to see. "So," he said.

"Yes?"

A stifling silence rose up between them, as though the creek were rising and filling his nose. She'd called him asking to talk. It hadn't been the other way around this time.

"Listen," she finally said. "I know this is awkward."

"What happened with Wade?"

She avoided his eyes.

"I think I made things worse. He's angry. Understandably, I suppose. I wasn't sure how to start talking to him. I wanted to do it in person. That seemed right, but I wasn't prepared."

"What did you say?"

"Well, I really only wanted to let him know why I was in Minden. But he didn't want to listen to anything. And I ended up saying something about my case against Green Energy, just trying to get him to slow down. That was the wrong thing to do."

No wonder Wade had shut down. Jack also couldn't figure what in fact she cared about. Her law work? Her land? She hugged herself, rubbing her hands up and down her arms. Cold was the word for her. Why hadn't he seen this when he visited her office?

He picked up a stone and tossed it into the creek, watching the rings move outward, one after another. He would share something personal with her. She needed to have a clue that for him, asking her to Minden was more than legal advice.

"I'm thinking of leasing. My wife and I have been trying to have a baby for a long time. The money might help."

She appraised him with wide eyes. He appreciated her

surprise and discomfort. "We're separated. I'm hoping the gas money will give us a way to reconcile."

Stella continued to meet his gaze. "There are things you should know, then."

She stood and paced in front of him. Muddy water oozed up from the crusty ground and splashed her shoes as she described the water-contamination problems of several families west of Minden. There'd been sickness. Property values had tumbled.

"Why hasn't this been on the news?"

She stopped pacing and sat back down beside him.

"The case was settled out of court. So details remain closed. But I wanted you and Wade to know, I've seen the other side of the drilling, and it can be ugly."

"People around here are farmers and hardworking folks who have been struggling for decades. Leasing makes practical sense for most of us."

"Gas drilling brings problems. Even if it's safe most of the time, it's not foolproof, Jack. That's what I've learned after doing more than a year's worth of hard work investigating."

He balled his hands and then opened them slowly, aching for a fight. She'd left, just like Wade, and expected, just like Wade, to come back here and tell people what they should do.

Beside them, Silver Creek rushed past. He closed his eyes to listen, hoping the sound would calm him as it usually did. "I heard the fracking fluid is ninety-nine percent water," he said.

"Even at one percent, that's a few hundred gallons of chemicals per well. We don't know all the chemicals in the fracking fluid, but we do know that some are carcinogens. We don't know enough. I've talked with people who sold their gas rights for a pittance and now they're left with property that is virtually worthless. I think I mentioned the case I settled with Green Energy involved toxic trespass. Neighbors who never leased in the first place wound up with water they couldn't drink."

The confident way she spoke pissed him off. She'd failed her family so completely and now she hid behind her law words and purpose. She committed toxic trespass now, showing up in Minden with no explanation for why she'd abandoned her family for a cause.

"People won't care about what you have to say," he said. "They've got bigger problems."

"Most won't. I hoped you might. Isn't this why you asked me here? You seemed concerned, too. Why are you being argumentative?"

She glanced at the tree again, seeming less sure of herself.

"I'm just trying to sort through all this. I don't know how I feel." He crossed his arms. He had asked her here, that was true. But she'd taken her time getting to Minden. And she sounded more interested in Green Energy than in helping him or Wade. "Anybody ask you to lease yet?"

"I got a letter."

"You don't need the money, I guess."

"I've been in debt most of my life, despite my degree. The firm I run with my husband is in trouble. More money would be welcome. But not this kind. Not for me anyway."

Her shoes, not to mention her car, spoke of a cushioned life. She had no idea about real need. "What if we decide to drill? You gonna stand in our way, being right next door?"

"I don't want my land harmed."

"Your land. Your cause. Why do you even pretend to care about your property? You never came here."

"I've always thought of it as my connection back here."

"Connection to what?"

She shifted uncomfortably.

"I've been taking care of your place all these years. Keeping the weeds down and whatnot. Watching it for you. I've protected it," he said, bitter tears coming to his eyes that he quickly wiped away.

"Tell me. Do you love this land, Jack?"

His laugh came out like a bark and for one wild moment he wanted to keep laughing that way until he scared her the hell off his orchard. "I stayed, didn't I? I've sacrificed more than you could possibly know."

"Then don't you want to keep your water safe? Protect what you have? This gas drilling is the biggest threat to clean land, water, and air that I've seen in my career."

Her career. Enough already. "I've saved every penny to keep this place alive. And I'm still barely, barely, hanging onto it," he said, voice shaking. "My wife and I couldn't have a baby. And since we have no money or insurance to help us, she left me. This isn't a matter of what's right for nature. It's what's right for the people like us who have been scraping by and doing without while we watch our lives crumble."

"Sounds like it's been difficult," she said softly, looking sorry for the first time.

She'd finally heard him, maybe. About time.

Then she turned into a lawyer again. "But Green Energy won't mention the risks, which are very much real. Even if there's no physical damage, you'll lose the sound of the country to the noise of drill rigs. Lights will run day and night. Each well—your well, should you decide to allow drilling—requires hundreds of trips by truck."

Four wheelers, jake brakes, and chain saws were as much a part of the country as the breeze through the trees. Jack shook his head. She had no idea about the life he had.

"This town is scarred from the coal mining days, just like so many other places. Fracking will bring new scars."

"This town wouldn't even be here if it weren't for the coal."

"Things go wrong. We're human," she said.

"Human beings stay where they're needed. Human beings admit to their mistakes."

She looked toward the creek, just like in the photo.

Were there tears in her eyes? Good, he thought. "From

far away, the answers might seem pretty clear. When you're right here and the drilling is about the only hope you can see, you don't want that taken away, too."

He'd always figured his family and the orchard were two things he could count on. Pierson family life before Stella and Steve had been steady and prosperous. But the orchard had become the place his mother abandoned. His father was shot. Wade had left him alone here. And now LeeAnn. The land meant loss, too. It took as much as it gave. Still it could allow him and LeeAnn a baby that just might save their marriage.

She stood. "I'd be happy to talk more about it, if you like. You know how to reach me."

Crossing her arms, she turned toward her car. After taking a couple steps, she stopped. With her back still toward him, she said, "I know I'm not giving you the answers you need. But if this is the last time we see each other, you should know I've thought about you and your brother over the years, even if I never reached out to you."

"Do you know how Dad died?"

The randomness of the gunshot that day, like a lightning bolt. It was a poison within him as potent as any potential gas leak could be.

"Yes. I'm sorry," she said.

"You *knew?*"

She appeared as torn open as he felt. Finally, he glimpsed more than a lawyer on a mission.

Stella walked on toward her car and he stayed by the creek. When she drove past him, he raised his hand to her at the last moment. He hoped she would see it for what it was—that he also didn't want to be shut down anymore. That if she wanted, she could try again.

The glare of the sunlight on her window prevented him from knowing her response.

MARCH

CHAPTER 19

Wade

GABRIEL AND WADE stood next to the dairy barn and watched as a loader pushed over fifty-year-old trees like sticks. Budded spring branches lay strewn about. The March morning, warm and thawed wet, smelled of promise. But the sign next to them said GREEN ENERGY in bold letters at the top, as though the property no longer belonged to Gabriel. At the bottom, the word WARNING was printed in red letters, followed by CONSTRUCTION SITE AHEAD. A bulldozer roared past so close they had to take a step back. It leveled and scraped an area four or five football fields in size. Smeared tire tracks ran through Rose's flower gardens.

The men operating the machinery worked fast. Gas prices had reached an all-time high and Minden was the new frontier. Overseas interest had the company eager to erase what had always been there to make way for the new.

Preliminary exploration of the Moore land showed potential. Green Energy wanted success with this first well to gain traction and spur on international investors.

Wade stole a glance at Gabriel. The older man's fists were clenched, his jaw set. Thank God LeeAnn wasn't there. Ever since Jack had withdrawn completely, things had been going well between them over the last few months, when work hadn't kept him away. They'd grown closer over dinners together, but Wade wanted more, and he'd hoped that night, when she came over for drinks, she would want more, too.

This mess, however, would upset her, just like it upset Gabriel.

"They have fifty acres to work with and they want to put a well in here?" Gabriel sounded pained, as though speaking these words aloud was more than he could do.

"How about I call them?"

Gabriel turned to him. "Did you tell them about Rose like we agreed? We shook on that."

"I'll tell them again."

Gabriel walked off toward the house. Wade didn't follow. He couldn't. He didn't want to hear the decibel level from inside. He didn't want to see the land violated from their windows. He didn't want to be reminded of how sick Rose had become, so thin now with bruised-looking eyes.

When he'd seen the plans for the drilling on paper, it hadn't seemed this close to the house. He hadn't envisioned the conversion of this farm into an industrial place it wasn't meant to be. He hadn't thought about the racket of the heavy machinery, the crack of wood against blade, the roar of engines and incessant backup beepers. The whole scene left him feeling hollow and wooden, like he wasn't part of his own body.

He stepped into the barn where it was slightly quieter and closed the door, cutting off the smell of diesel and exposed dirt to the pungent scent of manure mixed with fresh hay. Gabriel's cows, penned up behind him, moved in his direction, curious. He avoided their deep, questioning eyes and went into Gabriel's office.

He dialed Harrington Price's number at Green Energy

and described how close to the house they were, how Rose's cancer had grown worse. "Gabriel says she's got asthma now, too, and this prep work could kick up dust when it dries out. Can't we move the drill site even a few hundred feet?"

"What are you doing at the Moore's, Wade? We're paying you to get leases, not monitor drilling."

He'd done well in Minden and so Green Energy had sent him to new territory. They'd even allowed him to work out of the Red Leaf most days of the week.

"These are my friends. When they agreed to sign the lease, I told them the drilling would be done so it didn't bother Rose. I mentioned that to you."

"You know as well as I do, we have to go where the geologists tell us. And there were no stipulations in their lease agreement."

Wade ran his hand through his hair. He'd wanted the deal to go through and stipulations took time. "Listen, this is the first well. Everybody's watching. Jack and Elzer are still holding out. They aren't going to agree to a lease if we're going to drill so close to the house."

"The Moores want to make money and so do we. We're drilling where we have the best chance of getting the most gas. Gabriel and Rose will have royalties before anyone else in Minden. You've said they have medical bills. The faster we get the well in the ground, the faster the money flows. The real money comes with the royalties. We only have to get through this messy, loud phase."

Wade nodded his head, wanting to be convinced. Harrington had a way of turning Green Energy into the white horse Wade wanted so much to ride. "I know. I know. It just looks really bad."

"Remember, once the drilling is done, and it doesn't take long in the scheme of things, we reseed. And after it's all over, there's one small pipe coming out of the ground. Remind the Moores of that. While you're at it, remind Elzer and your brother. You're going to have to do what's difficult and courageous. You're going to have to stand by and take the long view. These people are going to thank you in the end."

"It's just hard seeing it for the first time. Especially here."

"All the more reason to head north where you're supposed to be working. I'm glad you're still thinking strategy about how to get Jack and Elzer's leases. That's why we sent you to Minden, after all. But you have new territory to cover. We need to make our move, just like you did in Minden, or someone else will."

Wade came out of the barn and looked once more at the Moores' closed front door. Then he left the farm in his rear view mirror. Harrington was right. They would thank him later.

That night he waited for LeeAnn to arrive and wondered if she'd spoken to her parents since he'd left the farm.

He took down the map of Minden hanging on his wall and stashed it away.

A short while later, when LeeAnn knocked on the door, he braced himself for the worst.

She handed him a warm apple pie. "For you." She closed the door behind her and slipped out of her coat.

So she hadn't talked to her parents yet.

"Come sit." He invited her to the small couch. He'd lit candles around the room since she liked them.

He poured her a glass of beer and handed it to her, then sat beside her. Their knees touched. Her eyes were beautiful in the candlelight.

"Some days this job seems more right than others. I'm assuming you haven't talked to your folks?"

She shook her head and frowned. "Did it start?"

"They're clearing and leveling. Your dad's having a hard

time. But it won't last long. Still, it's hard to watch."

Leaning back, she crossed her arms in front of her, and he worried their night would end early.

"How bad is it? What's got Dad upset?"

"Worrying about your mom, mostly."

She nodded, then covered her face with her hands. He put his arm around her and stayed quiet.

"I know my parents need the money," she said, "but I still don't know how to feel about all of it, I guess. Even now."

"Nothing wrong with being able to pay bills and stay afloat, is there?"

"But what happens when all this ends? People already seem different."

"In what way?"

"You haven't noticed? Folks wanting to find out who leased and with what company and for how much. Back when we were all just trying to get by, everyone was on even footing. Now those who don't have land or who haven't leased are poor and those who've sold gas rights are rich. Old friends are testy around each other."

"But most people are better off."

"Maybe." LeeAnn leaned forward and his arm slid from her shoulder. She reached for her drink and turned toward him. "I'm sorry," she said, shaking her head. "I'm worried about Mom and Dad. I shouldn't talk about any of this until I talk to them." She tried to smile.

He took her hand. "I want your folks to keep their home. I asked Green Energy to start with them, so they could get the money they need right away. I thought that's what you wanted." He needed her reassurance, not more questions and doubt.

"It is. I'm sorry." She let out a long sigh. "Once my mom . . . I just don't know how Dad will go on."

"At least they've had a chance to love each other all these years."

She met his eyes. "That's true," she said, managing a

real smile.

He took a long drink of his beer. "I wanted to love someone like that. But then life took a turn none of us were ready for."

Standing, he poured himself another full glass of beer and then sat down beside her.

LeeAnn reached over and took his hand. "We've needed to talk about this together. Tell me what you remember."

The stress of the day and now her tenderness broke him. That moment was where everything had stopped for them, for him. He wanted this confession. "I've always wondered what you were thinking. You know, after."

"I didn't know what to think."

"Dad. He never saw me, except when I put on my orange cap and hunting vest. That's when I felt like his son. The rest of the time I was in Jack's shadow."

"I know that's how you felt."

The details of those moments in the woods had never faded and had, in fact, only gotten stronger.

"The rack on that buck would've made the paper. I kept thinking how proud Dad would be when I brought it down. But the deer stood too far away and I didn't want to take the chance of missing."

She squeezed his hand, encouraging him.

"I heard footsteps in the distance. I thought it might be you. I wanted you to see the deer because I thought you'd be impressed. I had that pink stone in my hand, thinking it would bring me good luck. I wanted you to see that, too."

He stopped talking.

"What then?" she said, quietly.

He had all her attention. She'd been waiting for this as much as he had.

"The deer stepped into my line of shot. Then I saw Dad's orange vest. He nodded to me. I knew what he was telling me. 'Take the shot. This is what we've trained for. You can do it.'" Wade's voice cracked. "In that instant I thought he was so smart—that he'd seen this coming and I never should have doubted."

LeeAnn pressed his hand to her lips. "Jack told me about your dad and his target practice. Jesus, Wade. You were sixteen years old."

He had to tell her the rest. Now or never.

"I had so little time. I worried Dad would see the stone in my hand and know we were sneaking around behind his back. Things had been so difficult between me and him. It all happened so fast. *So fast.* I tried to put the stone back in my pocket. The gun slipped. It went off.

I saw Dad's orange vest in the leaves. He . . . he didn't move."

LeeAnn wiped away the tears on his face. She put both arms around him, hugging him to her breast.

He continued in a whisper. "I knew he was dead." He closed his eyes, once more trying to block the image of his father on the ground, so still.

"When I saw all the blood—I couldn't think. I would have taken any sort of abuse over his dead stare. It's haunted me. You have no idea."

She hugged him closer.

"Sometimes at night, I can still feel pressure on my trigger finger. The smell of gunpowder fills my nose. All of my senses get turned up times ten and I remember every detail, as if I could ever forget. The memory is part of me, growing more powerful and destructive over time. Sometimes, I think it will drive me crazy."

He started to tremble in her arms.

"Shush," she said. "Shush, now. It's all right, Wade."

He needed her to know everything. "I could hear you asking me to help get him down the mountain. But I couldn't move. When I came off that mountain with Elzer and your dad I wasn't the person who'd started up the gap that morning. I'm still not. Guess I hoped to find the old me by coming back here."

She drew away from him and cradled his face in her

hands. "I'm so sorry, Wade, that I left you there alone. I didn't know what else to do."

If only he hadn't been left alone. "I felt so far away I didn't figure I could get back. There was no human warmth. No forgiveness. I was so desperate."

"Oh, Wade. I need to—"

He put a finger gently to her lips. "Let me say the rest."

She nodded.

"After you and Jack left with Dad, time stretched out, even though the sun seemed to stay in the same place in the sky. I thought for a while that I'd shot myself and not Dad. That's how out of it I was. But then I would see the matted leaves and blood where Dad had fallen and I would check and realize that my fingers still moved. A self-loathing took over. So I prayed. Sent the message straight to Stella, bypassing God. Because God left me, and would never be with me because of what I'd done. I was sure Stella would be able to hear me. Half out of my mind, I know that now, but back then I believed she and I had a special bond. I thought she'd left that message on the sycamore for me and Jack as a promise to return. I'd passed it that morning on my way up the gap. I always thought she would come back."

"Dear God," LeeAnn said, holding him and rubbing his back. "I'm sorry. I—"

"But Stella didn't come."

"Wade . . ."

He wiped at his eyes. "I called her later to ask her for help." He laughed bitterly. "But Dad was right all along. She didn't care."

"But—"

He pulled her to him and kissed her. Her lips were so soft, just like he remembered.

When they parted, she said, "I'm so sorry we've never talked before this. We've both been carrying this around for too long."

"I know leaving before the funeral looked bad. It

seemed like I didn't care. But I couldn't face myself, let alone anyone else. Sitting up there alone, I found that pink stone I'd dropped and put it back in my pocket. I remember thinking that it represented who I was before the gunshot and if I held onto it I could hold onto that part of myself. Because I knew I'd become someone else, someone who'd just shot his father."

"Oh, Wade," she whispered.

"Being back here again and feeling like I'm finally doing good—it helps. I owe Elzer and your dad a lot for talking me down the mountain that day, but I've never really been thankful until I came back here and found a second chance."

"I'm so glad you're back."

"You were the one I came back for. Jack blames me for that day. But you know who I was. You understand."

"It was an accident, Wade. Absolutely an accident. Not your fault."

His shoulders collapsed. She hugged him closer, her breast damp with his tears.

"That moment has haunted me too," she said. "I'm sorry you've had these questions all this time."

He pulled her close. "Help me forget. Please. For a little while. Being with you helps me so much."

She bent and slowly kissed the tears on his face. She moved to brush his lips lightly with hers. He pulled her close. His desire for absolution heightened his long-held desire for her.

"I love you." These were words he'd never said. He hadn't planned to say them.

He unbuttoned her shirt. The primal part of him wanted her so bad. To taste what he'd left behind. He'd dreamed of little else.

He stopped unbuttoning her shirt to focus on kissing her. He wanted them to take their time. He pulled her onto his lap and took her hair into both hands, kissing her and groaning with desire.

She pulled away from his lips and whispered in his ear, "I want us to be a family."

He closed his eyes like he'd closed them on the mountain that day, the bond he'd felt with her just a moment before faltered.

When he opened his eyes, LeeAnn had undone the rest of the buttons on her shirt to reveal a sheer black bra.

He hesitated. Her bra turned him on and off at the same time. It was sexy as hell, with the pink of her nipple visible through the thin dark fabric. But the sheer blackness of it made him second-guess her. As much as he wanted to be with her, he now wondered how many times Jack had seen that same bra. How many different ways had Jack had her?

He'd bared everything to her. But was she really the pure soul he'd imagined? Still he wanted desperately to hold onto the closeness they'd just shared.

The smell of her clean, warm skin pulled him back into the moment. He pushed away the offending fabric and took a nipple in his mouth. He'd wanted this for so long.

She pulled away from him and stood up. Did she feel the same hesitation he did?

No. She began to take her clothes off, slowly, much as she had all those years ago while he watched through her bedroom window. He couldn't look away. She revealed herself to him one layer at a time. She had on black panties that matched the bra. Had she put those on intentionally? Had she planned what was happening between them?

He searched her face and felt at odds with the woman he'd been drawn to all his life. She stood beautiful and naked before him, and he ached for her like he was sixteen again. This time he could have her. But was she only after the family she'd never gotten with Jack?

He couldn't meet her eyes—the ones he'd sought salvation from just a moment before—and instead stared at her breasts. He could not deny the hunger of his body for hers.

She reached for his belt buckle. He closed his eyes again. She was making this happen. He felt as emptied as he had at the Moore farm earlier that day. But he let the thought go as he stood to let her take off his pants. She pushed him gently back onto the chair and climbed on top of him. He was powerless against her.

He lost his angel as he lost himself inside her.

CHAPTER 20

LeeAnn

When they closed for the day, Jack sent the harvest crew home early. He helped her lock up the fruit barn.

"We picked over an acre. I'm beat," he said, shutting off the lights and stretching his back. "My whole body aches."

She put her arm around his waist. "I know a cure for that. Come with me." She started off away from the house.

"LeeAnn. I want to go to bed."

She came back to him and pulled him by the arm. "Trust me. You need this."

"Need what?"

"It's our anniversary, so you have to do what I say."

He smiled despite himself and followed her, pretending to drag his feet.

She ran ahead of him toward the creek. "Catch me if you can," she yelled over her shoulder.

"I'm too tired to run. I've been trying to tell you that," he said, jogging after her anyway.

When they reached the edge of the swimming hole they'd played in as kids, LeeAnn took off her pants.

"That water is gonna to be freezing," he said.

"It's a warm evening." She pulled off her shirt and bra. She had his attention.

"Your turn," she said, smiling at him. He took his shirt off and then the rest of his clothes.

She whistled at him and then jumped into the water and went under. When she came to the surface, her hair was slicked back, leaving her collarbone and shoulders exposed white in the moonlight. "Come on. Jump."

He stepped in at the edge to his ankles. He gasped and then dove in and surfaced next to her.

"Doesn't it feel wonderful?"

"It feels cold."

She wrapped her arms and legs around him.

"Okay, now that feels wonderful," he said as she pressed against him. "If it wasn't for you, I'd wake up every day, work myself to the bone, sleep, and do it over again. You give me a life worth living."

"Big speech."

"It's a full moon," he said, tilting his head toward the reflection in the water.

He nuzzled her neck and kissed her.

"We've never done it in Silver Creek," she whispered.

The memory receded. LeeAnn opened her eyes and saw the raven tattooed on Wade's forearm. For a long moment she struggled for orientation.

Turning toward the window she lay staring at the moon. She heard a crinkling noise, like paper flapping. The heater for the room under the window blew warm air. Behind a chair next to the window, an edge of something fluttered in the moonlight. She got out of bed and looked behind her. Wade still slept. She slipped on her clothes and then went to the chair. Behind it she found a board tacked with a paper map. She pulled it out and stared. So many pins. Two colors. A green one pierced her parents' farm. A red one was stuck in the middle of the orchard.

She let the board slip from her hands onto the chair. She put on her shoes and let herself out of Wade's room.

CHAPTER 21

Jack

March 15 – Spring. Ides of March. Maybe that's what's under my skin.

A COCKY KID half Jack's age stepped into the ring and peered down at Jack. He saw an old guy who wasn't even dressed for a fight, wearing no shirt and a pair of jeans stained with the mud of a day's work.

The kid had the stance of someone who fought with gloves. Built like a boxer, he probably practiced with a punching bag and sparring partner a few times a week. Jack tried to convince himself it would be okay to fight him. But the kid's eyes said different.

The longer he stood watching Jack, the clearer it became he was new to fistfights. A little scared, but excited, too. Maybe here to impress one of the women in the audience. Maybe for the thrill. To see what it was like. He wouldn't be back. They never were.

Jack searched for some sign of the badger in the young man's eyes, but there was none. Gradually, as they stood there, the cockiness faded. His opponent glimpsed the animal inside Jack. The crowd began chanting Jack's name. Jack wished, as before, that an audience didn't have to be a part of this deal. He only wanted the fight.

LeeAnn hadn't spoken to him for many weeks. She kept her distance at the orchard. Her silence was worse than not seeing her at all. She'd moved on. With Wade, if the rumors were true. He heard people talk, at the Feed and Seed and the Stop-N-Go. He walked into conversations that stopped when people saw him. Stu had finally come to the orchard. "I don't know if it's true, Jack. I've only seen them together in the Tic-Toc. But they seem . . . close. That's all I'll say."

Jack hoped it was gossip, or at least not much more than that. The thought of Wade and LeeAnn together tortured him. Thursday nights brought the only relief.

Bob, the man who owned the barn, came into the center of the ring with a thick wad of cash in his hands. He held it high. "Bets have been placed."

The crowd cheered loud, beer bottles clinked. "Jack! Jack! Jack!"

Bob held up his dirty John Deere hat with the other hand. The ready signal.

Jack didn't want to take punches, not anymore. He only wanted to hit. Hit Wade, hit Dad, smash that tree with Stella's useless words, fight every fucking ghost in his life that had pushed LeeAnn away from him and into his brother's arms.

Bob kept telling him to take it easy on the others. "People won't come and fight no more, Jack. Word's gettin' around. I won't say it's not drawing the crowds. People love to see you like that. But we need fighters willing to go against you. Don't scare 'em all away."

But he hadn't been able to go easy, and now all he had was this guy who looked like he was about to pee his pants and the hat hadn't even dropped.

Jack rolled his shoulders. *Don't hit too hard,* a small voice said in his head. He didn't want to hear it. This was meant to be. Him alone, with the ghosts.

The hat came down and Jack stepped toward the man so scared he didn't move. Jack drew back his arm needing the release. To his left, he heard a woman scream, "William! Oh, God, please don't hurt him." Jack rarely saw, let alone heard, anything from the crowd once the hat was thrown, but he heard this woman's plea as though she'd spoken directly into his ear. His fist was still raised. The man in front of him, William, cowered, with his hands up.

"Please no! Don't hurt him."

Jack lowered his fist and stepped back. He glanced to his left and saw the woman standing at the edge of the ring. She stepped inside and reached out to Jack, taking the hand that had threatened her man a moment before. She was crying and shaking. "Thank you," she said. "This wasn't what we thought."

She stepped away from him and went to William, who'd fallen to his knees.

Bob was there again, talking loud over the booing crowd about getting a replacement. Soon another man stood before Jack. So like the one who'd just left.

Jack stepped out of the ring, pulled on his shirt and walked out of the barn into the night. The badger still clawed. But now he saw he'd been fighting all wrong.

CHAPTER 22

Stella

PATRICK STOOD FROWNING in the doorway of Stella's office. "What are you doing?"

"Cleaning."

The stacks of files that had always covered her floor were now gone. She labeled file folders to organize papers into the cabinets she'd never much bothered with before. If she could get herself organized, then maybe she would find a way to get interested in work again. Maybe she could get her mind back on the law firm.

Since she'd made the trip to Minden four months ago, intruding on Jack and Wade the way she'd promised herself she never would, she'd lost the ability to focus. No longer feeling like the highly capable lawyer she'd been, she spent her energy trying to appear like one instead.

And today, like most days, Patrick wasn't buying it. He didn't know that since drilling at the Moore place began, she'd been making a trip to Morrigan Gap once a week. Or how she spent most of her hours worrying about Minden. The town was transforming. The Tic-Toc had a new awning and storefront. Wood, once stored in piles and tarped, was now tucked beneath new pole barns with shiny metal roofs. Delivery trucks carrying new appliances were as common on the roads as water trucks. Campers and four wheelers appeared in driveways. New roads led toward new drill sites. And the support complex next to the church neared completion.

She kept tabs from Table Rock, where the distance between her land and the drilling at Gabriel's seemed almost nonexistent. She waited for what might go wrong, hoping nothing did.

"How did that meeting about the land easement go?" Patrick asked. "Wasn't that today, over at the coffee shop?"

Stella dropped the folder on her desk. "Damn. I forgot."

"Again?"

"I'll call them right away." She picked up the phone on her desk.

Patrick crossed the room and took the phone from her.

He put his hands on her face and turned it toward him. "Look at me."

She couldn't.

"Look. At. Me."

She turned her eyes to his and held them with considerable force of will. She'd lost all sense of purpose. She didn't want him to see that in her eyes, but of course he already had.

"This is not working for us. Sunrise Solar is more than a full-time job right now. The merger is turning into a hostile takeover and I have no idea what that means for us—maybe the end of our law firm if we lose them as a client. And you never ask about it."

"I forgot a meeting, Patrick."

"It's the fourth one, that I know about. How many more have there been? This is not you, Stella."

"Maybe I need to see a doctor." Another excuse that might buy her some of Patrick's dwindling good graces.

"Or maybe you need to deal with your issues in Minden."

He was right, but she'd already tried and failed. She felt foggy-headed, like she did so often now. She lifted her arms and let them fall. "Too much time has passed. I don't even know why I thought I could help. It was a mistake."

"Was it?"

"It didn't make any difference—probably made things worse. You didn't think it was a particularly great idea at the time. What's changed?" She hated that her eyes filled with tears.

"Do you love me, Stella?"

"You know I do," she said. "What does that have to do with anything?"

"Deal with Minden so we can move on. Go to a therapist, or go back there, or both. Figure out your stuff."

"I don't know how." She wished her voice wouldn't shake, that she didn't sound pathetic.

"Get help," he said, making it clear that help could not come from him.

No, her issues with Minden were hers to handle. Alone, as she'd ensured with her secret keeping. No one even wanted her involved.

Except maybe Jack.

CHAPTER 23

LeeAnn

"THEY GO. DAY and night," her mother said, wheezing with asthma. "Your . . . your poor father."

"Shush," LeeAnn said, smoothing balm on her mother's lips, which felt rough to the touch. LeeAnn held up a glass of water and steadied the straw for her mom.

"I'll get more water," said Franny, leaving the room with the empty pitcher.

Her mother closed her eyes, wincing a little, the latest dose of morphine still taking hold.

LeeAnn set the glass on the bedside table and walked over to the window.

"How's . . .Wade?"

Surprised, LeeAnn turned back toward the bed. How did she always know? "He's fine, I guess."

"You. Share. So much past. Memories that change a life . . ."

Her words were beginning to slur as she drifted toward sleep.

LeeAnn sat on her mom's bed and smoothed her forehead. "We'll talk later, Mom."

"So long ago. Jack's here now . . ." She trailed off.

LeeAnn turned back to the window. Jack. He'd been on her mind so much.

Franny returned with the water pitcher and joined her at the window.

"Want a sandwich or anything?"

LeeAnn shook her head. The thought of food made her stomach turn. Watching her mother day after day like this wore on her. She never felt rested these days.

A three-person crew welded steel together in the dusk a few hundred feet from the house. The yard, tracked with hardened deep ruts, stockpiled cargo containers of water for the fracking that would follow the drilling. Green shoots of grass and the first sprouts of her mother's flowers dotted the ruined soil. Spring trying to make its way, and losing.

LeeAnn bent down and picked up her cat Itch as she looked toward the orchard in the failing light. Red branches reached upward toward the sky already beginning to fulfill the promise of what they'd become. At least they waited for her.

"Seems like she's finally getting some rest," Franny said.

Her mother's eyes were closed. For the moment she was at peace. "Thanks for coming today. It helps."

"Of course, honey. Anytime. You know that." Franny scratched behind Itch's ear and watched the men working outside. "When are they supposed to finish?"

"It's gonna be a few more weeks, at least. I wish I'd never mentioned leasing to Dad."

"Was there another choice?"

Her mother's gentle snores told her she was deeply asleep. "Maybe not, but my God, look at this place." Why hadn't she figured out another way so that her mother didn't have to witness the ruin of her home in her last days? "I can't help but think that my parents would have been better off leaving things as they were."

"Is this the way they feel, or is this about you and Wade?"

"There isn't any me and Wade," LeeAnn snapped. Sometimes Franny didn't know as much as she thought she did.

LeeAnn's lips pressed into a thin line. Beyond that first day, Wade had not come by the Moore farm once since the drilling started. He'd disappeared from LeeAnn's life since their night together.

LeeAnn glanced toward the bed. Her mother still slept, the lines on her face smooth under the relative peace that only sleep and morphine offered. How many more days did she have? LeeAnn prayed they wouldn't all be filled with metallic grind.

A crashing, clanking racket came from outside, jolting her mom awake.

"Jesus Christ," Franny said. "Where do they get these clowns?" A newly arrived truck had just dumped a load of steel pipe on the ground.

"It's nothing, Mom. Try to rest." *Damn Wade Pierson for talking her parents into this. And damn herself for asking him to.*

"We need to block this noise," Franny said. "I'll get some towels from the bathroom for the windowsills. You go get some cotton balls for your mom's ears."

LeeAnn felt ridiculous following through with these lame suggestions, but she went after the cotton balls in the bathroom downstairs.

While she was there she picked up the phone and called Elzer at his office.

"Have you seen what's happening out here?"

"I've heard."

"The noise is so loud you can't hear yourself think. And it's twenty-four hours a day. Mom's too sick to move anywhere. I've called Green Energy twice to see if they'll drill elsewhere, even if only until after Mom . . . but the answer has been no. Can you do anything, *please*?"

"Have you talked to Wade?"

"I can't get a hold of him," LeeAnn said, hoping she didn't sound as hurt about that fact as she felt. After their night together his interest in Minden seemed as false as his feelings for her.

"I'll see what I can do. But honestly, LeeAnn, there may not be much from a legal standpoint."

LeeAnn went back upstairs. Franny had already tucked towels as best she could around the windows. LeeAnn helped her mother with the cotton balls. A short while later her mom's eyes closed and she began to breathe more evenly, too exhausted to stay awake any longer.

They heard a knock on the front door.

"I'll stay with your mom. Go ahead," Franny said.

LeeAnn hurried back downstairs, hoping the knocking wouldn't reawaken her mom.

Jack stood in the doorway. She felt sure he must know everything, just by looking at her. Her face reddened—damn it, the way her every feeling had to be so obvious. He had his hands in his front pockets. His face was rigid and angry, like she imagined him before one of his fights.

They hadn't talked in so long. Hadn't stood face-to-face since the meeting in the barn with Wade, when she'd found out about his keeping Stella's land a secret from her. She'd kept her distance, but he'd also stayed away. And since her night with Wade, she'd been too ashamed to reach out.

His first words to her in all that time were spoken with quiet fury. "I didn't think you'd do it, LeeAnn—start seeing Wade without telling me."

"It's nothing," she said, looking down at his muddy shoes. Her cheeks burned. He could surely read her thoughts. All of what she'd thought she'd felt for Wade—fueled by memories of being young and every apology she thought she owed him—burned up that night with him. Now she was left with ash and guilt.

"*Everyone* in town feels the need to tell me it's *not* nothing. Everyone, except you," Jack said.

Jack would never forgive her. She couldn't forgive herself. She'd tried to climb through what had seemed like an opening in her life and it had led to another dead end. She had no right to keep Jack there, too. Because that's what she'd been doing, wasn't it? So obsessed with having a baby all these years. She'd felt entitled to a family and wanted him to feel bad for failing to provide one. The kindest thing was to let go.

"We should move on, Jack."

Still, as she said the words, she realized she'd never considered closing up forever what was between them. Was that what her mother meant before she fell asleep? That her relationship with Wade was about what they'd once shared. But she and Jack had years between them and the hardship and understanding that went with those years. That she should have fought harder for their marriage. God, they both should have.

He turned and walked away before she could say more. When he reached the end of the lane, he stumbled and caught himself. She closed the door and slid to the floor.

Franny, who'd probably heard everything, sat down beside her and held her while she cried. "You love broken things," Franny said. "Jack, your stupid Charlie Brown Christmas trees, Minden, Wade, Itch. But you get frustrated after a while that they're still broken, no matter what you do. Except for Itch. You seem to have unconditional love for the cat."

LeeAnn smiled even though Franny's honesty pained her even more.

The next morning she found a note that had been pushed through the mail slot lying on her kitchen floor. She opened it and the rose quartz pebble tumbled out and fell to the ground. She picked it up. Why had he left it with her?

LeeAnn,

I'm going to be out of town for a few more

weeks. I expect to be busy. Green Energy is breathing down my neck. I'll be thinking about you.

Wade

She crumpled the paper but held on to it. Every choice she'd made had driven her away from the family she'd always wanted.

At the sound of the knock on her door, she wasn't sure which man she hoped to find on the other side.

She flung it open. But it wasn't Jack or Wade. It was Stella. LeeAnn hadn't seen her since she was a kid, but the resemblance to Jack was unmistakable. Here was the absent mother returned. What kind of woman left her two children with nothing more than a hasty message about love? Did she ever consider what those two boys would grow up thinking love meant?

"What are you doing here?" LeeAnn snapped.

"I hoped I could have a few minutes of your time."

"Why?"

"I need advice. I hoped maybe . . ."

"I don't have advice for you. Your sons avoid love. And you're a big part of the reason."

"I tried in November, but neither one wanted to talk to me."

"What did you think would happen, having left them so young? Then you did like they expected. You left again. For God's sake, they want answers. And then you disappeared at the first sign of trouble? It was the worst possible thing you could have done."

Stella shivered in the cool March air, looking terribly lost. Itch stood at Stella's feet and meowed, as though protesting LeeAnn's harsh words. LeeAnn let out a long breath and stepped aside. "You'd better come in a minute."

Stella took a seat, but kept her coat on, perhaps thinking that taking it off was too bold. LeeAnn noticed the pot of violets she'd brought from home and turned on the tap.

"I want to try again with Wade and Jack," said Stella.

LeeAnn turned off the water and let the violets drain in the sink. A wave of dizziness made her sit and she reminded herself she needed to eat.

She spoke as much to herself as to Stella. "If you're not here because you care about them, then stay away. If you can't make the situation better, it may be best to do nothing."

"I'll do whatever is in my power to not screw up this time. But I need help figuring out how. You know them."

LeeAnn studied Stella, wanting to trust. Stella did not turn away.

"Start with Jack. Ask him if you can work at the orchard one day a week. He'll think you're out of your mind. Keep at it. Eventually, that might be a way in with him. Or he might never agree."

"Jack asked me to come to Minden last November, you know."

LeeAnn sat back in her chair. "I didn't know."

"He thought my being in Minden might help mend things between him and Wade. Between all of us."

Jack had more courage than she'd given him credit for.

PART TWO

JUNE

CHAPTER 24

Jack

June 9 – Damn strawberries are ripe.

JACK BENT DOWN to inspect the berries in the early morning light. The warm, dry weather over the last weeks hadn't bothered them. Franny had already warned Jack that LeeAnn couldn't deal with the harvest and processing, given her mom's condition. The berries were ready to pick any day now, though, and people kept asking about LeeAnn's jam. He'd have to find the recipe.

Next door, an occasional muffled boom underlay the low roar of the skeletal drill rig. Quivers from underground explosions reverberated through the soles of his feet as the underbelly of the land cracked apart. Fracking had begun.

The tremors he felt in his own family were bigger, the epicenter moving ever closer. LeeAnn was gone from his life, he'd pitted himself against his brother, and he'd found no answers from Stella. The idea of Wade and LeeAnn together made him feel like the land he stood on, buckled and splitting under pressure.

Jack's cell rang in his shirt pocket.

"My cows are loose," Gabriel said. "Can you help? I'm in the high field."

Jack walked toward the Moore farm, his boots kicking up dust in the road, grateful to be able to help his neighbor. Since the latest trouble with LeeAnn he'd kept to the orchard. He'd even stopped going to church, since seeing LeeAnn there made him feel lonelier. Plus, he didn't want to be there the day she walked in with Wade.

Jack knew little about how the Moores were dealing with Rose's illness or the drilling. When he went in town for supplies, people asked him how they were, and he'd developed a series of vague replies he hoped didn't let on how little he knew.

On his way to Gabriel's pasture, Jack watched the men mixing water with frack fluid and blasting the stuff down the well, where it was pushed into the shale bed far below ground through perforations in a horizontal pipe. Each ground quiver meant another high-pressure blast of the mix into the rock, fracturing it so that the embedded gas would travel the path of least resistance along the horizontal pipe in the shale and then up the well to the surface. Right now gas bubbled out of the well along with leftover frack fluid, which diverted into a holding pond dug by the Green Energy crew. Even from this distance, Jack could smell its stink. A stagnating, milky gray mix of water, chemicals, oil-laced mud, and the noxious stuff in deep rock that was never meant to see the light of day. The June-green hills of Minden appeared so normal in comparison.

Jack crossed over what had once been Rose and Gabriel's yard, now mostly covered in erosion control matting and layered with dust. The constant drum of the rig had replaced birdcalls and lowing cows. Stella had been hard to take, but she'd also been right.

Green Energy went about the drilling as though it was inevitable. A practiced pattern they'd established over many years. Erase history to make way for progress.

When he reached Gabriel, who waited with his dog, the rig suddenly shut off. The immediate quiet made for a new kind of sound that converged around them like an embrace. Jack could hear Silver Creek again. He turned his head toward the beech trees, with leaves rattling like parchment paper in the wind. In the distance, the flute-like song of a wood thrush carried down from the mountain.

"This is sure welcome," Jack said.

Gabriel nodded and both men stood still a moment, taking in the regular sounds of a June day they'd almost forgotten.

"How many are loose?" Jack asked.

"All fifteen. The old barbed wire snapped. Ground vibrations haven't helped." Gabriel pointed to the gap in the fence. "You know how the cows are about staying together. They went toward the road. You go after them with Nell and push them this way. I'll stay here and call them back. They know my voice. Gerty's the one I'm most worried about. She's about to calf."

Jack smiled. "Again? That must be a record. What's this one make?"

"Six. Probably her last."

"Still your favorite?"

Gabriel nodded. "I won't be able to part with her, even when she's done milking."

Jack called the dog, and after looking to Gabriel for a sign to follow, Nell obediently came to his side. Jack walked through the woods in a long arc around the cows until he and Nell were on the downward side of them. As they began walking back toward Gabriel, the rig rumbled to life again and Nell jumped. That rig stood closer to the house than Jack would have agreed to, had it been his property. He guessed Gabriel hadn't had a say in the matter.

Jack raised his arms high in the air. "Hah! Get going!" The cows scurried up the hill toward Gabriel's voice.

Nell barked and helped him urge the small herd onward, crossing behind them, back and forth, keeping them together.

It didn't take long. The cows were eager to return to the familiar.

As Nell kept watch and the rig thundered on, Jack helped Gabriel mend the fence. Gabriel twisted the wire back together with needle nose pliers while Jack held the fence post straight and the wire in position.

"Damn thing," Gabriel said, struggling with the wire. He dropped his pliers.

Jack picked them up and handed them over. "How you holding up?"

Gabriel glanced up and shrugged.

"That rig. It's going on three months now. I'm not sleeping. And Rose . . ."

"How is she?"

"The doctor says maybe a few more weeks. LeeAnn's been with her when I can't be."

Jack looked away. LeeAnn had said so little, even about this. "I'm sorry," Jack said. "I haven't been around because I didn't want you and Rose to feel like you had to choose sides."

"We don't feel that way, Jack. You're family. That doesn't change."

Gabriel finished one string of fence and started on the next. "All this dust and mess and noise. It can't have done Rose any good. What really gets me is wondering if without the racket and the damned dust, would she have a little longer?"

"Tell Green Energy they're done."

"I've tried. So has LeeAnn. But they hold the lease." Gabriel sat back and rested on the ground. "They've got to be getting near the end. And then it will be quiet again." He let out a long breath. "The lease money let us keep the farm. That's what Rose wanted, although I don't suppose at this cost."

Gabriel squeezed the ends of the wire. Jack looked over

his shoulder and saw that Nell kept the cows in a cluster.

"Do you need more money, Gabriel? We could still lease the orchard."

"Honestly, I can't keep track of it all right now. And I don't know what the royalties will bring. Best to wait and see how this turns out." He nodded toward the rig. "I wouldn't wish this on anybody unless absolutely necessary."

Jack held the fence taut while Gabriel finished twisting the last of the wire.

"It's Rose and the animals I worry about. You and LeeAnn, too, of course. At least I can do something for the animals."

Gabriel wrapped his big hands around the fence post and gave it a tug, then stood. "I think that should hold," he said. He surveyed his small herd once more. "Jack."

"Yeah?"

"I've hoped you and LeeAnn would be able to sort yourselves out."

"Doesn't seem like that's going to happen."

Gabriel got a sheepish look Jack had never seen on his father-in-law. "Maybe not. But I think whatever was between her and Wade is over."

Jack felt a sad relief. Even if it was over, it probably wouldn't change much.

Gabriel studied him. "Doesn't look like you've been fighting."

Jack met his eye, for the first time not embarrassed to discuss the subject. "I haven't been in a few weeks."

Another fracking explosion made the ground shake slightly. Gabriel grabbed the fence post. "It always feels like an earthquake's about to start."

"Stella said the fracking would change Minden," Jack said. "At least we know there's an end to it on your land if they're almost done."

Gabriel slipped his pliers in his shirt pocket and cleared his throat. "I never asked about Stella's visit. I meant to."

"Not much to tell."

"Was she here just the one time in November?"

Jack nodded. "Not even sure why she came. She only wanted to talk about the drilling. Lately she's started calling, asking to help out at the orchard. Of all things. I don't answer. What would be the point?"

Gabriel watched the two men working the rig below. "I knew her some, when she lived here in Minden."

"Stella?"

"She had her reasons for leaving. I'm not excusing her, just saying there were reasons."

"You want to tell me what they were?"

"Doesn't feel like my place."

"No one else has offered an explanation."

Gabriel bent to stroke Nell's head.

"There were days when she couldn't get out of bed. Me and Rose felt sorry for her. It was probably some kind of depression, although no one called it that back then. Stella tried to take care of you boys, but she had a real hard time. And your dad wasn't any better suited to mothering. We all thought when you both got a little older she'd be okay, but she never came out of the dark place. After a while me and Rose didn't figure she ever would."

"Plenty of mothers get depressed and don't leave their kids."

"The orchard wasn't the place for her. She was skin and bones, nervous about everything. And you know your dad. Busy to distraction. He insisted she buck up." Gabriel stared off toward Morrigan Mountain. "She was drying up, Jack."

Old tension coiled in his stomach. He and Wade had made her miserable.

"One day I found Stella walking to the bus station and I drove her the rest of the way. I gave her all the money from my wallet and I felt like I helped save a life. I went to see your dad after I came back and told him what happened. He never forgave me. Felt like me and Rose pushed her away. But we were thinking about you and your brother, too. I still believe we did right."

"Is that what was between you and Dad?"

"Your dad felt betrayed. And you know he could hold a grudge."

"Her leaving us with dad didn't exactly work out."

"When Stella left, your dad changed. Back then he was kind, just as he was hard. In fact, when he and Stella were together, he was at his best. I didn't expect losing her to turn him the way it did."

"Well she sure didn't look back, did she?"

"We don't know that. I think your dad couldn't forgive Stella and over time it turned him bad. He loved her. But he couldn't accept her for who she was."

Jack scuffed his boot, kinking the grass enough to reveal the dirt beneath. "But how does a mother leave her kids?"

"When she had a good day, she could sound like a lawyer even before she probably ever had the idea she would become one. Where would she have gotten talking to fruit trees?"

Gabriel pulled the pliers from his pocket and looked at them, considering his next words.

"Of course leaving you boys came at a price. I figure it's torn her up ever since."

"Now you're defending her," Jack said.

"Just saying things aren't always as black and white as they seem."

All of the sudden a pop, loud as a gunshot, came from the direction of the orchard, followed by a surging gush. Gabriel and Jack turned toward the sound.

"Good God! Look at that," Gabriel said.

A geyser of water some forty feet in the air rose near the sycamore tree on Stella's property.

"Tell those guys to shut down," Gabriel yelled.

Jack raced down the hill toward the drillers, waving his hands. When he reached them, he shouted as loud as he could over the noise of the rig. "Stop! Shut down!" The carbide drill screamed and drowned his voice. He tapped one of the men on the shoulder, who seemed to be standing stiff as a board as though bracing against the sound even with earplugs. He turned, and Jack pointed to the geyser. Both drillers looked to where he pointed. Eyes widening, they scrambled to turn valves and levers.

Gabriel joined Jack, and they watched the geyser fall and disappear as the rig went quiet.

The drillers packed themselves in their truck without a word and got on the phone.

"Let's check it out," said Jack. The two of them crossed the fields toward Silver Creek. Grass lay matted all around the sycamore. They searched the ground for signs of where the water had burst through the ground.

"Look here, Jack," Gabriel said.

Jack bent down to study the hole Gabriel pointed to. It was small, maybe four inches in diameter. Jack picked up a rock and dropped it into the opening. They listened and heard nothing.

"Could be an old well. There's some deep ones around here, from way back."

Jack looked up and his eyes came to rest on the sycamore standing next to them. "Damn," he said. Gabriel followed his gaze to the tree, its leaves withered around Stella's message.

"That didn't happen today." Gabriel said. "Maybe the fracking has broken through more rock than they were planning. Gas could have been leaking over here little by little for a while now, and maybe some bigger connection to this old well broke through today."

Gabriel reached up and pulled on a low branch of the sycamore. The brittle wood broke off in his hand.

Across the creek, Jack's closest fruit trees sat only about two hundred feet away. Were they being poisoned right now? Jack felt the eyes of family's ghosts on his back. He turned and saw no one, yet an eerie gust of wind rustled the leaves of the apple trees.

Jack took his cell out of his pocket and dialed.

"It's Jack," he said when Stella answered. "You've been wanting to come to the orchard to help. It's time."

CHAPTER 25

Stella

STELLA CANCELED HER afternoon meetings and drove directly to the orchard. As she passed the Moore farm, she took in the three Green Energy trucks parked there and the small crowd of people gathered around a map spread out on the hood of one of the trucks. Only two of the men were drillers. Executives and geologists made up the others. Something had gone wrong.

When she got out of the car, Jack waved to her from her side of the creek, calling her name. Her stomach twisted as she hurried toward him, her feet intuitively finding the stones across the water.

"What happened?" she asked, taking in the matted grasses.

He showed her the hole and told her about the geyser. "Green Energy thinks it's related to an abandoned well. That's what Gabriel guessed. Probably a deep one—connected with the one at the Moore farm by the fracking. This tree's dead." He pointed to her sycamore.

Slow-witted and confused by what he told her, she

couldn't stop staring at the hole, as deep and connected as her silence had been all these years. Grasping, desperate not to be at fault she became indignant, a tactic that had served her well in the law. "You let them on my property?"

Jack looked stung and she was immediately sorry.

"We're trying to figure out what happened."

Someone yelled Jack's name and they both turned to see Wade approaching.

"I got here quick as I could. Gabriel and Rose all right?"

"Scared. But okay, I suppose," Jack said.

"What happened?"

"Frack water on my property is what happened," Stella said. She hadn't tried hard enough to warn them and now look.

Wade crossed his arms in front of him. "You don't know this is Green Energy's fault."

Jack told Wade what he and Gabriel had seen. "The geyser stopped as soon as they shut down the rig," Jack said.

Wade peered into the hole. "How were we supposed to know about an old well?"

"Shouldn't Green Energy make it their business to know?" Stella replied.

Wade's cell rang and he answered.

"They're going to turn the rig back on, so they can see what happens. They want us to step away."

"They're going to force more frack water onto my property?" Stella said.

Wade rolled his eyes and Stella suppressed the impulse to lash out again.

"The only people who've seen what happened are the two drillers over there," he said.

"And me and Gabriel," Jack said.

"Come this way," Wade beckoned.

Stella and Jack followed him back across the creek. Despite her protest, Stella wanted to see it for herself.

They stood beside Jack's house. Stella pulled her cell phone out of her pocket, keeping her eye on the abandoned well.

The rig across the road rumbled to life and in a matter of moments water began to bubble up from the abandoned well. It sputtered and then rose higher. Ten, twenty, more than thirty feet high–liquid filled with gas and who knew what else spewed into the air and onto Stella's land.

Stella strode toward the geyser.

"What are you doing?" Wade yelled from behind her.

When she reached the edge of the creek, the hiss of the spraying water drowned the noise of the rig. She turned on her phone's video camera and filmed the water erupting from the ground. She pointed the camera toward the creek, which also bubbled with frack water and gas. A fish floated to the surface, and then another. She scanned the water downstream and saw more, probably dead from before, caught in an eddy.

She kept her camera on Silver Creek as she glanced over her shoulder to see Wade rushing toward her, followed by Jack.

"Tell them to turn off the rig!" she yelled. "The fish are dying."

Wade stood beside her dumbfounded. More fish rose to the surface. He shook his head as if to deny what was happening. Jack turned toward the men at the rig and gave them a signal to shut down.

Stella took advantage of the silence that followed to make sure Wade heard her every word. "If my land is contaminated, Green Energy will be held responsible." Her anger uncapped like the geyser. "That sycamore was alive last fall. What about Jack's trees?"

All three of them turned toward the orchard.

"The trees will be fine. It's an accident is all," Wade said.

"You trying to convince me or yourself? I'm not going away until this is settled."

Wade leaned toward her until his face was inches from hers. "It would be a mistake to blow this out of proportion."

"Don't stand in Green Energy's way, you mean," she said.

"Green Energy is helping people here. That's more than anybody can say for you."

How could these words be coming from her son about his own home? Even if he'd chosen to walk away, it had to mean at least as much to him as it did to her. "I tried to warn you. I tried to warn you both," Stella said, eyeing them.

Jack gave a slight nod.

"It was an *accident*," Wade said. "No one could have seen this coming."

Her professional shield wavered, but she held fast. "I'm getting the soil and water tested today."

"Green Energy will cover the costs," said Wade.

"I'll do my own investigation."

"Why are you being so defensive?" Wade said.

"My property has been infringed upon. I never agreed to that. Neither has Jack. This is a toxic-trespass case if I ever saw one."

"Your specialty," Wade said. "How convenient."

"I'll be in touch with your boss."

"It's all about you, isn't it?" Wade said. "You're pretending to care about the orchard, so you can help build a case to add to your war chest. I'll be blamed for this already. Don't you, of all people, make things worse."

"I'm trying to do what's right."

"Then stay out of our lives, like you always have." He turned and stalked away.

She watched him leave, and with each step he took away from her, her anger faded and she wanted to call him back. What if she'd ended any possibility of speaking to him again? If an abandoned well had polluted her ground, it was a reminder of the way she'd polluted her sons' lives. LeeAnn's words about Wade and Jack not knowing how to love echoed in her mind.

The dead fish continued to gather in a bend at the edge of the creek. She turned her eyes to the 'X' carved into the sycamore.

"He gouged it deep," Jack said. "I'm surprised the tree hasn't already died from its wounds back then."

Her eyes prickled. Jack stood next to her, peering at her with openness that hadn't been there last time. Before was before. She glanced at the group from Green Energy, still huddled together. "Back when?"

"When Dad died."

Stella felt as if the X was slashed into her own heart. She turned again in Wade's direction, but he was hidden among the group from Green Energy.

"It's just like you said," Jack whispered, staring at the dead fish in the water.

Stella took in a long breath. It was now or never. "I'm sorry I left you and Wade and never gave you any reasons."

After a long moment he said, "I remember the day you left. Some of it anyway."

She didn't know how to begin. "I'd hoped you wouldn't remember." Was his memory like hers? She looked back at the house to the window of the bedroom she'd once shared with Steve. She could recall every detail of that afternoon.

It had been this time of day and she'd been in her bedroom as usual.

Through a small opening in the blinds of her window, Stella could see the Moore dairy farm, catty corner across the road. Rose and four-year-old LeeAnn lay barefoot in the grass lawn, hands clasped, faces toward the sun. LeeAnn held the baby doll she was never without in her other hand. Rose's beloved zinnias grew in a colorful spray behind them.

Stella shut her eyes tight against the tears. Rose and her daughter delighted in each other, whereas she tried to survive one day to the next while her own children argued downstairs.

Their voices carried from the kitchen. Jack, age five, was trying to make lunch for Wade.

"We've got peanut butter but no jelly," Jack said.

"I don't want that again," Wade said.

"It's all we have."

Never enough food in the house, never enough of herself.

LeeAnn's laughter carried across the road—it was the only laughter in their house—and Stella stared again out the window at the Moore's dairy. Rose swung LeeAnn in a circle, her legs out straight in the air. Rose's flowers, her love, made the place beautiful. The girl's giggle reinforced to Stella that she only burdened her sons.

On days that Stella made it out of bed, she would sometimes take her boys to visit Rose and LeeAnn. Stella felt a connection to the little girl that she didn't have with her sons. Maybe it was simply that LeeAnn wasn't her responsibility.

The one reason she was glad her father had left her in Minden was that he couldn't see how she'd failed like he'd predicted. Her mind—the one thing she had—wasted at the orchard, rotting like fallen apples.

Stella pushed herself into a sitting position. This took much more effort than it should have. The nightgown, like all her clothes, was now much too big. She smelled bad, unwashed for days. She went into the bathroom and splashed cold water on her face. She took off her nightgown and put on one that was cleaner. Then she went downstairs slowly, not because she wanted to go, but because she should. How many days had it been since she'd last been down?

The two boys sat at the kitchen table, each with a sandwich. Jack had put them on napkins. Stella saw the tall stack of dishes piled in the sink next to the empty cupboards where the clean dishes should have been. If she didn't love her sons as much as Rose Moore loved her daughter, it wouldn't matter. But her sons were in fact all she cared about. She hadn't been prepared for them, and could never seem to accommodate them, not in Minden, and for this they all suffered. Both boys looked at her—

Wade with a flush of excitement in his cheeks and Jack as pale as if he were seeing a ghost.

She could feel the question in her older son's mind. Why had she come down? What else would he have to worry about? Wade, on the other hand held his hands out to her. "Mama."

She preferred Jack's questions and anxiety.

"Do you want a sandwich?" Jack asked, moving toward the last of the bread.

"No. You eat."

She stood apart from them, by the refrigerator, in her bare feet.

"Will you sit by me?" Wade asked, still with his hands stretched toward her.

"Maybe in a minute," she told him, unable to close the distance between them.

Steve came charging in through the kitchen door. He didn't see her at first. She'd become invisible in her own home.

"Jack," he said, "I need your help with the sprayer again."

"Be right out," Jack replied in his high child's voice, one much too young to be helping his father the way he did every day, but she could also hear his eagerness. He loved the orchard. He seemed to be born from it instead of her. When she thought of leaving and taking the boys with her, the thought of taking Jack from his beloved fruit trees stopped her.

"You're up," Steve said, finally noticing her. He started toward her with a look of hope on his face so like Wade's.

Then as if he could read her thoughts, he stopped and instead turned back to the boys at the table. His fleeting look of hope wasn't about her anyway, it was about his dreams and wishes. He couldn't understand why she wouldn't adjust to this life. He wanted the dark mood brought on by the birth of each son to lift. She'd hoped for this, too, with all her heart. But now she was tired of wanting something that wouldn't be.

"I'm thirsty," said Wade, staring up at her.

"Your mama will get you a drink. I see she already got you some lunch."

From the table he picked up the pruners he must have sharpened that morning and turned back toward the door. "Come out after you're done, Jack."

She went to the sink and washed two glasses. She opened the refrigerator to see just enough milk left. Gabriel or Rose must have brought it over. She poured and set the glasses down in front of the two boys.

"Mommy?" Wade said, patting the seat next to him.

Why didn't he hate her?

He reached up to pull on her arm and knocked over his milk. The glass shattered on the floor.

Wade screamed at the explosive sound.

Jack jumped up and started picking up pieces of glass before Stella could move. She bent down next to him to help, more aware than ever that she needed a shower. When her hand brushed his by accident, he flinched, jerking his hand away and cutting it on a piece of glass.

He curled his fingers around the wound.

"How bad are you hurt?" she asked.

"It's nothing," he replied, as blood dripped onto the floor.

"Can I have more milk?" asked Wade, still eating his sandwich.

"Have mine," Jack told him.

"Let me get this," he said to her, not unkindly. Jack tried to protect her from herself. His smallness, beside her, trying so hard—it was just wrong.

Standing and turning back toward the stairway, she knew what she needed to do.

The first time she'd planned to leave the orchard Stella had bought a small suitcase, but she didn't have the nerve to use it when she learned she was pregnant again. She went up to her closet and took it down. Searching through her dresser, she realized she wanted nothing. She returned the suitcase to its shelf.

While she dressed she heard Jack go out the door to help Steve. She called down to Wade and told him to take the empty milk container over to the Moore's for a refill. Rose would keep him occupied for a while, as she was kind enough to do when she thought Stella was having a bad day. She'd been occupying him a lot lately.

After she heard Wade leave, Stella went downstairs, dropped Steve's pocketknife in her purse, and went out the door. She scanned for signs of her sons or neighbors and saw no one.

She crossed the road and stepped over the jutting stones of Silver Creek.

Pressing her cheek to the bark of the young sycamore tree growing there, she held on for dear life, as though she too might grow roots strong enough to make her stay. But the flowing water had the stronger pull: going, going, gone.

When she could no longer resist, she'd walked over to the stream and dropped a leaf, watching it twirl and bump along the surface as it floated. If it could float away free and clear, she would take it as a sign she could also make her escape. But the leaf hung up on a rock and then got swept underneath.

Still it was time to go, just like the creek, no matter how difficult the path. If her children felt her as concrete around their legs, no amount of love would ever be enough to keep them afloat.

She took the knife out of her purse and knelt in front of a small tree.

On good days, she'd brought her sons to this place. She watched the creek while they played in the shallow pools near the stream bank. Perhaps they would remember this was the one place in Minden, besides the Moore house, where they shared some peace. She pulled out the knife. She would leave her message for them here.

Someday she would come back and make it up to them.

She would return when she had something to offer them besides heartache. Keep her land, as a promise.

"What are you doing?" said a small voice behind her, as she finished.

Stella spun around to find LeeAnn watching her from across the creek.

"Making a promise. You go on home now. Your mother will worry."

She watched the little girl turn and head back toward her house.

"Wait, LeeAnn," she called.

The girl faced her, hugging her doll.

"Watch over them, will you. Jack and Wade?"

LeeAnn nodded slowly and then was gone back to her house.

Back then LeeAnn stood where Jack and Stella were now. Jack watched as more dead fish crowded the inside bend of the creek. "What do you remember?" she asked him.

"You were sad a lot. I knew you'd decided something after Dad came into the kitchen asking for me to help in the orchard. I could tell by the way you were looking at him that you didn't want to be with us anymore. He could see it, too."

"I stayed for a lot longer than I thought I could, if you can believe that. But the details don't matter. What you need to know is that it had nothing to do with you and Wade. Nothing. It had everything to do with me and your father."

Jack, jaw clenched, stared at the creek and said nothing for almost a minute. "Dad could be hard."

"He didn't get what he bargained for either. I wasn't prepared for that life. Every possible threat to you and Wade loomed so large in my mind. I'd see a car coming and have a horrible vision of you boys lying on the road in its path. I worried about every moment to the point that I couldn't sleep. Barely ate. I was essentially paralyzed, for years. I couldn't stay, but I didn't want to leave you and Wade. In the end I didn't see any other way."

"And so you left."

"I wandered for a while, caught between regret and trying to find a direction. By the time I had enough clarity and money to go to college and then law school and find a job, you and Wade were well into middle school. I wanted to come back then to see you both, but I just didn't know how. I've thought about both of you so much. But I've never let you know that. And I'm terribly sorry."

She reached out to touch his arm, but he pulled away.

"What did you say to Wade on the phone, that night after Dad died, when he asked you to come to Minden? I heard his part of the conversation, before I took the phone from him. It seemed like the call was only making things worse."

"That night was complicated."

"I'm just a farm boy, but I'll try to understand."

Stella turned to him. "He called during my engagement party—for me and Patrick. When I answered the phone I thought it was the caterer who was running late. I hear this man talking so fast on the other end, saying his name is Wade, but the only Wade I'd ever known was a four-year-old boy. For me, Minden was suspended in memory. You have to understand, a room full of people were staring at me, including Patrick. It took me a few moments to realize I had my grown son on the line, and even longer to figure out what he was asking."

Jack nodded, seeming to understand how disorienting that would be. "By the time I could make any sense of who he was and what he wanted, the conversation had already taken its toll on Wade."

"I shouldn't have interfered," Jack said. "I heard Wade on the phone with you, so upset, and then I took the phone after he dropped it. You'd never so much as called and he believed in you and I figured we'd been hurt enough already."

"I said I'd come, but I didn't think I could really help. I regret not coming then, yes. But I let you talk me out of it and I stuffed the pain down deep, where I keep all my feelings about Minden, and tried to make a life with Patrick. And honestly, I probably wasn't capable of helping Wade back then."

He buttoned his jacket and Stella worried he would walk away like Wade had.

"LeeAnn told me once," he said, "that she remembers you carving that message into the sycamore. She thinks you asked her to watch out for me and Wade."

"She remembers that?"

Jack turned to her. "Why did you put that on her?"

"LeeAnn had love in her house, every day. I hoped that maybe there was enough to share with you and Wade."

"What am I supposed to take from your story?" Jack said.

"You say your dad was a hard man, but he was more capable of raising you and Wade. And I couldn't take you away from here. Even at five I knew you belonged to the orchard. Don't you see, Jack, that's why I'm here now. To help you protect what's important to you."

Jack didn't seem convinced. Maybe he was right not to. She'd done little to find out what kind of a father Steve had been. She hadn't wanted to know.

"We grew up thinking we weren't worth staying around for."

Just like her father she'd left the family that needed her, never there for them in the first place. Her courage was always too thin. Her new life with Patrick had been hard won and she'd wanted comfort. So she'd taken the easy route. But now, as she stood with Jack, both of their properties facing the same threats, she knew they needed each other. And she would do everything she could for him, no matter the difficulty.

Two days later, back in her office, Stella shared what she knew with Patrick.

The tree evidence suggested that gas could have been leaking ever since the fracking began weeks ago, although most dramatically when the geyser appeared. She'd passed on what she'd witnessed to the Department of Environmental Protection and after a visit, they'd ordered a halt to the fracking at the Moore place until they had more information.

"What are you going to do next?" Patrick asked, making himself a cup of coffee in her office.

"Green Energy will want to seal the abandoned well on my property with cement. I still have to think that through. From there, I'm not sure."

Patrick stirred sugar into his coffee. "What do your sons want?"

"Wade wants me to walk away. Jack's worried about the orchard, of course. And he should be."

He sat down on the chair in her office, crossing one leg over the other. "Would you walk away?"

"I can't." She put her elbows on her desk and leaned toward him.

"Then you should stay focused in Minden."

His phone rang down the hall. "That's Sunrise Solar. Finally, some details about this takeover."

He ran to his office to answer and she listened from her desk. At first she could only hear Patrick's muted voice and then he got louder.

"What? Christ!"

Her heart raced. Patrick didn't swear. She stood up and walked quickly to his office.

"My wife—my law partner—may be involved in a new case against them," Patrick was saying.

Was Green Energy behind the hostile takeover? Had they figured out she and Patrick were married, then made a move to throw her off in Minden?

Patrick sat at his desk with his hand over his eyes. He

listened for a moment and said, "We need to sort it out on this end. I'll take the first flight out in the morning. I'm still your lawyer. You can count on that much."

He hung up the phone and looked at her.

"You heard?" he said.

"Yes." Their practice depended on Sunrise Solar's business. "I don't know what they're trying to pull. I'm not going to let this go."

"Who knows if they're trying to pull anything? Sunrise is primed for takeover. In a lot of ways this makes perfect sense and probably has nothing to do with you."

Her back stiffened. "It's not a coincidence."

"We need to figure out the best way forward, Stella."

That was true. They needed to pay the bills. She could be practical, too.

"I don't see how you can be involved in Minden now. It's a conflict of interest if you're investigating or negotiating with Green Energy. Without Sunrise we can't operate. When Green Energy takes over, one of us has to give up what we're doing."

Stella's heart raced. "There's another possibility." She feared her voice sounded too high. She was about to propose something crazy that would sound like she didn't care about their marriage.

"What's that?" he said, eyebrows raised.

"An Ethical Wall, Cone of Silence, whatever name you want to give it. It's perfectly legal. We agree not to speak to each other about our respective cases and clients. We'll keep our work lives separate. It's been used plenty of times before in other law firms."

Patrick shook his head slowly. Dismissing her proposal. "Sure, in big firms with lawyers who barely speak to one another. But we're a law practice of two. And we're married."

"Can you think of another solution?" She let her question hang in the air.

CHAPTER 26

Jack

June 11 – The sun, this morning, like three suns rising. A sun dog.

ON THURSDAY EVENING Jack stood outside in the shadows, peering through the barn window at the fighters inside. He wanted to go in, he did. He craved the fight as much as he ever had. But it hadn't helped, not beyond the moments when punches were thrown. He turned away and got into his truck to go Stella's office to find out more about her while she was occupied in Minden, with the soil and water sampling.

When he reached the stone building marked with the BRANTLEY & BRANTLEY sign, he walked inside, surprised to find the door open given the hour. He'd been prepared to sleep in his truck until the next morning if he found the place empty.

The bell at the door dinged, but no one came.

"Hello?" Jack called out.

"First door on your left," a man's voice called.

Jack walked down the hallway and found a rumpled

Patrick Brantley sitting behind his desk.

"Mr. Brantley, can we talk for a moment?"

He nodded and picked up a bottle of pills from his desk, dumped one onto his palm and swallowed it dry.

He studied Jack, his face expressionless. After a moment he said, "You look just like her. Funny I didn't see it at first."

Jack tried to think of something to say that would put them both more at ease. But there was nothing.

"These pills," Patrick said, motioning to the bottle. Prozac. "I haven't had one for years. Until now."

"Oh?"

"And this bracelet," he said, holding his wrist up so Jack could see the braided leather, "it's what she gave me when we got married, instead of a ring. I've never taken it off. But last week, it fell apart because of rot. I've done what I can to repair it, but who knows if it'll hold."

Jack stared at the frayed leather.

"My wife is committed to Minden. More than I understand."

"She wants to win against Green Energy," Jack said.

"There's more to it."

Patrick folded his hands on his desk. "I love Stella. Our marriage is foundational to everything in my life. Stella's passionate about her causes. But in Minden it's about you and your brother. Her efforts there take her away from our life together. So please, give her a chance. Because I need her back."

Two days later, Jack walked along the apple trees closest to Stella's abandoned well. Withered leaves and baby apples littered the ground.

"I wish we'd taken more samples," Stella said when he called her on his cell, pacing the rows between his trees.

This had to do with her land as much as his. Talking to her now, feeling like she was on his side, gave him hope that maybe the orchard could be saved.

"High methane in the soil could be causing damage to your trees," she said.

Jack stopped walking and looked up at the clouds scudding past. He closed his eyes. She would tell it to him straight, unlike Green Energy. "Can it be fixed, or is the orchard done for?"

"If it's only methane, then the harmful effects will resolve once they seal off the source from Gabriel's well. To do that, they'll pour cement down the abandoned well to create a block. They'll hope to cut off the gas leaking onto our properties."

"And if it's more than just methane? Or if they can't seal it off?"

"It gets complicated. There could be long-term groundwater contamination."

Jack reached up to touch a cluster of small apples hanging from the limb above his head. Two of them broke off and fell to the ground. He bent and picked them up, cradling them in his hand. "How could it be only methane? What about the fracking chemicals you mentioned?"

"Methane moves more easily through soil and water than the other chemicals. It's the canary we first notice. I'm still waiting on the water-sample results. I should have them later today."

Jack placed the two apples in the crook of the tree and walked toward the creek. "Was it only methane that killed the fish?"

"Possibly."

When he reached the creek's edge he scanned the surface. He didn't see any more fish bodies. "I suppose you're planning a lawsuit."

"I don't see another choice."

Jack sat down on a rock at the creek's edge, where he and Stella had been when she'd first come. He wished he could talk to her in person now. "Would it involve me and LeeAnn?"

"Ideally, yes. We have the best chance of restoring your property if we work together. But it's up to you two."

He looked at the abandoned well across the creek that had caused so much damage. "I'd rather not get involved. Not with the way it is between me and LeeAnn."

"You'll have to discuss that with her."

He'd have to talk to her about what had happened to the orchard anyway. She'd want to do whatever they could for the place.

"I appreciate your advice. Thank you," he told Stella. She didn't reply for a long moment, but when she said goodbye, he didn't miss the emotion in her voice.

Next he called Wade. Years ago they'd planted the trees that were now dying. It wasn't about fault, but about the family orchard. It would take all of them to get through this.

"Apples are dropping from the trees closest to Silver Creek. Can you come out and take a look?"

"I'll let the boss know. We'll be there soon."

Wade sounded ready to do his part. In a matter of hours Jack stood at his kitchen window watching a team from Green Energy take measurements and samples of the soil around his trees. Wade was among them and yet his brother didn't come to the house to discuss what they were doing or planning. Instead he kept his distance.

It was after dark when the knock finally came.

"Mr. Pierson, I'm Harrington Price, a project manager for Green Energy." The man held out his hand and Jack shook it automatically, looking past him for his brother. But another younger man came behind Harrington carrying a sophisticated-looking instrument with a narrow tube on the end. His face was that of a kid whose baseball had just gone through the window. Wade was last inside, dragging his feet as though his boss had forced him, seeming barely interested in the house where he'd been raised.

"Mr. Pierson, I'm sorry to bother you so late," Harrington said. "I'd hoped to talk to you sooner, but I wanted to know what we're dealing with first. Given the situation, we'd like to test the air in your basement. I also need to take a water sample from your tap."

Jack looked at Wade for an explanation, but Wade avoided his eyes.

"Why?" he asked Harrington.

"It's not uncommon for the rock close to the surface to be more fractured than it is deeper underground. So gas may be leaking through the soil in places other than at the well itself. We need to check to make sure it's not leaking into your basement, in case there's some remote danger of explosion. And we need to check your water to make sure it's okay to drink. I'm sorry about this, but until we get the results back, we're going to supply you with bottled water for drinking. I don't want to worry you unnecessarily. It's all probably fine, but we like to take precautions in this type of situation. You should be fine to bathe and wash clothes with your tap water."

Harrington patronized him. Jack guessed his regular voice was a full octave higher. "So this has happened before?"

"Accidents happen." Harrington smiled wider, selling the snake oil.

Jack turned again to Wade. "What about the soil around the trees? How high is the methane?"

"We're keeping an eye on it," Harrington said.

"But the gas is harming my trees, isn't it?"

"It's possible," Harrington said. "I'm not trying to keep information from you. We don't know enough yet. That's why we need the samples."

Jack glared at Wade waiting for a real answer and since his brother continued to avoid his eyes, Jack knew his worst suspicions were true. The gas had gotten to his trees and the men in this kitchen were not on his side.

"Basement's here," Jack said, pointing to the stairway

off the kitchen. The man carrying the measuring device went downstairs.

Harrington pointed to the sink and held up a plastic bottle with a label that read PIERSON, WATER. "Do you mind?" he asked Jack.

"Doesn't sound like I have much choice."

Jack didn't make any effort to move dirty dishes out of the way, except for LeeAnn's red mug, which he placed in the cupboard. Harrington put the bottle on the counter and took disposable plastic gloves from his pocket. He put them on, removed the dishes, and turned on the tap. "I need to let this run for a few minutes."

"You worried about your hands touching my water?"

Harrington laughed, like they were friends talking about the Friday night football game at the high school. "Not at all. Wearing gloves is standard procedure."

Even if that were true, his answers came too easily.

Jack crossed his arms and glanced again at Wade. He'd moved closer to the door. "What do you think you're going to find?" Jack asked Harrington.

"Nothing, I hope. And even if we find a little methane, it may well be unrelated to the drilling. It occurs naturally in this part of the state."

Jack stepped toward Harrington to make sure they were eye to eye. "Uh huh. Except that my trees just started dying."

Harrington put up his hands. "Let's take things one at a time. You should know we mean to set things right here. We would feel that way anywhere, but it's even more important to us given that Wade's your brother. I hired him myself and he's part of our family, too. We care about what happens and we'll take care of you," Harrington said.

Jack glared at his brother until Wade met his eyes.

"What happened here has nothing to do with me," Wade finally said. "No one could have known about that abandoned well."

Turning back toward Harrington, still at the sink, Jack

said. "Has my brother told you who owns the abandoned well?" Stella would have to help him fight this, and her involvement wasn't his secret to keep.

"I thought you owned the well, Jack," Harrington said, still forcing a smile, but looking to Wade for an answer.

Wade shot Jack a warning glance.

"Stella Brantley," Jack said. "I suspect you know her name. She used to be a Pierson. Our dad gave her the ground when they married."

Harrington dropped the bottle he'd been filling. "Stella Brantley is your mother?"

"She was here just yesterday," Jack said.

"Wade?"

Wade took a step back toward the door. "There was no reason to mention her before now. I didn't know about her owning the land until fairly recently myself. I planned to tell you, of course. There hasn't been a moment to talk."

Footfalls came up the basement stairs. The man gave Harrington a small nod, showing him the number on his instrument.

Harrington ran both hands though his hair. "You'll have to find somewhere else to stay tonight," he said, as though he were in charge of Jack's house. "We'll get your basement cleared out, but it's going to take a few days."

"What are you talking about?"

"The level of methane in your basement is too high for you to stay here."

Jack looked from Harrington to Wade and back again. "It's June. One of the busiest times. I've got hundreds of strawberries to pick. And I can't leave my trees right now. Especially if they're in danger."

Harrington spoke in a low tone, probably meant to calm Jack, but all it did was incite him. "There's enough methane in your basement to cause an explosion. We need to set up aeration equipment immediately. You can probably work at the orchard during the day, but you can't be in the house. I promise it won't be long. We'll get you back in as soon as possible." Harrington went to the door and grabbed the knob. "Let's take this conversation outside."

Jesus. This guy didn't want to spend another minute, like the whole place was about to blow. Jack stayed where he was. "Where am I supposed to go?"

"We'll pay for a room in town," Harrington said.

"There are no rooms in town," Jack said.

"You could stay at my place," Wade said. "I'm headed back up north tonight anyway."

All his brother could offer was the room he'd probably invited LeeAnn to more than once if rumors could be believed. Talk about rubbing his nose in it. "I'll find a place on my own."

An hour later, Jack sat in his truck next to a bag filled with a change of clothes and his notebook that he'd grabbed at the last minute. He'd parked in the lot behind LeeAnn's apartment, hoping that Gabriel had been right when he'd said whatever had been between Wade and LeeAnn was over. Wade's truck wasn't in the lot. Jack had been watching the windows for about thirty minutes and he'd only seen her shadow.

His phone rang. It was Stella.

"I got the groundwater results back."

"And?"

"Methane's been seeping onto my property. I've shared this evidence with the Department of Environmental Protection. But a series of samples from Silver Creek showed methane levels decreasing since the rig was turned off. You should get your water tested, too."

"Green Energy took soil and water samples from the orchard today. The methane levels in my basement are so high, they told me I had to stay someplace else tonight in case my house explodes."

"Holy shit, Jack."

"They weren't saying much else." He would leave Wade's name out of it for now.

"They'll have to seal off the well on my property right

away," Stella said.

"What about Gabriel? He needs the cash the gas royalties will bring, but first the well has to produce. He could lose his farm otherwise."

"His well has to sit idle until the contamination is dealt with. A lawsuit could help Gabriel as much as anything. Talk to LeeAnn. If you both want to go forward with it, I'll ask for a meeting with Green Energy as soon as you give me the go ahead. If you don't want to do it, I'll see what I can do on my own, but honestly, we would lose a lot of leverage."

LeeAnn's shadow stopped in front of her window and he wondered for a moment if she saw his truck.

Putting his phone in his pocket, he pulled his bag off the seat, and walked up the steps until he stood outside her door. He listened for the sound of voices. When he heard none, he knocked, instantly wishing he could take it back. Why hadn't he called first? What if Wade hadn't decided to go north like he said, and was there right now?

She opened the door wearing pale pink pajamas, her hair mussed, her cheeks a little fuller than the last time he'd seen her up close. When had that been?

"Are you all right?" she asked, opening the door wider. "Dad called and told me what happened."

"Are you alone?"

She nodded, seeming annoyed.

"There's methane gas in the basement. It's getting at the apples, too. Green Energy won't let me stay at the house. I didn't want to bother your folks. Can I have your couch or the floor for a night or two?"

She opened the door wide for him.

"I'll get some blankets," she said, disappearing down the hall.

Jack stood waiting, taking in the bare walls. The boxes she'd moved from the house still lined the kitchen walls, all these months later. The pot of violets he'd brought her at the orchard sat on the windowsill. He hadn't known she'd brought those with her.

She returned with her arms full of pillows and bedding. "I've worried the drilling wouldn't be good for Minden." She unfurled a sheet and began tucking it into the couch cushions with angry motions.

"Stella was at the orchard today. Wade, too."

"Wade?" She looked up.

Jack tried his best to hide the flare of jealousy. He told her what Stella had proposed about the lawsuit.

She spread out a top sheet and smoothed the wrinkles. "What do you think?" she said.

"It's a good idea, but I don't know that I'm ready to line up with Stella against Wade, which is what it would seem like," he said.

"But that's not what we'd actually be doing," LeeAnn said.

His brother didn't seem to want any responsibility for what had happened, but Jack didn't know if Harrington might have forced him to stay quiet so that he could do the talking at the house. Harrington was certainly the type. Anyway, he and Wade shouldn't be fighting each other. They needed to work together one way or another to make sure the orchard survived. "We'd do it for the orchard, your parents, and for Minden."

"And those are good reasons," she said. "We could explain it to Wade. Maybe at this point he would feel the same way. Maybe he would understand and even want to help us."

He took one end of the comforter and LeeAnn took the other. They spread it out over the couch.

She handed him a pillow. "Can they fix the damage?"

The anguish on her face softened him. She really did love the orchard.

"I don't know."

Itch jumped in his arms, purring loudly.

"She misses you," LeeAnn said.

Jack settled onto the couch with the cat. LeeAnn turned

off the light and went down the hall to her bedroom. Even in this apartment, and with all that had gone wrong between them, she still smelled like home.

CHAPTER 27

LeeAnn

LEEANN CREPT INTO the living room and found no trace of Jack. Itch stood on the floor meowing in the direction of the couch, now empty, with the bedding neatly folded into a pile. It was as though he'd never been there.

Her apartment seemed as foreign as ever. The night before she'd wanted to reach out to Jack, wanted them to comfort each other. Their orchard was possibly poisoned. But she'd not only lost the right to touch him, she'd also lost the sense of whether she could.

She wrapped herself in the afghan he'd used, lay on the couch with Itch, and slept. When she woke, the extra rest had done little to relieve her weariness. Lately, she couldn't seem to get enough sleep. Even caring for her apples required too much. Probably stress, given how much she'd been under.

Just to be sure, she picked up the phone and called Doc Black.

"You can come right now," said his wife, who was also his nurse. "We've had a cancellation."

She walked the few blocks to his office hoping the fresh air would provide some relief.

The welcome warmth of the sun reminded her of walks in the woods she and her mother usually took in June to see spring flowers—dame's rocket, violets, and lady's slipper. This year it felt particularly important to walk those same places so she could share with her mother what she saw, one last time. But the thought of walking more than to the doctor's office seemed out of the question.

"You're feeling tired?" Doc Black sat perched on a stool in his examining room.

"To the bone."

"Anything else?"

"I feel lightheaded every time I stand up too fast. Probably because I don't have much interest in food right now. I'm so worried about Mom."

"Have your periods been regular?"

"You're the one who diagnosed perimenopause. Lately it's been hit and miss."

He smiled kindly. "Could be anemia or stress or both. I'll take some blood. Come back in a couple days and we'll discuss the results."

Two days later LeeAnn returned. She'd driven this time, too tired to walk.

Back in the examining room, Doc's stern look did nothing to quiet her. She tried to quell the panic that welled inside. She couldn't take anything else going wrong.

"What is it?" she finally asked him, when he couldn't seem to find any words.

"You're pregnant, LeeAnn."

Her vision faded to black.

The next thing she knew Doc knelt beside her holding her upright in the chair. "Do you want to lie down?"

"No."

"Put your head between your legs."

She did as he said and the darkness clouding her mind began to clear.

"Slow and steady breaths," he said.

"It's . . . it's not what I expected to hear," she managed.

He put his hand on her arm. "You've waited for this for a long time."

He knew how badly she'd wanted this. And he of all people had no right to give her false hope.

She sat up and dried her eyes on the tissue he offered.

"Should we see if we can hear a heartbeat?"

"Now?" she asked. "Already?"

"Come over here and lie down," he said, pointing to the examining table.

"I wonder if we shouldn't wait."

"No need." He patted the table.

She lay down. She'd go through the motions and then she would tell him where to go.

"Lift up your shirt."

Cold fear mixed with anticipation she didn't want. She gasped as he dabbed gel on her belly.

"I'm sorry," Doc said. About the chill, or lying to her?

She would not watch. If love and years of concerted effort couldn't make a baby, a one-night affair at her age surely wouldn't. Life was a goddamned joke. She focused her eyes on the vast white ceiling above her, as empty as she was. He probed with an ultrasound scope. She peeked at him. His furrowed brow said it all.

She reached for her shirt. Time to put a stop to this nonsense.

"Hold still." Doc Black continued moving the probe around. "Perhaps it's too early."

Or too late.

"There!" he said.

He adjusted the volume on the machine and LeeAnn heard it, too. A rapid swish, swish, swish.

She blinked, disbelieving. But her own heart raced, as though trying to match the one she now heard beating inside her. She looked at him—she would draw no conclusions.

"That's your baby, LeeAnn."

Her eyes filled with tears. She shook her head back and forth. She would not recover from more false hope.

But the heartbeat kept on and Doc kept peering at her with a small smile and tears in his eyes. This helped her begin to believe. "Is it real?" she whispered.

"Yes. It really is." He took her hand and squeezed. "This baby came to you when it was good and ready."

"Thank you," she said, wiping her eyes.

He sat with her a long time and reviewed her prenatal care. She made him say it all twice. "You can't work like you're used to—not at both the Tic-Toc and the orchard. You need to get some help around the house, too, so you'll be able to rest. We aren't going to take any chances."

She was still in shock. And joy. And confusion. And shock.

When she left the doctor's office, her legs shook so badly she was glad she'd decided to drive.

On her way to her car she passed Elzer's office. He opened the door and stuck his head out. "LeeAnn, I heard about the orchard. Let's talk later. I'd like to help if I can."

She managed a nod. At the mention of the orchard, she thought of Jack. How would she tell him?

Doc had ordered the pregnancy test, making the same assumption everyone else had about her and Wade. People wouldn't be as generous as Doc when they found out about the baby. She wrapped her arms around her belly, wanting the child to know love from the start. She would apologize to no one. But when she thought of trying to explain it all to Jack, she swayed.

In two long steps Elzer caught her by the elbow. "Here. Let me get you to the car. You're under too much stress lately. You need to take a day." He helped her inside and closed the door.

She wanted only to lie down in her apartment and

think things through. There was so much now to consider. She looked out the car window. She hadn't yet put the key in the ignition. Elzer peered at her from outside, concerned. She rolled down the window.

"Let me drive you home. You really don't look well," he said.

She took steady breaths in and out. "I'll be okay. I'll get someone to cover for me at the Tic-Toc. So I can stay home tomorrow and rest."

"You're sure?"

She nodded and drove herself home.

When she arrived at her apartment door, she heard a crash inside, followed by a yelp. She pushed the door open and stood back before peeking in.

Jack leaned on the small kitchen counter, surrounded by quarts of strawberries. Jam ran onto the counter in front of him and dripped from several overturned jars.

He glanced up at her, sweat dripping from his face. "How do you get it in the jars?"

She kept her smile minimal. "A funnel."

"A funnel?"

Jam made a slow crawl toward the edge of the counter. "People keep asking for it. I figured with your recipe I could do it, but . . ."

LeeAnn's nerves were stretched so taut she felt half hysterical and pressed her lips together to keep it contained. Jam dribbled over the edge onto his shoes. She giggled.

"Is it supposed to be this runny?"

"No," she squeaked.

"So maybe it's best that it's on the floor?" he said, still serious.

"Probably. For the best," she managed to get out.

"This is the second batch. But nothing in the jars." He rubbed his forehead, leaving behind a swath of red jam. LeeAnn burst into a fit of giggles. She had to sit on the floor.

"What's so funny?" he said, finally grinning, too.

His smile. How long had it been since she'd seen it? This man who'd grown up so fast and serious his whole life, trying to make his way. When it had been good between them, she had made him laugh often. She'd forgotten how much she liked being the one to bring it out in him.

The rush of feelings made her dizzy and she put her forehead onto her hand.

"Are you all right?" he asked.

He walked over to her and bent down. He smelled strongly of strawberries.

"Just overtired," she said.

"Let me help you up."

He reached down and offered her his hand. So warm and rough, calloused by work. The work she'd shared with him for so long that made him real and substantial. Hands so unlike Wade's. She blushed and when he pulled her up to standing, she had to turn away. "I'll help you clean up. And then I'll show you how to get the jam in the jars."

"I've made a mess of your kitchen. I'm sorry."

She wet a towel in the sink. "I'm glad you're here."

How would she ever tell him?

"I'm still not allowed in the house, but they tell me by tonight it should be okay. Let me get this mess. I'll just get myself cleaned up first."

Taking off his jam-covered shoes by the door, he headed down the hallway toward the bathroom. "Be right back."

He returned, clean except for the jam on his face, which he must not have noticed, and this made her smile again. She took the towel and wiped the streak off his face, and he peered down at her, his eyes soft on hers.

"Whatever happened between you and Wade . . ."

She shook her head.

"Your dad said he thought it was over. If that's right, I'm not ready to give up on us."

"Jack," she said. She wiped her eyes, wishing what he'd

said could be true. Now she'd never find out.

"You don't need to decide now. Think about it."

She turned away, unable to meet his eye any longer. He took the towel from her hand and cleaned away the rest of the mess.

She forced herself to clear her mind and focused on the jam still remaining in the pot. She put it back on the stove and pulled out a thermometer and her funnel from one of the boxes. A short time later, jars were sealing themselves on the counter with little pops.

Just like LeeAnn had done for their customers every year, Jack held a jar up to the window, sun lighting the jam like stained glass. "That's more like it," he said.

They worked together hulling strawberries for another batch. Then her phone rang.

"It's your mom. You'd better come," her dad said.

Jack drove. When they arrived her mother's eyes fluttered open taking in Jack and LeeAnn standing side by side. She smiled, before drifting into a fitful sleep. They stayed the night at the foot of her bed, LeeAnn holding her mom's hand, Jack sitting beside her.

When the hospice worker came in with Doc Black the next day, her mother wouldn't eat. Out in the hallway, Doc said, "Sleep and lack of appetite is her body's way of saying it's almost time."

Jack put his arm around LeeAnn, a silent reassurance that he'd be there when the time came.

CHAPTER 28

Wade

"WHAT'S THE LATEST?" Harrington asked over the phone.

"Leases are hard to come by right now and you know why," Wade said, picking a piece of mud off the bedcover in his room.

"The geologists tell me the Moore well will be worth all the headaches. That means your brother's land is more valuable than ever. We need our momentum back. You should have had Jack's acreage in the bag before this mess."

Wade had done so much other work for them, but this job had gone about as bad as it could lately. People from all over had heard about the Moore place, with the story on TV many times. How could he make a sale when folks didn't even meet his eye?

"I need you to keep pushing for those properties," Harrington said. "Spend some time in Minden again. You did great there before."

Wade knew it wasn't the right time, but Harrington wouldn't listen. "I'll try again today."

"There's something else we haven't spoken about,"

Harrington said. "Stella Brantley."

"I was a kid last time I saw her, until she showed up here. But maybe our relationship will do Green Energy some good." Wade didn't let on how unlikely this seemed.

"That hope is the only reason you still have a job," Harrington said.

Lying back on his bed, he thought about LeeAnn. That one evening had spoiled their promising relationship. But it had only been one evening. And if nothing else, Minden had shown him second chances were possible.

After work and a stop at the Red Leaf for a shower, he went to LeeAnn's apartment and knocked. She wasn't glad to see him.

"I want to talk," he told her.

She came outside, pulled the door closed behind her, and crossed her arms. "I'm listening."

"I haven't been acting the way I feel. I care about you. I got way off track. I'm sorry."

"Don't you think you're a little late?"

"I feel terrible about your dad's place, and the orchard, too. I should have called you the minute we knew something was wrong. I'm ashamed." He hung his head.

He wanted her to invite him inside. He wanted to put their last night together out of his mind. Erase it. He wanted them to start as though they were just meeting for the first time, without all the history and mistakes. But in his absence she seemed to have grown into a woman with expectations.

"How long are you planning to be in town?"

"A while," he said.

"Have you thought about another job, like we talked about?"

He lowered his voice, hoping she would, too. "I think about it. It might be time. But I'm not sure what I'd do."

He glanced over his shoulder, hoping locals he'd talked to about leasing were well out of earshot. He didn't need people to start talking. He hadn't made any decisions.

"Are you planning to stay around? I'd like to be able to count on that."

"I've missed you. I don't want to think about the what-ifs. Can't we just start over?"

"Start over? You left and stopped calling me right after we slept together. What am I supposed to expect if we start again?"

He wished she would lower her voice. "Did you get my note? I left the stone as a promise I'd be back. Give me another chance."

"Why?"

"Because I love you." He took a deep breath. Did he really mean it? "I do. I let other stuff get in the way."

"I'm pregnant," she said.

He looked away, disoriented, feeling like he'd split in two. He watched a large semi roll by, carrying materials for the complex going in next to the church. She probably blamed for him for that, too.

Raising her hands in exasperation, she said, "You can't even look at me."

He tried his best to meet her eyes. "What are you going to do?"

"I'm going to have this baby and I'm going to raise it the best I can."

He wanted to say something helpful, but this was the last thing he'd expected.

"I thought you might want to be a part of the baby's life," she said, her voice softer.

"I . . . I need time to think."

She shook her head. "And yet you say you love me. Don't come back until you're sure what you want."

She walked back into her apartment, leaving the door open.

Standing motionless, he was caught between the desire

to walk away and the desire to hold her. But he knew more about the man he wasn't than the kind of man he was.

He turned and went down the apartment stairs, holding tight to the railing. A baby took away options. Was Minden really where he wanted to end up? Part of him wanted to turn tail and leave town right then. And part of him wondered what it would be like to be a father. He could be better than his parents had been. He could make up for what they'd withheld. Still, this wasn't a choice he'd made. It was a circumstance he'd fallen into, like so many. One that LeeAnn wanted. But did he?

CHAPTER 29

LeeAnn

IN THE DARKENED room, her mother's breathing became more irregular. At times there were long breaks between gasps. LeeAnn called her father in and they sat close to each other.

Hours passed.

Her father, pale-skinned, looked thin and slack. If there was anything more exhausting than the anticipation of death, she didn't know what it was.

LeeAnn went to the kitchen and brought up sandwiches and glasses of iced tea, which neither of them touched.

Her dad rested his hand gently on her mother's arm. Closeness was important now, not words.

LeeAnn turned off the overhead lights and lit candles on the nightstand by her mother's bed.

All the while time ran thin, and now there was a baby she would never meet. But at least she knew about the child.

The day before, while her mother slept, LeeAnn stood

at the bedroom window, in the shadow of the rig momentarily standing idle. Green Energy had finished cementing the well on Stella's land, and preliminary tests showed that the seal held.

"You're pregnant," her mother said in a hoarse voice.

LeeAnn walked across the room to sit beside her, so shrunken beneath the blankets she seemed like a small child herself.

"How did you know?"

"I rubbed my stomach like that . . . when I was pregnant with you."

LeeAnn felt her face redden.

"You're also. Starting to show," she said, struggling with so many words. Her breathing was irregular.

"I've only known a short while."

Her mom reached for her hand. "Told anyone?"

"Wade. I'm not sure how he feels. Obviously it's a shock."

"And Jack?"

"I don't know how . . ."

Her mother nodded feebly and soon her eyes grew heavy. LeeAnn held her mother's hand in both of hers, trying to warm them.

"Mom?"

"Hmmm?"

"I only hope to be as good a mother as you've been to me."

She squeezed LeeAnn's hand with surprising strength.

It wasn't the suffering she'd endured over so many years that showed on her face now, but the laugh lines around her eyes and mouth and a glow of grace that had only increased as she'd grown sicker. She wasn't angry or fighting it this time.

How was it possible to feel even closer to her mom as she slipped away? This last shared secret connected them to each other and to the child. The bond between LeeAnn and her mother was strong because her mother knew her.

It was a gift to be seen clearly and to be loved so completely anyway. Her mom let her live her life, including mistakes. Even when Rose Moore could see a better way, she hadn't interfered. This is what LeeAnn wanted to give her child. This feeling of being known, loved, and set free. That is how she would honor her mother.

Near midnight, her mother's breathing became even more labored. Each gasp seemed like her last. A short time later she let out a long exhale and was still.

LeeAnn knew her mom was gone. Her father must have felt it, too, because he began to weep.

LeeAnn put her hand softly on her dad's back.

He brought his wife's hand to his lips and sobbed. The sound of his heart breaking almost ripped her in two. She let the tears come and did what her mother would've done. She stayed so her dad wouldn't be alone.

The funeral took place three days later. LeeAnn and Gabriel waited in Jack's truck outside, as Reverend Joe suggested, while friends, family, and acquaintances entered the church.

LeeAnn kept her eyes fixed on them, trying her best to block out the odd complex that Green Energy had created next door. Right now, LeeAnn wanted only the people and place she'd known her whole life around her. She wished all signs of Green Energy would disappear for one day while she had this time with those who mattered and cared about Rose Moore.

She turned to her father. "Dad?"

"Yes?"

"There's something I want to tell you. Something I told Mom just before she died."

He turned to her, his eyes red but dry. They were both so raw, and yet the baby gave LeeAnn something to look forward to. Her father needed that, too.

"I'm gonna have a baby."

He smiled and cried at the same time and hugged her.

"It's not Jack's," she said, pulling away.

"LeeAnn," he said gently.

She met his eyes.

"I'm glad for you. And happy your mother knew. That's a comfort."

Reverend Joe knocked on the window and motioned for them.

It was time.

She took her father's arm and they walked toward the church. The June day, scented with honeysuckle, felt too fine for the occasion. But all those crowding the pews and folding metal chairs in the aisles were a solid reminder of why she loved this small town, where the roots of her life ran deep and wide.

They followed the reverend to a seat in the front pew. Jack sat behind them and he put a hand briefly on LeeAnn's shoulder. She half turned to give him a grateful look. He'd been the one she'd called in the middle of the night. And he'd been the one to help with the arrangements.

Franny and Stu sat behind Jack. Stella was also there.

Reverend Joe called them to prayer. A water truck rumbled by outside.

LeeAnn lowered her head and closed her eyes, trying to resurrect that closeness she and her mother shared a few days before.

Reverend Joe called her father to the podium. He stood and LeeAnn reached up and squeezed his arm.

Facing the crowd, he appeared shrunken and old to her for the first time.

He cleared his throat. "This is hard."

He paused for a long time. He wiped tears away. LeeAnn felt anxious. She scooted forward to stand—she'd prepared something to read, just in case—but Jack put his hand on her shoulder. "Give him a minute," he whispered.

"Ours is a love story," he began, in a shaky voice. "One

made of holding onto each other, no matter what. But it didn't start out that way. I'm going to tell you about our early marriage because it will tell you about Rose."

LeeAnn looked back at Jack and he gave her a small reassuring nod. She pressed her hands together in her lap.

"When we were first married I didn't know how to be a husband. I loved the farm and Rose from the start, but the truth is I didn't feel like I deserved her or her family's land. So I left her soon after we were married, more than once. I went running off with my friends or back home, scared off by little stuff."

This was not a story LeeAnn had ever heard. Why would he tell it now?

"Rose was pregnant with LeeAnn the last time I left. When I came home, after having been gone for a week or so, I finally saw in her eyes how she believed in me. And I saw it for what it was—her gift to me. She forgave me for leaving, like she'd done before. I finally realized what Rose already knew—all we needed to be happy was to show up for each other."

Sunlight streamed in the window behind him.

"Acceptance and forgiveness. That's how love grows. Rose taught me that." His voice broke and he looked down before starting again.

"If she were here now, she'd say that life carries on if you're patient and open." He gazed at LeeAnn. "She would tell me to show up for the people and the place I love. I intend to keep doing that."

He moved away from the podium, sat down next to LeeAnn, and put his arm around her.

Later, in the receiving line, LeeAnn searched for Jack, but he'd drifted to the back of the church.

She and her father greeted one person after another, many of them seeking condolences as much as they offered consolation. She'd been dreading this part, but instead felt grateful to have so many people to focus on. She heard one story after another about her mom. Some she knew and many she didn't. As a teenager, Rose Moore had won the local cow-milking contest three years in a row. Over the last twenty years, she'd taken flowers from her garden to the cemetery and left them on the graves of those with no family. Franny told her Rose had once rescued a bat from Stu's garage while Stu and his mechanic hid under a table. That story brought an actual smile. The memories helped fill the emptiness.

LeeAnn glimpsed Jack still near the back, talking to people. Even now, trying to be there. For her mother. For her.

Wade appeared jittery as he came through the line, and, hugged her tighter and longer than necessary. His aftershave caused her to stifle a gag. LeeAnn did not look at her father or Jack after Wade released her from the embrace. "I'm so sorry," he said. He bent close to her and said quietly, "I'm sorry about before, too. Let me know when you're ready to talk again."

She nodded and he walked on.

Jack came last through the line. Her dad gave him a long hug.

Then Jack took LeeAnn in his arms. They'd shared so much. Why hadn't they held onto each other like her parents had? Was Jack thinking the same? He smelled of motor oil and strawberries, which probably should have made her sick, but didn't.

As he held her she worried that he would sense the change in her body, which he knew so well. *You're starting to show*. He shouldn't find out this way. As much as she longed for his hug, she pulled away.

CHAPTER 30

Jack

June 20 – God Speed, Rose Moore.

SINCE GABRIEL AND LeeAnn were still visiting with the few people left in the church, Reverend Joe handed the urn to Jack. Holding the remains of the woman who'd been more of a mother to him than his own had the unwanted effect of making him feel more distant from her and Gabriel and LeeAnn.

Death divided people. It had been true with Dad and it was true now. He went outside into the overly bright sunlight and wedged the urn safely behind the seats in his truck. When LeeAnn and Gabriel came out, he opened the car door for them without a word. As it had been all day, he wasn't entirely sure whether he was helping or in the way.

LeeAnn sat close, but he sensed tension in her as though she wished otherwise.

Then she let her head fall on his shoulder and what had felt so wrong a moment before was suddenly right. He relaxed for the first time all day.

At Gabriel's house the sun sat near the horizon among low clouds. Gabriel went inside, exhausted. LeeAnn, leaning against the back of Jack's truck, lingered outside. He sensed she wanted to talk.

"Thanks for today," she said. "You were strong for everyone."

She seemed open to him again, finally.

The setting sun broke through the clouds and illuminated her dress showing the silhouette of her body.

His gut told him what he saw before his mind could process it. He staggered back.

Pointing a shaking finger at her, he sputtered a few times before he could get the words out. "When were you gonna tell me?"

Her hand went to her swollen belly. *It was true.*

"I was waiting for the right time."

"Wade's?" He spat the word.

"It happened, Jack. I won't even call it a mistake because it doesn't need naming. It's over between me and him. I don't regret this child, though."

Hot tears came and he angrily wiped them away. "But I loved you."

She shook her head, crying too. "You quit on us."

"You're the one who left," he shouted.

"You left me a long time before I walked out the door."

He kicked the ground, sending up a cloud of dust. "You asked me to choose between you and the orchard. Don't you think that was unfair, given how much I loved both?"

"I never asked you to choose. You made your choice by doing nothing."

Anger mounted inside him. He climbed into his truck and slammed the door against everything that had gone wrong and sped to his house without looking back. LeeAnn had crawled into the arms of his brother to get the baby she'd wanted. Did she ever consider how worthless that would make him feel?

And Wade made it perfectly clear how little regard he

had for Jack by staying away all those years, leaving him stranded on an island of grief and regret. One that had slowly undermined his marriage. So he could come back to reclaim the only person Jack had ever loved, right here in Minden where he'd be forced to bear witness to the happy family day after fucking day.

In his driveway, Jack pulled out his cell and dialed, keeping his voice as steady and easy as he could. "I'm ready to talk about the lease now. Why don't you come over?"

Wade agreed. Even sounded eager.

When Jack hung up, his breathing came in heaves. The ferocity inside had never been stronger.

All during their marriage Jack worried she'd wished he were Wade, even though Jack had been the one to stand by the orchard. And her. And Minden. He'd believed in those things. He still did, goddamn it. He wished he didn't. It would make what he was about to do easier.

Inside his house he opened the closet where he kept Wade's old rifle, the one that had taken Dad's life. It hadn't come out since. He pulled it from the back corner and took down a box of shells from the shelf, loaded the gun, then went back outside.

He walked into the orchard and climbed a tree close enough to give him a clear shot of his front door. He couldn't take LeeAnn carrying Wade's baby. Christ. Anything but that. Anything.

His breath came fast and shallow. His mind wouldn't stop. His brother fucking his wife. The baby *they'd* made.

Dusk settled and it started to rain when a car pulled into the drive. But it wasn't Wade's. LeeAnn got out. She walked to his front door and knocked. Her shoulders were slumped. The funeral and now this, but he couldn't think about that now. When he didn't answer, she pounded. "Jack! Let me in. Let's talk. Please." She tried the door and found it locked.

Too late now. There was nothing to say.

Wade's truck arrived next. Jack started to tremble at

the sight of it.

"What are you doing here?" LeeAnn asked him.

Jack could hear them both clearly. He was close enough to get in a good shot, even if he hadn't shot a gun in twenty years.

"Jack called. Told me he wanted to talk about the lease."

LeeAnn looked around and then backed away toward her car. "I hope he's not thinking crazy. That's not like him, but . . ."

"What do you mean?" Wade said, taking a step toward her.

"He found out about the baby. He's upset. I came here to talk."

"You told him?"

"I wanted to wait for the right time. Instead he figured it out for himself."

The wind kicked up and brought more rain. Jack's grip slipped as he raised the barrel of the gun. He steadied himself and set his sights on Wade's head.

In the crosshairs, he could see Wade's face clearly. His brother didn't go to LeeAnn. He didn't insist she get in her car and leave. He didn't seem like he wanted anything to do with her or the baby. Jack grimaced at the irony. Rage shook his hands and he pulled his finger away from the trigger slightly as he panned over to LeeAnn. He'd loved her even back when he'd had to help hide Wade and LeeAnn's relationship from their dad. She seemed oblivious to the rain coming down, wetting her hair around her face and her dress close to her body. He pointed the scope to her belly. Surprising it had taken him until now to notice.

He turned the rifle back to his brother's head.

"We should go. Maybe you should come stay with me," Wade told her.

"I don't get the idea you want this baby. Or me."

"I want a family like you had growing up, LeeAnn. You want that, too, don't you?"

Jack had wanted the same thing. Hearing his brother

say his deepest wish made him ease his finger off the trigger.

"You heard my dad today. Loving me and the baby would have to be enough for you."

Maybe he was scared of the same thing Wade was: a child he might leave miserable. Jack lowered the gun.

"I want to be with you. If my job takes me out of town, you could come with me," Wade said. "Leave this place for somewhere better."

Wade knew she'd never leave. Jack raised the gun and pointed it again at his brother.

"If you really cared for me, you would know better than to suggest that."

"What you're asking isn't fair, LeeAnn."

"Not fair to who?"

This was the same conversation he and LeeAnn had for years. Wade held his job between them just like Jack held the orchard. He and Wade were more scared of family than they were of being alone. They knew what it was to survive on their own, but neither had the courage to love. Not like Gabriel and Rose. He and his brother shared more than Jack realized and it made him feel oddly sympathetic, a feeling he didn't want but couldn't deny.

LeeAnn walked back toward her car and Wade followed. She opened her car door. She'd wanted a family, and now she had one.

"I don't want to lose you," Wade said.

She ignored him and got in her car. After a sputter the engine caught, and she drove back to Gabriel's. In the darkness, lightning arched across the sky, followed by cracking thunder. In a moment, Wade's taillights headed toward town. The sky opened up, soaking Jack, but he didn't move from his position in the apple tree. Lightning and thunder rolled through the orchard. A loud thwack came from the direction of Stella's property. The dead sycamore sparked and split in two.

Jack climbed down from where he was. He went into

his house and, still dripping wet, called Stella.

CHAPTER 31

Stella

THE CONE OF Silence agreement between Stella and Patrick required Stella to move all files related to Green Energy to her car, so Patrick wouldn't accidentally see something he shouldn't. She now worked in the local library in a small closed room with no window, when it was available.

Lately, she and Patrick had little to say to each other beyond dishes and laundry. Every word had to be carefully considered, the consequences parsed, before one of them spoke. A tiring task neither of them felt up to at the end of a long day.

On this June night their bedroom window was open and the cool night air raised goose bumps on her arms. She lay beside Patrick, their disconnection like a line drawn between them that neither knew how to cross. Lawyers instead of lovers, in bed with their work between them. She turned toward him. He stared at the ceiling, but took her hand.

"Patrick?"

"Hmm?"

"I went to a funeral yesterday in Minden. For someone I once knew. I want to tell you about it."

"Isn't that against the rules?"

"It's personal, not professional."

Letting go of her hand, he said, "Thought maybe you wanted to talk about us. Not Minden."

"It is about us."

He looked at her for a moment and then back to the ceiling. "Go on."

"The funeral was for Rose Moore. She and her husband Gabriel were my neighbors in Minden. And my only friends."

"Was the service in your father's church?"

She considered him, fondly. "That's right." He'd been listening, trying to understand her.

"Was it difficult to be there?"

"Yes. But I want to tell you about Gabriel and Rose."

He gave a slight nod.

"Rose saw something in Gabriel he didn't see in himself. It made me think of you." Stella propped herself up on her pillow. "I know you think I've left our life. But I hope you trust that I'm trying to get back to you."

He let out a long breath and put his hand on her hip, pulling her closer. "It's hard to keep faith. I believe in you. But there's so much standing between us now. When do you think things will settle?"

"I don't know."

He quieted for a moment. "Is it worth it, Stella?"

"It's for us."

"I want that to be true," Patrick said, rolling on his back again. "But I can't wait forever for you to settle a past that might never be resolved. You may not be able to fix your relationship with your sons."

"Jack called me tonight. He wants to talk about how to move things forward tomorrow morning."

She looked over at Patrick when he said nothing. His

eyes were closed and he was either sleeping or pretending to be.

~

The next morning, Stella met Jack outside the apple barn, where he loaded fertilizer into his tractor.

"I know it's probably more than you and LeeAnn have been able to think about, but are you both willing to be a part of a suit against Green Energy?"

"When you mentioned it to me before, I thought it might be a good idea."

"But now?"

Jack tilted his face to the sun and closed his eyes for a moment. "I'm not sure what it would get us, except money. And that doesn't matter much to me."

Jack sounded wishy-washy again. "A lawsuit will be a way for the truth to come out. People beyond Minden should know what happened on the Moore property and here at the orchard. You asked me to come here to share this kind of information. Surely you don't want to help Green Energy sweep their flawed practices under the rug."

This time she would build a better case against them from the start so that they would not be able to buy their way out of responsibility.

Jack balled up the empty fertilizer bag and stuffed it into the trash. "I guess I don't see how it would help. People like the Moores will have more to fear, but they'll still need the money. I suppose if a lawsuit is successful then the drilling goes away altogether. And you get what you want. Isn't that right? You get to finally beat Green Energy?"

Stella shook her head. "I'm not here just to win a case. But if we were to find a way to stop the drilling, then the land stays the way it is, preserved."

"Like in a museum, behind glass? That's not what anyone who depends on their land wants. It feels wrong to take away a landowner's choices. Change isn't easy, but it's happening and all of it's not bad. What I'd like is for Minden

to have more of a say. I'd like to put the people, like my neighbors, first, instead of last."

Stella wondered how much of what Jack said tied into his feelings for LeeAnn. "You love this place and want to protect it. You asked me here to help you do that. I don't understand why you still have reservations."

Jack emptied the last of the bags of fertilizer into the tractor. "I've worked this orchard my whole life. I've taken from this ground and as long as I've cared for it, it's given back. I don't like what happened next door. The damage to the orchard breaks my heart. But Green Energy has done some good, too. So, I have to think there's another way. A lawsuit doesn't seem right. Can't we somehow work together to make the drilling safer? You know, make sure what's gone wrong at the Moore place doesn't happen again."

"But Green Energy already holds ninety percent of the lease contracts in this area. The same kind of contract as the Moore's."

Jack closed the hopper. "There's got to be a way to convince them."

"You mean an ultimatum?"

"Yeah, maybe."

Stella peered at her hands and linked them together. "Like?"

"Like . . . they either fix what happened at the orchard and next door and give better terms on their lease contracts in Minden, or they get sued, right along with a lot of bad PR. If they don't want to be sued, then maybe we have a chance to help ourselves *and* other people. Maybe we can do something here that can be an example for other places, like you want."

"Bad PR has never stopped them."

"But we can give them a chance to work with the people here so that everyone is better off in the end."

"Green Energy is a corporation. They're interested in the bottom line, not this community. Any civic effort they

show, like the donation to the school, is so that they can get more leases to bolster their bottom line. End of story."

"Well then, we'll have to talk them into using better methods. We can find a way, can't we?"

Stella opened her mouth to tell Jack the reasons his idea would not work, and then closed it as she thought of the possibilities. "If we take the course of action you're suggesting, the end result would be uncertain. There's a reasonable chance of failure."

Jack took off his ball cap and wiped his brow. "I want the drilling to be safer, and to make sure it's done in a way that protects Minden and people's relationships with each other. But I don't feel like we have a right to try to stop it altogether."

Stella's mind worked to sort through how Jack's idea could be put into action. "In order to get Green Energy to agree with this, we would have to threaten a lawsuit, as you've suggested. And if they didn't want to give people an option for new lease agreements, we would have to be prepared to follow through."

"I'm good with that plan," Jack said.

"I've set up a meeting with Green Energy tomorrow at the fire hall. The ball is in our court, and it's best if we move quickly. I think I can be ready to present this idea by then, but I want to meet you, LeeAnn, and Elzer before then to discuss details."

Jack replaced his hat. "LeeAnn and I aren't talking," he said. "If you need her to be involved, you'll have to speak to her. I can't be in the middle anymore."

"When did this happen? If we're going to meet with Green Energy, you'll have to present a united front. Both of your names have to be on the lawsuit. Green Energy will pick up on any issues and use it in their favor."

"You talk to her then," he said, climbing onto the tractor.

She found LeeAnn at home after checking the Tic-Toc first. LeeAnn, wearing an oversized shirt, looked tired. They sat on the stairs to her apartment and Stella told her Jack's idea.

"I want Wade to be asked to join us. He should know we're not doing this against him, but instead watching out for Minden," LeeAnn said.

"Agreed." The warm June sun came out from behind a cloud and felt overly hot. Stella decided to get right to the point. "Jack says you and he aren't talking to each other."

"Is that how he put it?"

"What's going on?"

"It's complicated."

"If something's about to erupt between you two then this isn't the time to go into a meeting with Green Energy."

LeeAnn turned her violet eyes on Stella, which appeared deeper than ever. "I'm pregnant. Wade's the father. Jack found out last night before I could tell him myself."

Stella saw in LeeAnn's face this wasn't something she'd planned.

"You and Wade?"

"That's right," LeeAnn said, now defiant, as though to reinforce that there was much Stella didn't know.

If it came down to it, how would Wade deal with a lawsuit threat against his company involving the mother of his child? And Jack? Would she be able to set aside the personal hurt, like he was apparently willing to? LeeAnn and he had wanted a child for years. Hadn't that been why they'd split up? Good God, it was all so much more complicated than she could have imagined. The lump in her throat made it burn.

"Is it hard? Being back here? Facing them?" LeeAnn asked, looking past Stella, out over Morrigan Mountain.

"Yes."

"I have to say it's hard for me, too. Neither wants a family. They're more alike than they are different. I always thought I could help them, but I haven't done that. Instead,

I wanted them to be people they aren't. I see that now. I'm going to raise the baby on my own." She stood and arched her back.

Stella wondered if LeeAnn had told Wade or Jack her plan. She thought for a moment, assembling an argument. "They must see something in you they need."

"What's in me right now is a baby and neither one of them is around," LeeAnn said.

Sidestepping the obvious parallel to her own history, Stella said, "If nothing else, the meeting tomorrow will help you sort through what to do with the orchard. I won't pursue anything you don't want. But we should at least address the damage on your property and your parents' place. The baby gives you another reason to make sure the land is healthy."

Stella stood and started down the steps. LeeAnn followed her to her car. "If this is going to happen, then you'll be spending a lot more time in Minden," LeeAnn said.

Stella nodded. "I'm not sure how to break it to my husband. Things are already difficult between us."

"Oh?"

"We can't discuss our work because of a legal agreement, and our work has always been at the heart of our marriage."

"Where will you stay, when you're working up here? You can't travel back and forth every day."

"I'm going to ask Elzer if I can use his office a few days a week. I'll find a hotel somewhere when I have to stay overnight."

"Stay here with me."

Stella felt unsure of how to respond and hesitated to say anything for a moment. "I'm surprised you'd offer."

"I am, too, to tell you the truth. But Doc Black told me I'll need help to give the baby the best chance. Maybe we can do each other a favor."

It hit Stella then: this woman carried her grandchild. "Are you sure?"

"All I have is a couch, but I think it's pretty comfortable. Think about it."

Stella covered LeeAnn's hand with her own. "Thank you."

Stella arrived before Jack at Elzer Hawk's house.

Elzer answered her knock right away.

"I need your help," she said.

He gave her a skeptical look. "Hello to you, too."

She stepped into his foyer. "Based on what happened with the Moore well, I believe I can get Green Energy to let go of all the leases they hold in and around Minden, and we can help the community get better deals for their land."

He chuckled. "Green Energy won't agree to that."

"I think they will. I spoke with Jack, and this is his idea. LeeAnn is also in favor. I've been thinking about how to make it work. If I can get Green Energy to release people from their contracts, I could develop a new lease agreement with restrictions that will offer more protections to landowners. A joint agreement that those already leasing as well as newcomers could sign. Then, ideally, once we have a lot of people on board, the new lease agreement will be offered to the three energy companies in town. Highest bidder wins."

Elzer reached for his tobacco sitting on the table and stuffed a wad into his lower lip. "With the exception of my land and the orchard, Green Energy owns almost all of the leases in town, thanks to Wade. Why would they let go of the properties they have in order to buy them back at a higher price, with, I assume, restrictions that will only hamper their profits?"

"I have something they won't want in the public domain: bad PR and a nasty, drawn-out lawsuit."

He turned and gestured toward the living room. "You may as well come in and sit down." Stella took a seat on the couch and he sat down across from her. "What kind of lease restrictions are you thinking about?"

"Protection of people's health, property, the water, forest land, and whatever else we think is smart. The market is at an all-time high right now. Green Energy is in the right place at the right time. But they need the land and they need to be able to move forward without a lawsuit and bad PR slowing them."

"You're capable of doing what you've described. Why do you need me?"

"This will only work if we can get enough landowners to sign on. In the end we need to represent a huge parcel of largely contiguous acreage, which is exactly what the energy companies all want."

"So have a meeting."

"It won't work that way. I'm not from here." The burning in her throat returned. "I'm worse than a stranger. But people trust you."

"Why should I help you now?"

"Because this is the right thing to do as mayor of this town."

He leaned toward her and cocked an eyebrow. "I suppose you'll need me to sign over my property for the lease agreement to be a go."

She straightened in her chair. "It wouldn't hurt."

"That's not going to happen. Like everyone, I'll wait until I've had a chance to decide for myself."

"Then at least help me explain this to your community. This new lease idea would give them options."

Elzer met Stella's eyes. "You can talk to people one-on-one all you want. I'll even help you. But no signatures until we hold a public meeting with Green Energy so they have a chance to say their piece. Then we'll let people decide. And I'm only agreeing because it's what Jack and LeeAnn want and only if you promise to see it out. No walking away this time, Stella."

"I promise," she said. But that did little to change the

doubtful look on his face. "I'll need space in your office to work over the next few months."

"You haven't even had your meeting with Green Energy yet. They may shoot you down before you start."

"Can I work in your office if they don't?"

He sighed. "Don't you have an office?"

"There's a Cone of Silence agreement with my law partner regarding Green Energy."

"You mean your husband?"

"I need a few days a week. I'll go home on the weekends."

Elzer studied her. She could almost hear his thoughts. Stella had left her sons, Steve—and now, perhaps, her current husband. Was she someone he could count on?

Her stomach fluttered with nerves—even she wished she knew the answer. But Stella Brantley was a name that had earned respect in the world of environmental law, and that circle should include Minden.

CHAPTER 32

Jack

June 25 – Can't save this orchard on my own.

THE FRESHNESS OF the cool morning air conflicted with what Jack saw as he walked down a tree row surveying the damage. This should have never happened. As many as six of his acres would produce no apples this year, and maybe never again. Far enough from the abandoned well, LeeAnn's trees were spared.

The sticky white paper sheets she'd hung weeks ago waved in the wind next to her developing fruit. Insect traps with pheromone lures. She monitored what got caught on the lures to figure the best time to apply organic sprays. They didn't kill the insects, but instead covered the fruit in a thin clay film to discourage the bugs from eating. He guessed she wouldn't be working at the orchard much now.

Climbing the tree, he studied the bugs and what got caught in the sticky paper. The usual stuff – oriental and codling moths. He knew nothing of the counts and calculations she did with the bugs. But he did know that the flower petals had fallen off weeks ago, a sign for him it was time to spray to make sure the fruit didn't become infested. Spraying her trees when he treated the rest of the orchard would be easiest.

He walked back down the tree row toward the apple barn. The spray tank, already filled with the chemicals his father had always used, sat attached to the tractor ready to roll. The risk of experimenting now, with so much already lost, was a reality he shouldn't ignore.

Except that the way he cared for LeeAnn's apples mattered, even if he didn't want it to.

He found the organic orcharding book she used in a corner behind the apple press. He turned to the index, trying to decide how the sticky white paper or the clay spray might be listed.

Later that day, when Jack arrived at the fire hall, Stella waited for him outside.

"Are the Green Energy people here?"

"Inside," she said. "We'll wait for LeeAnn and all go in together."

"How did she seem when you talked to her?"

"You'll need to put aside your personal issues today. This meeting is about the orchard and Minden, both of which you and LeeAnn care deeply about. Let's focus on that."

Despite what Patrick had said, Jack still couldn't be sure if Stella really wanted to help them, or if she was just out to settle the score with Green Energy. "I can't separate the orchard from my personal issues."

LeeAnn arrived a few minutes later, emerging from her car wearing a dress that accentuated the pregnancy she'd been hiding, as though to announce his brother's baby to the world. The knife dug into Jack's side a little deeper. Even so, he knew he needed to get past it. LeeAnn had gotten what would make her happy.

"Hello, LeeAnn," he said. Unlike before, when standing near was like a magnet pulling him toward her, he now felt pushed as though the magnet reversed. A physical force now separated them. The baby.

She nodded in his direction. "Jack."

"Can I talk to you in private for a moment?"

They walked a short distance away while Stella waited by the door.

"Listen," he said in a low voice. "I'm sorry about the other night. I was surprised and upset. I still am, to be honest. But I know this is what you've wanted."

"I've wanted a family, Jack. A mother, a baby—and a father."

He wondered what the child would be like. In the orchard, Red Delicious couldn't pollinate Red Delicious. Trees could only cross-pollinate, like Red Delicious with McIntosh. The host tree determined the fruit variety. Perhaps LeeAnn's baby would take after her, too. That's what he would hope for.

Stella called to them. "I'm sorry, but we need to go inside. Are you ready?"

"Wait," LeeAnn said, turning and walking toward her. "What about Wade?"

Jack bristled. He wasn't ready to see his brother.

"He didn't call me back." Stella put her hand on the doorknob. "Now, let's go in."

Jack nodded.

"Leave the talking to me," Stella said.

Inside the fire hall, two men from Green Energy waited for them at the rectangular folding table used for meetings. Both men stood.

"Stella, we meet again," said the man Jack recognized as Harrington Price. "You remember our counsel, Mr. Reynolds."

Jack could tell instantly that Stella and Mr. Reynolds didn't like each other. Stella introduced Reynolds to Jack and LeeAnn.

"LeeAnn, it's a pleasure," Harrington said. "I've met your husband, but not you. I see you're expecting. Congratulations to both of you."

"Let's get to business, shall we?" Stella said.

Jack took a seat between Stella and LeeAnn. Harrington and his lawyer sat at the opposite side of the table.

Stella began. "For the record, I'm representing myself as well as Jack and LeeAnn Pierson. We're offering a choice. Option one is a lawsuit I've drafted. You may look it over." She handed a copy to Mr. Reynolds.

He took it and began reading.

"And option two?" Harrington said.

"We have a proposal in mind. But let's start with the lawsuit. This is a toxic trespass case. Gas was found in my clients' house at levels high enough to cause an explosion. High concentrations of gas were also measured on their land and mine. Our property values have plummeted. The water's polluted. There is evidence of tree damage in their orchard that may prove catastrophic. We have all the data, gentlemen. The Piersons' livelihood is in question. Mrs. Pierson is expecting, as you've already noted. She will be right around full term when we take this case to trial. The jury will appreciate the potential impact . . . we'll sue for monetary compensation and we will not sign a nondisclosure agreement. The trial and all the information we have will become public. Nothing will remain hidden. You'll see in my write up, my clients are fully committed."

Jack shifted in his seat. Stella had not previously mentioned her history with these men. Rather than wanting to save the orchard and farmland in Minden, as she'd claimed, she sounded like she wanted to punish Green Energy. Jack hadn't agreed to go to trial "no matter what." He couldn't imagine LeeAnn had either. He looked at LeeAnn. She gave him a small nod, as though to say, let's see where this goes.

"And your other proposal?" said Harrington.

"Within a ten-mile radius of Minden proper, you will give everyone with whom you have a lease agreement the option of being released from their contract. They will be allowed to sign a new lease that I'll draft with a colleague. These terms will also be offered to anyone who has not yet leased. After people sign on, we'll put our joint landowner lease agreement up for sale to Green Energy and the two other companies in town."

Both men glanced at each other and laughed, heads thrown back, as though they'd practiced. "What kind of a lease are you talking about?" asked Harrington, in a patronizing tone.

"One that better protects the leaseholder, this community, and the land."

Reynolds frowned, put both hands on the table and leaned toward them. "This is preposterous," he said, spittle flying across the table and settling on Stella's briefcase. "I'm surprised at you, counselor. What you're proposing is out of the question. Why would we let go of the leases we have without the guarantee of getting them back, and for more money?"

Jack leaned back in his chair. This was bad business. He wondered if Stella was out of her league. But she didn't even hesitate.

"I have evidence you don't want in the public domain," she said. "In the courtroom, we'll have the Pennsylvania Department of Environmental Protection behind us. We have federal experts. Several movie stars and well-known musicians have offered to come and protest right here in Minden during the trial. Imagine a large media spectacle garnering national outrage with the spotlight on Green Energy and you'll have it about right. I wonder if the public will align with corporate greed or with what happened to poor Gabriel Moore, LeeAnn's father, just recently widowed. Asthma may have played a part in his wife's death and there was all that dust, with your chosen drilling location so close to the house. We have records of that, too, gentlemen."

Jack could see LeeAnn stiffen. Stella used her parents like chess pieces. But now he could see the hesitation in Harrington's eyes. The urgency to reassure LeeAnn, so that she didn't say anything to undo the progress he could now see Stella was making, allowed Jack put his hand on LeeAnn's arm and squeeze gently, hoping to offer the same reassurance she'd given him a moment ago. Stella might know what she was doing after all.

"I know as well as you do how much gas is under Minden," Stella said. "I know how much it's worth. The longer you stall, the longer the money waits. Gas prices aren't going to stay high forever."

This is what Stella did well, Jack thought. It was, in fact, a performance that made him weirdly proud to be on her side. This is what she'd been trying to tell him the whole time. That she could help them because she was a lawyer. And, maybe, because she also really did care.

"Numbers and scare tactics won't matter to the public," said Harrington, his cool demeanor beginning to slip.

"This will matter," Stella said, opening up her laptop and playing the video she'd taken of the geyser and dead fish bobbing to the surface in Silver Creek.

When the video ended, Stella said, "The choice is yours: a lawsuit or a compromise. In the meantime, you will supply my clients with water for drinking and household use until their water quality is back to normal, no matter how long that takes. You will give them fair-market compensation for loss at their property, given the toxic trespass. The value of their property has been compromised. This compensation will include rectifying damage incurred to the orchard on the property. You will also fully restore Silver Creek and my land to its original state, including restoration of the fish population. You will incur all of these costs and you will be bound to these terms by contract. Or, as a starting point, this video might find its way to YouTube."

"What timeframe are you talking about for this new lease agreement?"

"Five months. Time enough to write it up and discuss it with this community. We're going to have to go door to door and explain the options, maybe more than once. We won't ask people to sign right away. I've talked to the mayor and he's agreed to hold a public meeting in November. People will have the opportunity to sign on during or shortly after that meeting and not before. The mayor wants it that way. He wants all the energy companies there, particularly Green Energy, to answer people's questions so they understand their options."

"You don't give us much choice," Harrington said.

"Option two is your choice," Stella said, holding up a folder. "I have an agreement for you to sign, describing what we've discussed." She handed the folder to Green Energy's lawyer.

"I'll need time to go over this," Reynolds said.

"I'll expect it back tomorrow."

"Fine," Harrington said.

Stella stood. Jack and LeeAnn followed her lead, trailing her out of the building. As soon as the door closed behind them, Harrington came out and asked Stella to come back inside to answer some questions about the agreement she'd presented.

"Just a minute," she said. Harrington retreated back to the table to wait.

"You go on," she said to LeeAnn and Jack. "We've done what we came to do."

"One of us needs to talk to Wade about all this. At this point, it's best coming from you," LeeAnn said to Stella.

Stella nodded.

Jack couldn't feel bad for Wade. Not now. If what they were planning ruined the work he was doing for Green Energy, then so be it. He would still have so much—a new baby with LeeAnn.

"I'll see you later tonight, then?" LeeAnn said.

Jack thought LeeAnn might somehow be talking to him, but Stella nodded before going back inside.

"You'll see each other later? For what?" he asked.

"She's going to stay with me a few days a week while she works on the lease agreement and then shops it around over the next months."

A truck loaded with water for fracking thundered past.

"Did she ask to stay with you?"

"I invited her."

Jack glanced toward the overcast sky, a block of impenetrable white.

"Do you think that's best, considering the baby?"

"She needs a place to stay and she's willing to help me through this pregnancy. That's more than I can say for Wade, who doesn't seem to know what he wants. I can't very well ask my dad, not right now. I certainly don't expect you to offer."

It hurt that she would consider him a last resort.

"But Stella isn't capable of taking care of you."

"She's all I've got at the moment."

It made him sick to say it, but he had to: "It's Wade's child, too."

"It's my child. And I'll do what's best. Right now that means being on my own."

"But LeeAnn!"

She turned and put one hand on her hip. "What?"

Why did this woman, even now, take the words from his mouth, the breath from his chest? After a long moment he said, "If you need anything, let me know."

"I need you to let me be. I think that's best for both of us right now."

CHAPTER 33

Wade

"WE'VE GIVEN STELLA Brantley until November to work on the new lease agreement," Harrington told Wade over the phone. "We haven't agreed to stop our own efforts. So you're going to be working in Minden again full time. And you're going to offer more money, too. That gives you five months to hold and improve Green Energy's position. You still at the Red Leaf?"

"Yep." Wade tapped a couple of aspirin into his hand and washed them down with water he gulped directly from the sink. If he could focus only on Minden over the next few months, maybe it would give him the stability to fix his life.

"If people want to be released from an agreement with us, they'll have a year to pay back the signing money we gave them with no penalties," Harrington said. "Brantley thinks she can get them a better deal with her lease and they'll be able to pay us back. Your job will be to make sure that folks know her idea is risky. Tell them she may never get enough people to make this work. They'll have to pay us back, either way. And when she fails, they'll be stuck, and we may not be around anymore to offer another deal. That's the honest truth."

Stella would disappoint. He'd made relationships in Minden. He'd spent the time. Surely they would listen to him and not her.

"You said Jack and LeeAnn are involved?" Even if LeeAnn never liked the drilling, he hadn't expected her to side with Stella against him. What had Stella told her?

"Honestly," said Harrington. "We're talking about your brother here. You might have mentioned that you two weren't close when we gave you this job. Now I'm the one telling you he's got a knife in your back."

There was a knock. "Listen, I have to go. Someone's at the door."

"Think carefully about your next steps, Pierson. Your job hangs by a thread."

Wade hung up the phone and opened the door. Standing with her fist raised, ready to knock again, was Stella.

"Do you have a minute?" she asked, as if she hadn't recruited Jack and LeeAnn to ambush him. "I'd like to talk."

"I'm busy."

"I need to tell you something important. It won't take long."

He gripped the door to keep from shaking her senseless.

She spoke quickly. "I've just had a meeting with Green Energy."

"The boss already filled me in."

"We're trying to help people protect what they have. We're not going against you. You might even think about working with us."

He smiled wide. Good fucking God. What did she take him for? Whatever spell she'd cast over LeeAnn and Jack wasn't going to work. He spit and it landed next to her leather loafer.

She did not budge. "We'll be working on a lease agreement, but we're not in competition for leases. It's about offering a choice."

"You never offered me and Jack much choice."

Her eyes narrowed. "You and I are a lot the same. Both of us have a history of running away, instead of running toward what could be."

"Who in their right mind would take your advice?" he said, moving to close the door.

She put her hand out to stop him. "LeeAnn told me about the baby."

"That's none of your business."

"I'm going to stay with her over the next few months a few days a week, to help. I thought you should know."

"Liar."

"She asked me to."

He slammed the door shut. Light glinted off the pins stuck in the map hanging on his wall. He punched it. The map crumpled as the drywall cracked and bent inward. Blood dripped on the floor. He went, unhurried, into the bathroom and let cold water run over his hand. How had things become so fucked?

He would fight to keep the leases he'd won. He would make sure Stella failed. The sooner she slunk back where she came from, the better.

NOVEMBER

CHAPTER 34

Stella

FOR THE SECOND November day in a row, rain punished the roof of Elzer Hawk's office. Stella went over again what she would say in an hour at the public meeting. Over the last months, she and Elzer had met at least once with nearly every landowner who had more than a few acres in and around Minden. But she didn't know whether anyone would choose to sign their new lease agreement, at the public meeting or during the two-week period following. That was all the time they had.

After all, people forgot problems quickly, especially when money was involved. No traceable levels of gas remained in Silver Creek, in the soil on her land, or at the orchard. Green Energy had agreed to compensate her, Jack, and LeeAnn for their losses. The Moore well produced even more than expected, helping Gabriel manage his bills and even increase his herd. In the eyes of many, Green Energy had more than made up for what had happened.

The office door opened while Stella studied the notes

in front of her. Elzer said to meet her at the fire hall, but he must have changed his mind.

"Think we'll get enough signatures?" she asked him, still reading.

When he didn't respond, she looked up. Patrick stood there, white-faced and dripping with rain.

"What is it?" she said, standing and going to him.

Over the last five months she'd spent more time in Minden than at home and she hadn't been able to tell him why. Her worst fear: he was here now to tell her she'd lost him.

"Come home. No more excuses," he said.

"I just need tonight. Then, the Cone of Silence between us goes away." There would be no more secrets. For the first time in their relationship, she could just be herself with him. That's what it had all been for.

"Everything's imploding."

He appeared thinner. Gaunt, really. She knew what this probably meant for him. How had she missed it?

"What's happened?"

"So much that I haven't been able to tell you." Patrick raised his hands and let them fall. "I can't anymore. Green Energy, as the new owner of Sunrise Solar, has fired us. This is the final straw for our practice. It's rotten on Green Energy's part, but Sunrise has been a friend. They want to figure out a way to get me back on board, but you have to let go. Green Energy isn't buying the Cone of Silence deal and they've forced Sunrise's hand. We can't live this way any longer. Please. Come home now and help me save the firm. *Save us.*"

She looked away. "I'm so close here. You have no idea."

"I can't wait anymore, Stella."

Turning and walking back to her desk, she picked up her brief case and her raincoat. She could not lose him now. Tears threatened. But there was only this choice.

"I have to finish this," she said, walking past him out the door.

She hoped to God she could manage to get Patrick to understand later.

CHAPTER 35

Jack

November 19 – These last weeks I've been able to sit in my house and feel at ease.

JACK RAN IN the fading light to his truck, hunched against the downpour from the late-season hurricane making its way up the East Coast and currently stalled over Minden. The purl of the creek had grown into a low roar over the last several days.

He was on his way to the public meeting at the fire hall. He would see LeeAnn in her final month of pregnancy.

She'd asked him to let her be and he'd done his best to respect her wishes. Even caring for her apples the way she would have wanted, and selling them, too. He'd put the money away for her.

Doc Black reassured him that with Stella around, LeeAnn had the rest she needed. Just a week ago, Jack saw Stella in the grocery store studying a book open on top of her grocery cart. The header on the page said, BEST FOODS FOR A HEALTHY PREGNANCY.

"She's doing well," Stella said. Just those words and

Stella knowing he needed to hear them, left him choked.

As Jack drove down the drive toward the main road he saw movement out of the corner of his eye near Silver Creek. He stopped. The old trick of the eye. The ghosts that kept him from living his life. He no longer wanted them around.

Surveying the creek, he searched for reasons to dismiss what he'd seen. But the longer he looked, the more convinced he became that people stood near the rising water.

He turned off his lights, squinting into the rain. He made out two small figures and a larger one leaning against the remains of the sycamore. A small family standing on the bank of the flooded creek?

It seemed so unlikely and yet he could swear the three were gathered near the part of the sycamore that had been struck by lightning and fallen. The large limb bounced slowly, as the rising water tugged. The limb was so heavy Jack was sure it could not be dislodged. Still, these people should not be that close. The creek was beyond dangerous.

He pulled up the hood of his coat and got out of his truck. The rain chipped at his exposed face and hands. He hurried toward them, huffing in the chilly, damp air. As he approached he made out two children huddled by a woman.

He slowed, not wanting to startle them. He watched as the woman put her arms around the kids and pulled them close to her, but then in the next instant she pushed them toward the limb, half of which had now been dragged into the current. The children resisted. Then one slowly walked away from the woman and toward the limb.

"Stay back," Jack yelled to them, and started to run again. Water ran down his face into his eyes as he got closer. "It's too dangerous!" He wouldn't be able to cross the creek to stop them. God, he hoped they heard him over the water.

Jack wiped his eyes again as the rain came down even

harder. He stumbled on. When he reached the bank of the creek, the people had vanished. Only rocks and bushes stood at the creek's edge. The sycamore limb that had been lying on the ground was gone.

CHAPTER 36

Wade

THE POUNDING RAIN overpowered the sound of the television at the Red Leaf. Wade sat at the end of the bar in what had become his spot. He was usually alone, unless some roughneck or townie wanted to talk business. These days he wasn't much interested in talking business. He wasn't much interested in anything.

Over the last few months he'd had little luck getting a bead on what people were planning. More and more he stayed in the bar, the only friendly place where he was still part of the community.

People were in wait-and-see mode. Tonight's meeting would be the decision maker. His fate hung in the balance: either he would become a very busy man again or an unemployed one. He'd figured out early on people weren't going to decide one way or another until they could see what played out at the meeting. Green Energy didn't seem to understand that, but then what else was new.

If it weren't for Stella and her abandoned well, things would be different. His job wouldn't be in question. LeeAnn wouldn't have turned against him. Stella, the same piece of bad luck he kept rubbing against, like a cursed penny.

He would see LeeAnn tonight for the first time in months. By involving Stella with the baby, LeeAnn had made it clear she wanted it that way. *Their* baby. Stella would vanish as soon as the meeting concluded. After the meeting, no matter which way it went, Wade could fill the hole Stella would leave in LeeAnn's life. He could talk sense into her. They could leave Minden and raise the baby together. He could give the child what he'd never had.

Two beers would not be enough to soften the set jaws and hard edges of people's faces he encountered every time he emerged from the Red Leaf. Many still blamed him for what happened at Gabriel and Rose's place, not to mention the orchard. The public meeting was his last chance. If he played his cards right, maybe he could undo the mistrust. Elzer Hawk had been the only one from Minden to call and ask him to come and speak on behalf of Green Energy and the industry. "We want a fair representation," he said. Harrington had some other crisis to handle and, for once, agreed that Wade had the best chance of gaining leverage. They needed a local face.

Wade took his last swig of beer, pulling longer than he knew was smart. The bartender asked if he wanted another, but he shook his head. LeeAnn would be there and he needed to think straight.

He drove to the fire hall. In the fading light he saw that the creek had spilled out of its banks and now looked more like a swollen river.

Cars and trucks jammed the parking area. LeeAnn walked just ahead of him across the lot. He called out to her. She turned and waited under the overhang of the roof. She wore a scarf around her neck that matched her eyes.

"Can we can talk afterward?" he asked.

Even in the dim light, he could see her face redden. She spoke in a low tone he could barely hear over the rain. "I don't know what we'd talk about."

"I want another chance. I haven't been fair to you, I know."

"You want another chance with me? Or a new reason to start over?"

"Let's talk after. I have some things I want to share with you."

She turned, opened the door, and Wade rushed to hold it while she shook out her umbrella. Franny waited for LeeAnn inside, taking her from him, and guiding her past Doc Black and his wife to a seat she'd saved near the front. Otherwise it was standing room only.

Over four hundred people, Wade guessed, and he'd talked to all of them. Some nodded in his direction.

Elzer Hawk stood at the front of the room, his Stetson shadowing his face. Stella sat beside him. Jack faced them in the front row.

Wade angled his way through the crowd until he also stood near the front, in a place he could easily speak from when the time was right.

He scanned the crowd, sensing people's curiosity about Stella, and their mistrust. He knew the feeling well. She seemed undisturbed. Wade wondered if she knew that every person in the room judged her.

Elzer stood and called the meeting to order.

"I'm glad to see a good turnout. A lot of change is happening in our town as concerns gas leases and we need to know our options."

Wade checked over his shoulder for LeeAnn who had her hands folded over her swollen belly. In one month she'd be holding their child.

The crowd shifted in their seats and settled in as Elzer studied the paper in his hand. "We're going to hear from Stella Brantley first, and then Green Energy. After the presentations we'll get to questions."

Elzer put the paper down and cleared his throat. "Tonight is about options, not choosing sides. There's no right or wrong. So let's keep it respectful. When I first heard about the drilling, I saw it as a God-given opportunity for this town. And I still see it that way. Being a cautious type, I waited on signing anything. Some couldn't wait. Or some were braver than I am and signed early. Now most of us have an opportunity to start fresh. You all know I've worked with Stella Brantley to develop a lease agreement that protects our place in Minden while allowing us to profit from the drilling. But you should know I have not signed onto it and I won't. Not unless most of you decide to on your own. It may not be right for you and your family, and if it isn't, then you'll make a different choice. This meeting is your chance to ask any questions that have cropped up since we spoke to you individually. So Stella, the floor is yours."

This is why Elzer has been mayor all these years, thought Wade. He knew how to talk to people and he really cared. Everyone in the room was with him.

"I think you understand that this new lease offers a provision for setbacks from houses as well as protections for drinking water, farmland, and forests," Stella began. "The lease may mean more money, too, if enough people sign on. The more landowners that sign, the more bargaining power."

Wade caught Stella's eye and stared her down until she looked away. This town would never listen to her. People here valued loyalty and commitment. He could feel it in the room. Even with Elzer's backing, she was an outsider. Just wait, thought Wade.

"The plan we've put together is one anyone can sign on to, even if you've only got a few acres," she continued.

Wade studied the room. People were paying attention.

"I have a question," he said, interrupting her.

Elzer stood up and didn't hide his irritation at the disruption. "Yes?"

"It's no secret Mrs. Brantley put Minden in her rear view forty years ago. Does she really have Minden's best interest at heart? I would ask people to think before signing onto something that might set you back in terms of getting the best deal."

A murmur ran through the crowd and grew louder.

Elzer pounded his gavel and people quieted.

Stella spoke up, her voice strong. "Thanks for bringing up that point, Wade," she said, referring to him as though he were another person in the community that she'd talked to once over the last few months. People would notice that. She cared about him about as much as she did a stranger. The distance between her and this community was palpable.

"We've tried to make this lease agreement meet the needs of the people in Minden. Elzer has helped to shape it that way," Stella said. "We'd like to have a final agreement two weeks from now, so if what you hear tonight interests you, then please contact me as soon as you can. After we've answered what questions you have tonight, go home and ask some more. Our intent for the lease we've drafted is not to stop the drilling, but to make it more cooperative and safer for everyone here."

Wade mustered what he had left and gave it his best shot. Stella wasn't the only one who could make a good argument. "Options are good. We all want options. But for some perspective, think about this. At the end of the 1800s, Pennsylvania was one of the leading producers of oil in the world. Then coal. Energy is what built this state. The Marcellus shale is perhaps a more important energy boom. Stringent requirements packaged as 'protections' could end that. There's gas all over the country. Make it too hard for gas companies to do what they need to do and they'll take their money elsewhere."

Wade cleared his throat. People were listening to him, too. "I don't know how you put a lease agreement together that helps people's interests when you're against the industry in the first place. I have to think that kind of lease is so rigid no gas company will touch it."

There were shouts of support from the crowd at the

same time people were telling Wade to be quiet. Elzer called for order, but the room erupted.

"I don't want people telling me what to do on my property," said one man.

"They're trying to help us sort out the choices," Franny shot back.

"These people don't know us. How could they know what we need?"

"Green Energy has made this community better. No one can argue with that."

"How much money are we talking?"

People stood, trying to shout each other down. Elzer pounded the table with a gavel, but it was useless.

Jack caught Wade's eye and shook his head. Stella tried to speak, but her voice was drowned out.

LeeAnn stood up, put two fingers in her mouth and gave one of those loud whistles only she could do. That got people's attention. And when they found the whistle came from a very pregnant LeeAnn, they went from chaos to calm, as though she had some divine power.

"We've worked hard to get to the point of this meeting," she said. "Rather than fighting and nitpicking, why don't we take a show of hands, just to see how we feel as a community. No one is going to hold you to what you say now, but in order to go forward we need to see how most people are leaning." She didn't miss a beat. "Now, raise your hands if you think you'll sign the new lease contract."

More than three quarters of the room raised their hands.

Indoors, the chaos was over. Just like that. Outside it had just begun.

A few fire radios went off at once, and Franny made her way quickly to the front of the room and whispered into Elzer's ear.

Elzer banged his gavel to regain everyone's attention. "We have more to discuss, but emergency management says the rising creek is a flash-flood situation. We need everyone to get home. If you're headed toward the bridge, you'll have to find another way. It's been closed because of debris backup. All other roads are open, but please go home directly and stay out of harm's way."

People stood all at once. Wade began pushing toward LeeAnn. He could only see the top of her head.

"We'll resume this discussion at a later date," Elzer shouted. "Thank you for coming."

Wade edged closer to LeeAnn but she was already moving toward the door.

"Let's be orderly now. The people in the back leave first and then the rest will follow in line," Elzer said.

Wade pushed people out of the way so he could get to LeeAnn. He would get her and the baby home safely. But as he got closer he saw Jack already there, along with Gabriel.

"Dad, you go on ahead," she was saying. "Take the south road. You have to get to the cows in the barn."

"Are you sure, LeeAnn? You'll take care?"

"I'm going right home. It's so close."

Wade moved the last person out of his way.

Gabriel looked at Jack standing beside LeeAnn and then hurried toward the door. He was counting on someone to get his daughter home safely.

"I'll drive you," Jack said.

"I'll drive myself. I don't need your help."

"Listen to reason, LeeAnn. It may not be safe," Jack said.

"I'm going that way," Wade cut in.

"We both are," Jack said.

"It's only a mile," LeeAnn said. "If you want to help, go with my dad. He's going to have his hands full."

"I'll head to your dad's after I drive you home," Jack said.

"I insist, LeeAnn," Wade said.

She put up both hands in front of her. "Insist all you want, I'm driving myself. And I don't want either of you following me."

Wade took her by the arm.

"Don't!" she said, shaking him off.

"Leave her alone," Jack said. "You smell like the bar."

Stella arrived, took LeeAnn's arm, and led her toward the door. Wade turned on his brother.

"Your problem is you're always on the wrong side. Can't you see that?" Wade said.

"I take responsibility for my actions."

"You've always been a self-righteous son of a bitch," Wade said.

Jack looked around. "Where's LeeAnn?"

"She left with Stella while you were on your high horse," Wade replied, his fists balled. He took a swing at his brother.

CHAPTER 37

LeeAnn

LEEANN WANTED TO get home as soon as possible. The mild contractions she'd experienced off and on over the last few weeks had grown stronger during the meeting. She needed to rest, away from stress and excitement.

When she and Stella emerged from the fire hall, they stood under the cover of the roof overhang peering into the dark, wet parking lot that spanned the distance between them and the shelter of their cars.

LeeAnn put up her umbrella. Stella held it over them both, and put her other arm around LeeAnn.

"I'm parked right beside you," Stella said.

Before LeeAnn could reply, a cramp unlike anything she'd felt before took her breath away. Doc Black said cramping was normal. She just needed to lie down. She'd wanted to talk to him before he and his wife left the meeting, just to be sure. She'd almost reached Doc before Jack and Wade's argument about who would drive her home.

"Are you all right?" Stella asked, the rain and wind nearly drowning her voice.

"Just some cramping. Normal stuff, I think. I have an appointment in the morning."

"Normal or not, I'll follow you home. Then I'll call the doctor. I need to get home tonight, but I want to make sure you're safe first."

LeeAnn took Stella's arm.

The parking lot looked a muddy mess, with water coming from everywhere at once. When they reached her car, LeeAnn got in as quickly as her body would allow. She turned the key and the motor coughed for a moment in a half-hearted effort, then choked. She tried again: nothing.

Through the blurry window, Stella motioned for her. LeeAnn hauled herself from her car and into Stella's passenger seat, getting soaked in the process.

They drove slowly toward LeeAnn's apartment, the wipers against the driving rain the only sound between them. Another cramp overtook LeeAnn and she focused on breathing. She pulled out her cell and tried Doc Black's house, but got no answer.

"He probably hasn't made it home yet," Stella said. "We'll try again when we get to your apartment."

Maybe LeeAnn could convince Stella to stay one more night. Then she could drive her to Doc's, if needed.

Later, LeeAnn would remember hearing the alarm from the fire hall. But at the time they had no way of knowing that the closed bridge had become a dam, backing up logs, debris, and miles of waters. They had no way of knowing the hurricane, still hovering over Minden, was in the process of dumping five more inches of rain than predicted. They had no way of knowing that the bridge had splintered and broken under the weight of water and debris backed up behind it, releasing a monstrous surge right toward them.

It appeared instantly, surrounding them and overtaking their car. At first LeeAnn felt a gentle jostle and wondered if they were hydroplaning. She realized they were being lifted, floating. She looked desperately into the watery blackness, but she couldn't comprehend what she saw. It was too awful. She didn't scream until the first tree hit the car.

CHAPTER 38

Jack

JACK DIDN'T SEE Wade's punch coming and it caught him on the chin. He fell to the floor, his body automatically tensing for the fight. Wade stalked out of the building and Jack followed.

The parking lot was empty except for their trucks and LeeAnn's red car.

"She must gave gotten a ride after all," Jack said, relief replacing some of his anger.

"Maybe if you hadn't picked a fight we'd know that for sure," Wade said.

"Fuck you."

Wade swung at him again and this time Jack easily dodged it. Carried by the momentum of the swing, Wade fell to the muddy ground before rising on all fours. He charged Jack with his head down. Jack could have moved, but didn't. Wade rammed him in the stomach, knocking Jack on his butt. He lay back, sinking into the mud, trying to get his breath.

"Get up," Wade said.

Jack closed his eyes. He took one slow breath and then another. A sharp pain pierced his ribs. For a long time this had been the fight Jack wanted, but not anymore. Now he wanted to understand. Otherwise it was more time wasted. But there was still so much frustration. God, he wanted free of it. "Why'd you sleep with my wife? Why would you do that?" Jack said in an agonized cry.

"You thought nothing of marrying the woman I loved first."

Jack staggered to his feet. "I thought nothing of it? You don't know what I thought, or what I went through. What *we* went through. You left us, Wade. All we had was each other," he said above the sound of the driving rain. "Do you care? Do you care about anything?"

Wade slouched, the fight going out of him. "I'll be out of your life soon enough." His eyes went to LeeAnn's red Chevrolet. He turned and walked toward his truck. "I'm leaving town."

Jack stared after him. He would head out when his baby would be born in less than a month? "You can't."

"I'm going. It's past time."

Pain stabbed Jack on one side of his chest. He coughed. A broken rib, he guessed. But that wasn't the only cause of pain. Now that he was faced with it, he didn't want Wade to go. Couldn't regret lead to something better? Wade was a part of the puzzle Jack wanted to solve. The same ghosts haunted them both, whether Wade saw them or not.

Jack struggled to a stand. "Don't go. I'm sorry for blaming you all these years. I've been wrong. I see that now." If Wade went, Jack felt certain they would never see each other again.

Wade turned back to him, rain-drenched. "There's nothing here for me."

"There's something you need to know. I should have told you before."

Wade shook his head as rain streamed down his face, as though denying the words Jack needed to say.

"I invited Stella to Minden. I told myself after you left that if you came back I would get her here. Because when I took the phone from you that night after Dad died, she said she would come. You needed her, and she responded. It was me who kept her from coming. Me, Wade, who turned her away. When I took the phone from you, I told her you'd changed your mind."

"It makes no difference," Wade said.

"It makes *all* the difference! I thought by bringing her back to Minden, I could help make things right."

"It wouldn't have mattered if she had come after Dad died," Wade said, his voice oddly unemotional. "I was desperate at the time. She had nothing to give, anyway."

Jack stood up, favoring one side. "You're wrong."

Their relationship had cracks that went all the way down. They had to choose now whether to be brothers because of or in spite of those cracks. "I'm asking you not to leave. Things can be better between us. I've been an angry idiot. I'm sorry I've avoided you. You have a place here in this town and as part of this family. But only if you stay."

Wade opened the door to his truck. "I don't have it in me. I just didn't know it until now."

Ignoring the sharp pain in his ribs, Jack ran to Wade's passenger side door. He tried to open it, but Wade had it locked. He pounded on the door. "Open up!" Jack yelled at the closed window. "What about LeeAnn? You can't leave her like this. What about the baby? If you won't stay for me, stay for them!" He turned his guts out to scream as loud as he could.

Wade gave him one last cold, blurred look through the rain-streaked window. Wade put the truck into gear and backed up. Jack held on, running backwards, his hand on the door, feet slipping in the mud. He pounded on the window, trying to break it. "At least wait until morning!" he screamed.

Wade changed gears. His brother would not look his way. The truck lurched forward and Jack had to let go.

Wade's tires threw mud and water onto Jack's already soaked clothes. He watched his brother's taillights disappear.

Jack hobbled to his truck, wincing as each step caused jabbing rib pain. He would follow Wade, try to catch him and bring him back. Out of the corner of his eye, blue lights flashed through the downpour. He turned, squinting, straining to see. Another truck pulled into the parking lot. Franny.

She ran inside and he hurried after her as best he could. Someone else should know he was going after Wade. The pain in his ribs was like a knife, slowing him.

He limped inside the fire hall doors in time to watch her flip a switch. The siren blared around them.

"What happened?" he yelled over the noise.

"The bridge gave way. It's going to be a long night. Jack? What's wrong?"

"LeeAnn," he said, turning and running toward his truck.

CHAPTER 39

LeeAnn

"OH MY GOD, we're floating–" LeeAnn said, panic choking off the rest of her words. Stella shook her head, as if she could deny the creek rising around the car.

LeeAnn started to open her door.

"Don't," Stella yelled. "It's coming up too fast." She rolled down the windows and turned off the car.

LeeAnn let go of the door handle and a painful contraction took her breath away. Warm liquid soaked her underwear. *Jesus.*

Another tree hit, spinning the car around sideways. They both screamed.

Stella let go of the wheel. "We need to get on the roof." She looked over at LeeAnn's body and then at the window. LeeAnn didn't have to ask what she was thinking.

"I'll climb out first and help you."

LeeAnn would not lose this baby, not now. She could already feel another contraction coming on and braced herself.

Stella pulled her shoulders through the driver side

window and sat on the windowsill. She kicked off her shoes and hiked up her skirt. When the car started to pitch to the left, Stella quickly grabbed the top of the window, placed her feet where she'd been sitting, and then hoisted herself onto the roof. The roof bent overhead, where Stella was, and where LeeAnn needed to be if she and the baby were going to survive.

Water was all she could see or hear. The car bobbed in the current, scraping the bottom.

Stella's stocking feet appeared in the driver's side window. She wedged them inside the car for leverage before lying across the roof and leaning into LeeAnn's window. She extended her hand. "Come. There's no time."

LeeAnn grabbed Stella's hand. She tried to sit on the windowsill, as Stella had done, and realized that wasn't possible.

"Let me go, I can't make it that way."

Stella let go but stayed in position.

Water lapped at the window and would soon fill the car. LeeAnn reached out through the window with both hands this time, to make as much room for her midsection as possible. She squatted on the seat with trembling legs and grabbed the frame of the window.

Another contraction racked her body, and LeeAnn used every ounce of energy and will to squeeze herself through the window, the frame of it pressing painfully on her seizing belly.

Stella grabbed her hands and used the water to help float LeeAnn to the hood of the car. "Don't let go!"

The car tilted and water began pouring through the windows.

LeeAnn looked around and couldn't tell if they were moving or stopped. She could see nothing but water. Then something hit the car and the women lurched forward. Stella lost her grip on LeeAnn's hand momentarily and then clasped tightly again before LeeAnn could slide off the hood into the churn. In the dim light, LeeAnn saw they were jammed against something big, like a rock, with the full force of a raging Silver Creek pushing against them from upstream. The metal of the car squealed beneath them. Only a matter of minutes before the car flipped or crumpled.

LeeAnn shook all over. The night was cold and she was soaked. Her teeth chattered.

She made out shapes floating past them in the water. More branches. Barrels. Part of a roof. Furniture. She thought about the frack water undoubtedly washed into the creek from flooded holding ponds like the one at her dad's. Her body seized again.

"Contractions. Are. Bad," LeeAnn gasped. "And my water broke." No one would look for them. No one could. Stella was scared, too. "Help me get out of here," LeeAnn begged when the pain of the contraction ebbed.

An enormous limb floated toward them. LeeAnn stiffened. If this one hit the car, they would not be able to hold on.

Stella squeezed her hand and yelled over roar. "We're going to jump and grab that tree. I can't swim, so if I miss, you get there and hold on. You hear me?"

"But what if it hits us first? Maybe we should wait. What do you mean you can't swim?"

"We can't wait." Stella jumped into the water, pulling LeeAnn with her. LeeAnn's head instantly went under the surface and she lost hold of Stella's hand. The growl of the water muffled as it jostled her beneath the surface. She kicked and flailed, totally disoriented. The darkness outside offered no help. There was no way to tell up from down.

She kicked hard, but it seemed useless against the strong rushing water. Silver Creek was unrecognizable. She couldn't believe that her creek would take her life and the baby's. She was caught in the inevitable—the waters swollen like her body, trying to stake out a future. The creek would have its way. More powerful than she was or anything Green Energy could do, it would reclaim the land.

She hadn't been able to change Jack or Wade or her mother's cancer and she wasn't going to change this flood. She stopped struggling and felt her body being lifted.

Her head broke through and she gasped for air. Water splashed her mouth and nose so much she had a hard time getting her breath, but at least she wasn't underwater anymore.

A bloated cow carcass floated past, a hoof scraping against her arm, and she screamed Stella's name. PVC pipes and a Green Energy sign bobbed past her. She grabbed onto the sign to keep herself afloat as she searched blindly for Stella. The sign sank under her weight and she let it go. Had Stella made it to the tree? Or drowned?

"LeeAnn!"

She swam toward Stella's voice, the last of her strength ebbing in the cold water. Waves spilled onto her face. Her arms and legs grew heavy. Waterlogged clothes and shoes tried to sink her.

She felt a hand grab the back of her collar and pull. Stella.

"Hold on," Stella screamed. "And lift your legs up."

"I'm not going to be able to hold on for long," LeeAnn yelled, as another long, painful contraction hit her. The baby would soon be born. She felt an overwhelming need to push. Her body would push the baby out whether she wanted to or not.

"Lift your legs," Stella yelled to her again. LeeAnn lifted them as high as she dared. But she was afraid the baby would come out and drown.

Stella put one arm around LeeAnn, supporting her as much as she could. "We're close to the shore. Keep your legs up."

The water suddenly slowed and LeeAnn could make out trees standing upright. Land. Stella was right. She squeezed her eyes shut as another painful contraction took her breath completely. She bent in pain. The baby's head pushed apart her pelvic bones. "Get me out of this water," she said through her teeth.

The tree limb they'd been holding onto caught in the shallowing water. They let go of its dappled bark.

"Come now!" Stella said, helping her to her feet.

LeeAnn wrapped her arms around Stella and sagged, her face in Stella's neck.

"Plant your feet. Think of the baby."

LeeAnn stumbled in the water but regained her footing. They slogged together toward the bank and staggered out of the water, stepping over the mighty sycamore limb that had carried them.

Stella steered her toward a sheltered spot under a large willow a short distance away.

"The baby," LeeAnn said, her face screwed with pain.

"Just a few more steps," Stella told her.

Stella tripped, falling to the ground, pulling LeeAnn with her. LeeAnn threw her hands forward to catch herself. Stella lay motionless, her head bleeding where it had struck a tree root.

"Stella!" LeeAnn shouted. "Stella!" She did not wake.

LeeAnn let out an anguished cry. "God, no!"

CHAPTER 40

Jack

JACK DROVE AS fast as he dared toward LeeAnn's apartment, cursing himself for not following her home. "Please, please, please," he whispered against the bad feeling inside.

His wipers beat against the rain pounding his windshield, making it so difficult to see that he almost missed the road flares and orange cones blocking his way. He pulled over, confused. The creek was where the road should have been.

Broken bridge. Holy shit. He searched for his cell so he could call her, but didn't find it. Probably lost it while fighting with Wade. He searched the water ahead, looking for any sign of them. He stepped around the cones and hurried along the water's edge. Each time his foot hit the ground a sharp pain shot through his left side, but he hardly cared. He slogged on and on, dodging trees and brush relocated by the watery devastation around him. Please, God, let Stella be with her and let them have made it home.

He heard something and stopped to listen, working

hard to slow his labored breathing. Squinting against the downpour he scanned the creek ahead. Nothing. The rush of the water and his own breath filled his ears. But up ahead in the distance he saw something in the middle of the channel. Someone in the water downstream from where he stood? Another ghost, perhaps, or more debris. The stream now carried so much. He wiped water from his eyes and saw a flash of violet-blue. The scarf LeeAnn wore to the meeting. Stella was there, too. Good God.

Jack ran, slipping and falling on the uneven ground. He picked himself up and ran again, scrambling to reach them, willing them to safety. They were just ahead, stumbling together along the water's edge. He'd nearly reached them when Stella fell and pulled LeeAnn down with her.

His wife's desperate wail pierced his heart.

"LeeAnn!"

She didn't even turn toward him.

When he finally reached her, he took her hand, and helped her stand. She stared at him with glazed unrecognizing eyes. He glanced down at Stella. She was out cold with a nasty gash on her head but still breathing.

"The baby," LeeAnn begged.

He took off his wet coat and helped her lie on it. The rain, at least, had slowed to a fine mist.

"I'm here," he said, putting his hand on her belly.

"I don't want to have my baby here," she said, trying to focus. Her lips quivered.

It was too cold and wet. Too dirty. All of the old disappointments, the lost chances, threatened to overtake him. He would do all he could to make sure her baby would not be taken from her now.

He lifted her loose dress and helped her get her underwear off. He'd helped Gabriel with birthing cows. It wasn't much to go on, but it was something. He willed his hands to stop shaking.

LeeAnn watched his face.

He nodded. All he could do was give her hope. "I see

the baby's head. Push with the next contraction."

LeeAnn took a deep breath and pushed, straining forward.

"Do it again, LeeAnn. Then we can get the baby someplace warm."

Her teeth chattered and her whole body trembled. He could see her exhaustion, but she needed to fight. Her eyes became glassy and unfocused again. On pure instinct he reached up and slapped her face. She blinked rapidly. "You need to do this," he said, looking into her eyes, trying to pull her back.

LeeAnn fixed her gaze on him.

"Come on, LeeAnn."

She pushed, straining hard and calling out.

"The head is out now, honey. You did it. Push again, just like that."

LeeAnn reached out to him. "Hold my hands. I'm so tired. Keep me here!"

He held her hands tight as LeeAnn pushed again. Then Jack pulled the baby girl from her. The creek, the rain, his broken rib, even LeeAnn faded for a moment as he held the child in his arms, willing it to show signs of life. He broke down when the baby gave a weak cry.

He laid the little girl on LeeAnn's belly. "She needs you. I'm going for help."

"Her color—even in the dark I can see—"

"Keep her warm. Let her know you're here for her. That's what she needs. I'll be back as soon as I can."

He brushed his lips against her forehead and stood. The moon had come out and the water rushed past. Stopping only to pull Stella safely away from the torrent, he hurried back the way he'd come, praying he would find help in time.

CHAPTER 41

LeeAnn

"WE'RE TOGETHER," LeeAnn whispered to the baby wrapped in her arms, trying to cover all of her. "Stay here, baby girl. I'll never leave you."

Stella lay still on the ground only a few feet away.

LeeAnn shivered. The dark tiredness returned, threatening to pull her under. She rubbed the baby's skin. They both needed to keep warm. But how could she keep another body warm when she felt so cold? So very cold. Even as she trembled, she could feel her little girl breathing. As long as she could feel that, she would not close her eyes, no matter how heavy they felt. She bit her lip to stay awake.

CHAPTER 42

Jack

JACK LOOKED BACK at them only once. The baby and LeeAnn, slick with blood and afterbirth, the cord still connecting them, as though they'd both been born of the swollen creek and washed up on its banks. The sight of LeeAnn with her arms around the child pushed Jack to move faster. He raced back the way he'd come.

The ground was soaked and slippery. He fell several times, blindly grabbing onto rocks and trees, pulling and pushing anything that could move him forward. When he reached the cones across the road, his chest burned and his hands bled. Headlights came toward him and he stepped out into the middle of the road with his arms raised.

The car slowed. Gabriel jumped out. "Jack! I heard about the bridge and came right away. What's happened? You okay? Where's LeeAnn? I got no answer on her cell or at her apartment."

"Call nine-one-one. We need an ambulance. She's downstream, along the shore, straight ahead." Jack pointed the way. "Stella and the baby, too. They're alive, but there isn't much time. The baby's more blue than pink. I'm going back to wait with them."

"Take this," Gabriel said, removing off his coat and handing it to him after pulling his cell from its pocket.

Jack hurried. By the time he got to LeeAnn he could already hear the sirens.

LeeAnn was awake, her skin as chalk white as the sycamore in the moonlight. Her lower lip bled. "Hold on now, LeeAnn. Help is coming." The rapid, shallow rhythm of the baby's breath didn't seem right even to his untrained eye. He wrapped them both in Gabriel's coat and then went to Stella. When he shook her, her eyes flickered open. "Just lay still for now. Medics will be here in a few minutes."

He moved back over next to LeeAnn, stripped off his shirt, and lay down under the coat beside her and the baby, wrapping around them to offer what body warmth he could. "Your dad's waiting for the ambulance. They'll be here very soon," he said, kissing LeeAnn's forehead. "I'm here with you. That's all I've ever wanted," he said, muttering it over and over, hoping she heard.

"Jack?" came a voice in the distance. It was Franny.

He sat up. "Here! Hurry."

It seemed to take forever for Franny and the two paramedics to get to them. They carried stretchers and medical bags and other equipment.

"She's so cold," he said quietly to Franny. He wouldn't state the obvious about the baby, not with LeeAnn there.

Two of them set to work on LeeAnn and the child, while the third man took care of Stella. Soon all of them were wrapped in shiny blankets. More people arrived. Stella revived quickly. When Franny put a tiny oxygen mask on the baby's face, LeeAnn closed her eyes.

It seemed to take impossibly long to make their way back through the woods. In the light of the ambulance, LeeAnn's skin was gray and the baby's not much better. Stella, now fully alert with a gauze bandage on her forehead, sat next to Jack and Franny in the back.

On the way to the hospital LeeAnn did not respond, not even to the baby's weak cries or Franny's continued attempts to wake her.

Jack put his hand on her clammy forehead. Franny took his other hand in both of hers. "I radioed the hospital. They'll be ready."

When they reached the emergency room, a team of people awaited them. They whisked LeeAnn and the baby inside. Stella was taken in a wheelchair. Jack followed close behind.

LeeAnn went one way and the baby another. Stella was somewhere behind him, also being seen for treatment. LeeAnn would want him to stay with the baby. He hurried over to the doctor who was checking the infant's pulse and heart rate. The doctor nodded, as though he liked what he saw. "Her color's not bad considering," he said to the nurse standing beside him. "Let's get her in an incubator and then we'll see if she'll eat. I'll check back as soon as we get the mother stabilized."

Jack, still wrapped in an emergency blanket, followed the nurse upstairs. He stood next to the baby while she lay in the incubator. The nurse returned in a few moments with a dressing gown, a blanket and a warm bottle. He washed his hands at her direction and put on the gown, then she handed him the bottle. "Sit there," the nurse said motioning to a chair. She covered him with the blanket. He was grateful for the warmth. Then she gently handed him the baby. "This little girl looks much better. See if she'll eat. I'll come back in a few minutes and check on you both. We're short staffed, but I'll be able to dress those hands for you when we get a minute." She closed the curtain.

She was leaving him alone with the baby?

Jack stared down at the now pink-faced girl. He touched the center of her hand with his finger. Impossibly small fingers curled around his.

He tipped the bottle and let the nipple gently touch

the baby's lips. Unbelievably, her mouth opened and she began to suckle.

"Wait till your mama sees you now," he whispered.

Peace enveloped him. Anger had been replaced by a loving stillness he knew would last.

There'd been so much pain over the last hours. Wade leaving. Nearly losing LeeAnn and this baby. Stella, too.

All those years with LeeAnn, and even with Wade and Stella, he'd allowed love and heartbreak to happen with equal amounts of indifference. He'd never fought for what he wanted. Now, things were different.

After drinking most of the bottle, the baby fell asleep on Jack's lap. Franny came into the little room a short while later and smiled when she saw them.

"How is she?" he asked, encouraged by her smile.

"Still unconscious. Her temperature has shot up. Probably an infection."

"She needs to hold her little girl," Jack said, his voice hoarse.

CHAPTER 43

Stella

STELLA WENT TO LeeAnn's room to keep watch. Jack was already there with the baby she'd seen briefly in the ambulance but had not yet held. He stood with the child when she came into the room. The cuts on his hands had been taped, as well as the broken rib Franny told her about.

"Thank you for saving them," he said.

"I'm glad I could help," she said.

"How's your head?" he said, gesturing to the stitches above her eye.

"I'll be just fine."

Jack hesitated as though he wanted to say more, but turned and put the sleeping baby in the bassinet by LeeAnn's bed. "She'll be wanting her mother soon."

Stella looked toward LeeAnn, hooked up to oxygen and IVs.

"She'll come back for her daughter," Jack said. There was no doubt in his voice.

Stella searched for something to say. LeeAnn's color still seemed off.

"I'm going to get a shower," he said. "If you'll stay here with them?"

She nodded. He turned and headed toward the door.

"When you were born," she began. He stopped in the doorway, his back still to her. "I didn't expect to feel so much love the moment I saw you. It took me completely by surprise. That feeling has never gone."

He turned back and nodded. She went to him and touched his arm.

The nurse arrived and they stepped apart.

They waited as the nurse checked LeeAnn's vitals and took her temperature. "Her fever's broken."

Jack smiled at Stella before heading out the door.

Stella approached the bassinet where the baby slept and gazed at the little girl. A rapid, strong little heartbeat thrummed against her hand, which rose and fell with the tiny chest. Wade was the last baby she'd touched. LeeAnn's baby, awake now, grabbed a handful of her sleeve.

Here it was. A sense of belonging that didn't beg questions or lay blame, but only required her presence. She wanted to be in this child's life.

Stella picked up the phone in the room and placed a call.

"Patrick. Don't hang up—"

"Stella, I'm so glad. The news—"

"You need to know I'm ready now, for you and for me." She watched as LeeAnn's eyes fluttered. "But I had to have this time in Minden to get to this point."

"Stella, just come home. We can talk when you get here."

She laughed with relief. She could tell by his tone that his love hadn't waivered. "I have so much to tell you. Can you come to Minden and get me? My car isn't quite up to the trip. And there's someone here I'd like you to meet, even if it's just this once."

CHAPTER 44

Jack

WHEN LEEANN OPENED her eyes in the dawn light, Jack sat beside her, his head in his hands. He must have appeared as startled as she felt.

She looked around the room. She shook her head and squeezed her eyes shut. "God, no."

"The baby's okay. She's right here. Just sleeping." he said.

"Where?" she croaked, tears of relief filling her eyes.

He turned to the hospital crib behind him. Jack picked up the baby, swaddled in a pink blanket. He looked down at her and smiled. He already loved her, just like Stella had said. Her eyes fluttered open, as though she was ready now to meet her mom. He gently placed her in LeeAnn's arms.

"Is she really okay?"

"Perfectly fine. A fighter, like her mother."

LeeAnn held her daughter to her swollen breast. Her little girl was olive-skinned like Jack and Stella. Her hands, small, like her grandmother Rose's.

"Your dad brought these," he said, pointing to a vase of

zinnias, her mother's favorite.

LeeAnn sat looking down at her baby for a long moment, then leaned down and inhaled deeply.

"I'm going to call her Rose."

Jack nodded, overcome at the sight of them together.

"I wasn't ready before," he said. "All these years I was scared that I wouldn't be able to handle a family."

"And now?"

"I love you, I always have, and I always will. You are part of me, LeeAnn, and your baby is, too. I'm not fighting anymore. I don't need it. If you'll have me, you can count on me—after all that's happened, I know that's the truth. Stella is who she is. I am who I am. I want that to be enough for you."

LeeAnn looked down again at the baby. "It is. I needed this last year to know that. I needed to see you with Rose, just now. You're not scared anymore. I believe you—that you're ready. But if Wade wants to be involved, then he should be."

Jack turned from her and went to the window. The morning was clear blue. He watched the sidewalk below as a little girl fell and skinned her knee before running back to her dad for comfort.

"What is it? He's okay, Jack, isn't he?"

Jack nodded. "Wade had to leave town. For work. He may not be back for a while."

"You don't have to cover up for him. Maybe someday he won't have to run anymore and we'll see him again."

Jack sat back down beside her. Sick as she'd been, she looked so beautiful holding her child.

She squeezed his hand and wiped her eyes. "We'll be okay. Let's just give it some time."

Stella came into the room, her face lighting up at the sight of them. "I brought these from your apartment, LeeAnn." She carried a pot of violets Jack recognized. Stella set them down on the windowsill along with a small pink stone that caught the morning light. "Should I come back later?"

"No," LeeAnn said. "Stay." She patted the bed, offering Stella a place to sit.

"Thank you for everything," LeeAnn said.

The baby stirred; LeeAnn snuggled her, then handed her to Stella.

Looking first at Jack, who gave a nod, Stella took the child. She held the baby away from her, unsure.

"Hold her close," Jack said, watching as Stella settled the baby into the crook of her arm.

The tears in Stella's eyes warmed Jack. He'd had no clue what would be unleashed when he asked Stella to come to Minden, but if the only result was this moment, then he'd done right.

"I don't want to lease the orchard," LeeAnn said.

"We don't need to talk about that now," Stella said.

"But I do," LeeAnn said.

"Even now with the baby?" Jack said. "She could have anything she'd ever need."

"If we give her what we have now, that's enough."

Jack kissed the top of LeeAnn's head.

Acknowledgements

It takes so many to make a book. People are generous and willing to help, if you ask. The experience of creating this novel over seven years has shifted me from a realist to an idealist. People reached out to help me again and again when I could offer little in return. Along the way it didn't seem very realistic that I would ever hold this novel in my hands. And yet, it happened. The experience has shown me that dreams are made of vision, belief, and openness to possibility.

Any inaccuracies in this book are mine. That said, I'm grateful to those who gave me technical advice, including lawyer Chot Elliot, who took time years ago to meet me in Porters' Pub and help me understand the ideas of toxic trespass and a cone of silence, from the legal sense. I want to acknowledge THE ORCHARD, a wonderful memoir by Adele Crockett Robertson, where I learned some things about growing apples.

Thanks to early readers including Dianna Sinovic, Janet Robertson, Ian Kindle, and Becky Bartlett. Your comments helped me so much. Thanks also to Jenn Rossmann for your insightful criticism that gave me direction, more than once.

My deepest thanks to Kathryn Craft. When I started this book I didn't know how to tell a story and you taught me how to tell this one, and much more. Thanks for opening so many doors. Thanks also to the rest of my Weggie friends: Donna Galanti, Janice Bashman, Tori Bond, Karen Pokras, Lisa Papp, and Dana Schwartz. Your advice, support, and friendship have been invaluable.

I owe a great deal to Nancy Cleary at Wyatt-MacKenzie Publishing for taking a chance on this novel, at the eleventh hour. Your belief in my book was the turning point. Thank you. Thanks also to the whole team at Wyatt-MacKenzie for turning my loose pages into a beautiful book with all the finishing touches. It's been truly wonderful to work with you all.

I'm grateful to Katie Shea Boutillier, my agent, who finally said yes! Your keen comments and feedback were invaluable. I look forward to working on many more books with you.

Thanks to my dear friends at Nurture Nature Center, where I worked while writing most of this book. Can you guess my inspiration for the flood scene? Thanks also to my friends and family and especially, my mom, Joan, for being there and for asking how it was going.

Thanks most, to my sons, Owen and Sam, for the light you bring everyday to our home. Our world is so bright with you in it. And to my husband, David—thanks for helping me catch my dream. I'm not sure a partner can offer more to the one they love. XXOO